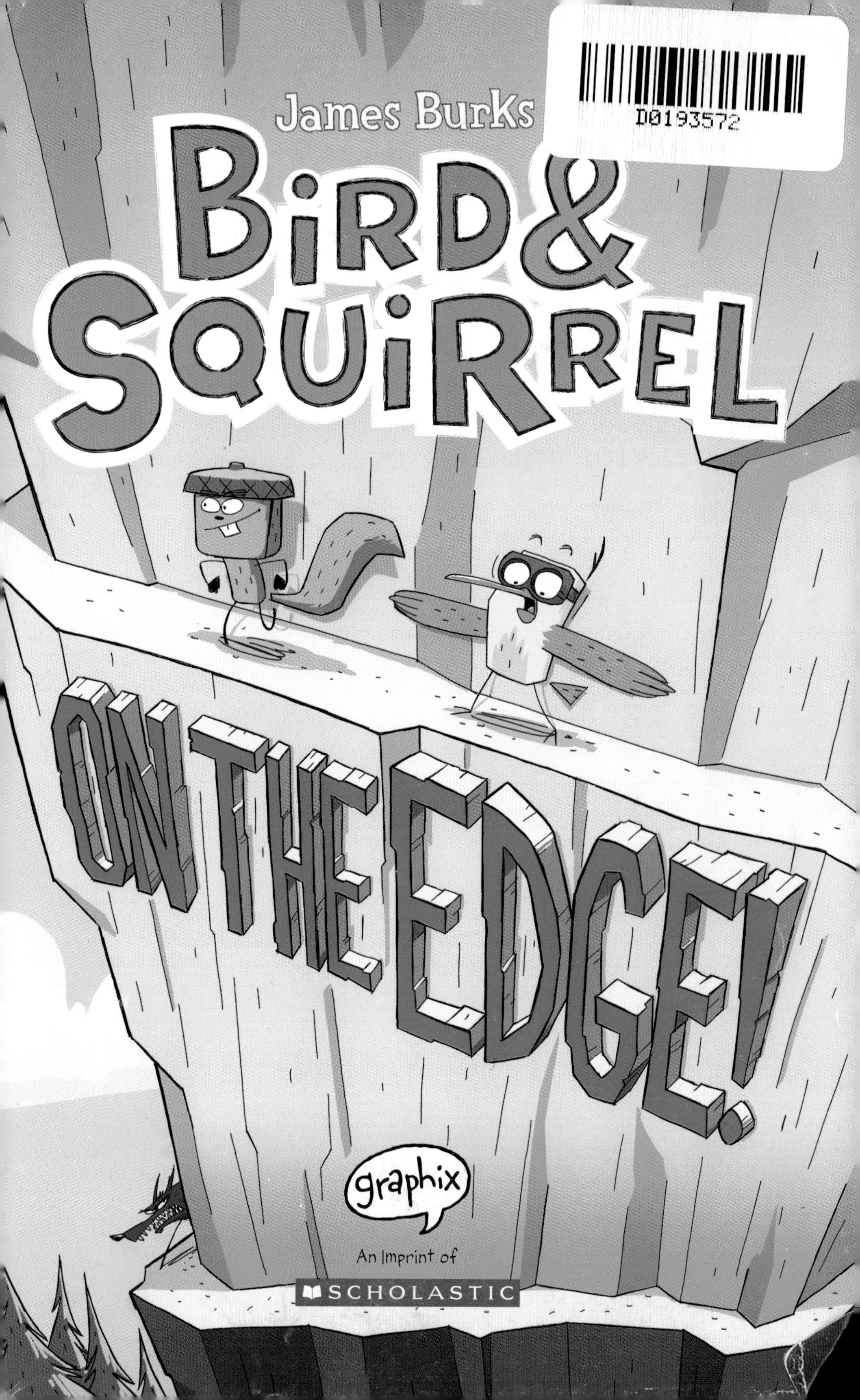
James Burks
Bird & Squirrel
On the Edge!
graphix
An Imprint of
SCHOLASTIC

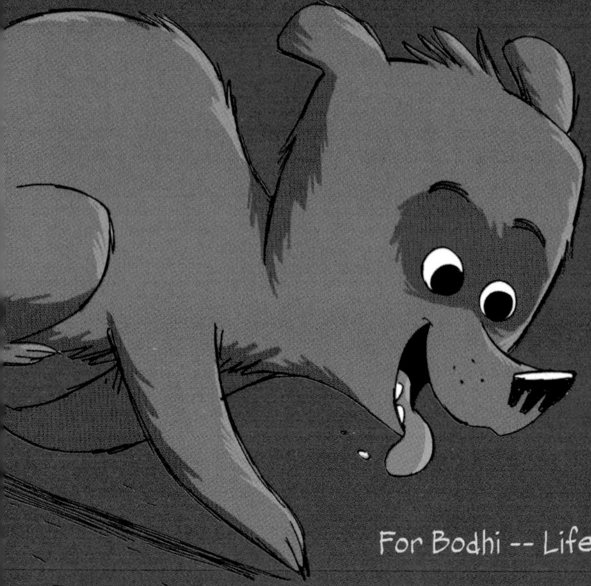

For Bodhi -- Life is an adventure. Have fun!

Library of Congress Control Number: 2014956158

ISBN 978-0-545-80425-7 (hardcover)
ISBN 978-0-545-80426-4 (paperback)

15 14 13 12 11 18 19 20 21 22/0
Printed in China 38

First edition, November 2015

Edited by Adam Rau
Book design by Phil Falco
Creative Director: David Saylor

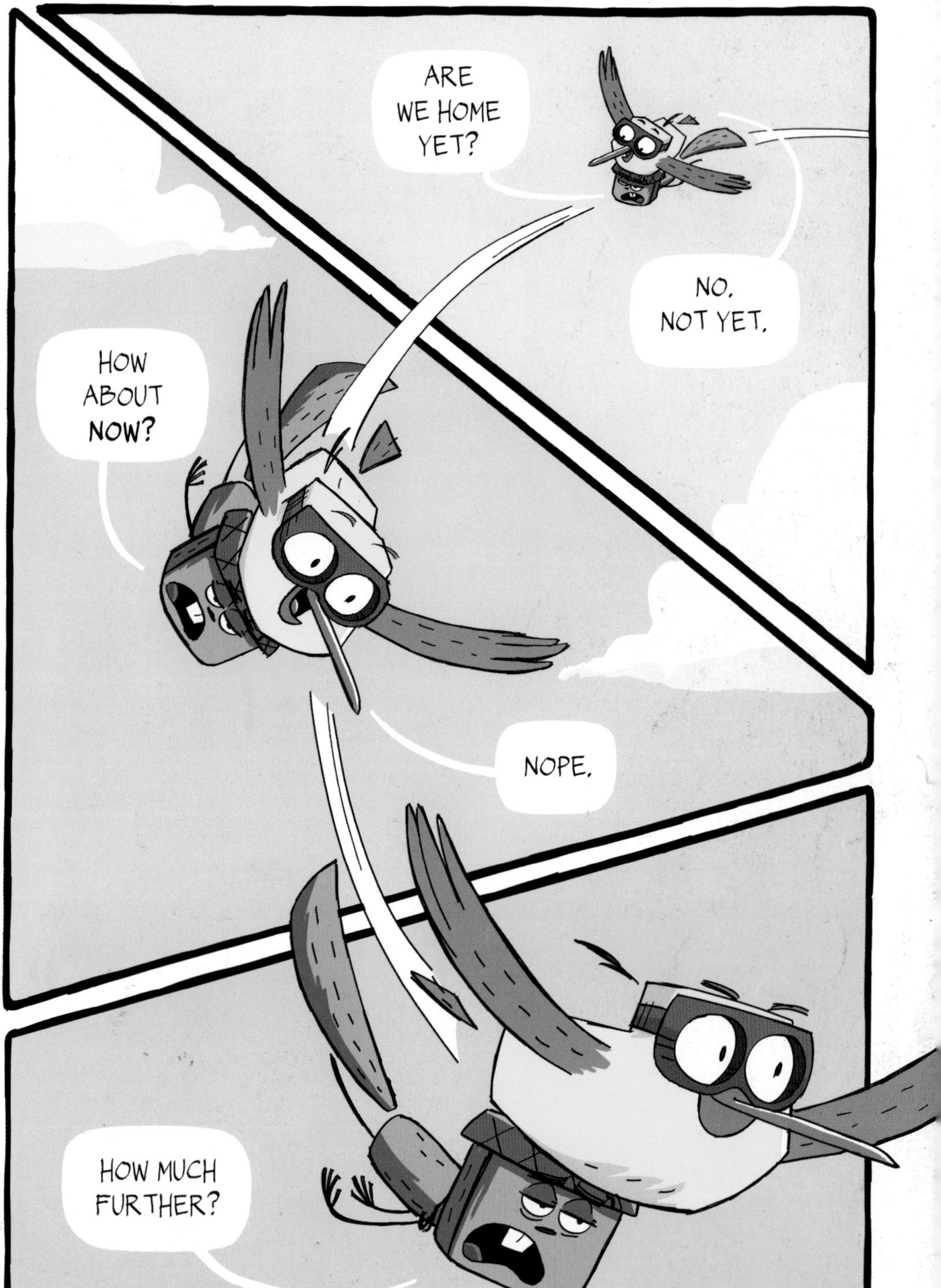
ARE WE HOME YET?
NO. NOT YET.
HOW ABOUT NOW?
NOPE.
HOW MUCH FURTHER?

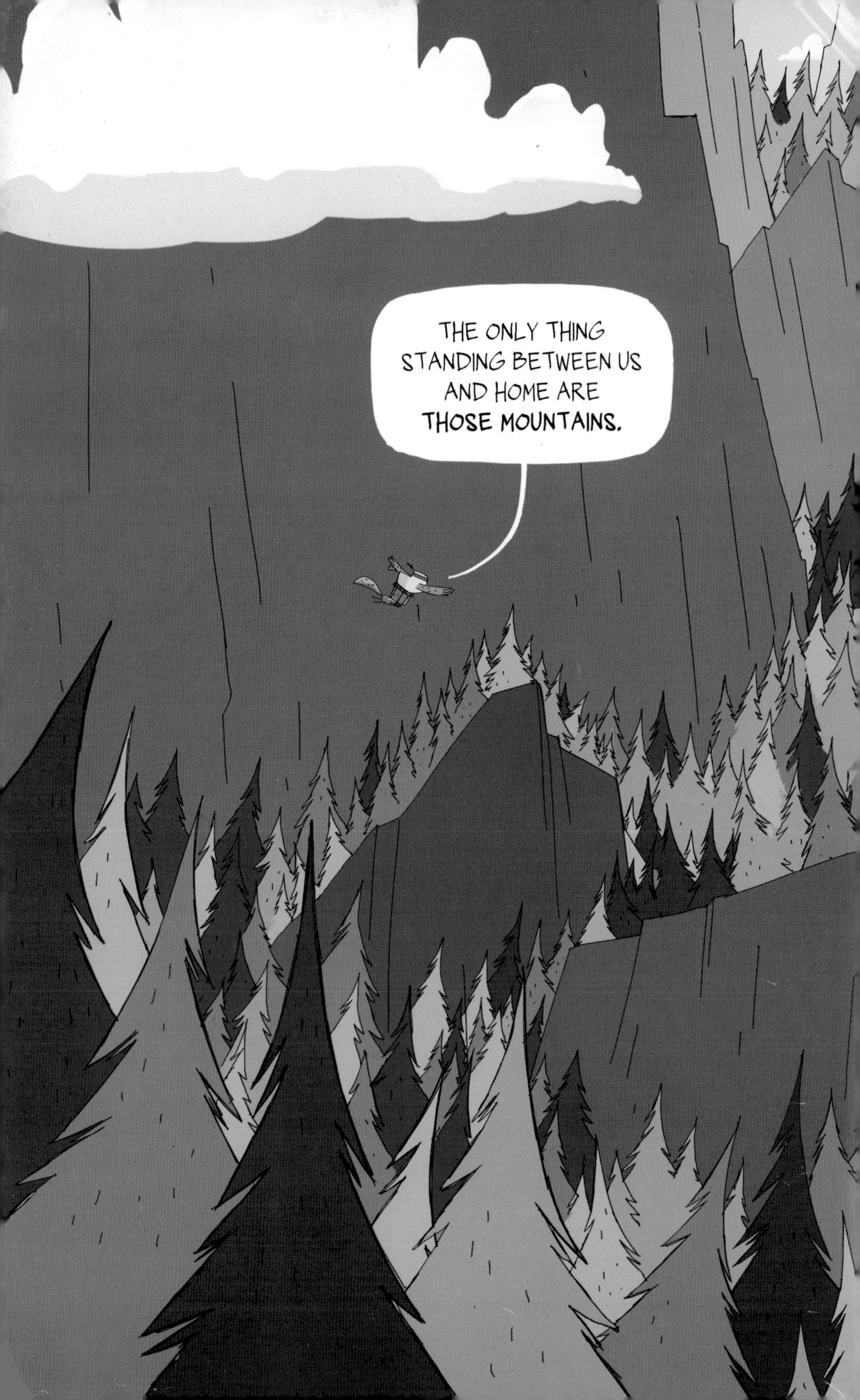
THE ONLY THING STANDING BETWEEN US AND HOME ARE THOSE MOUNTAINS.

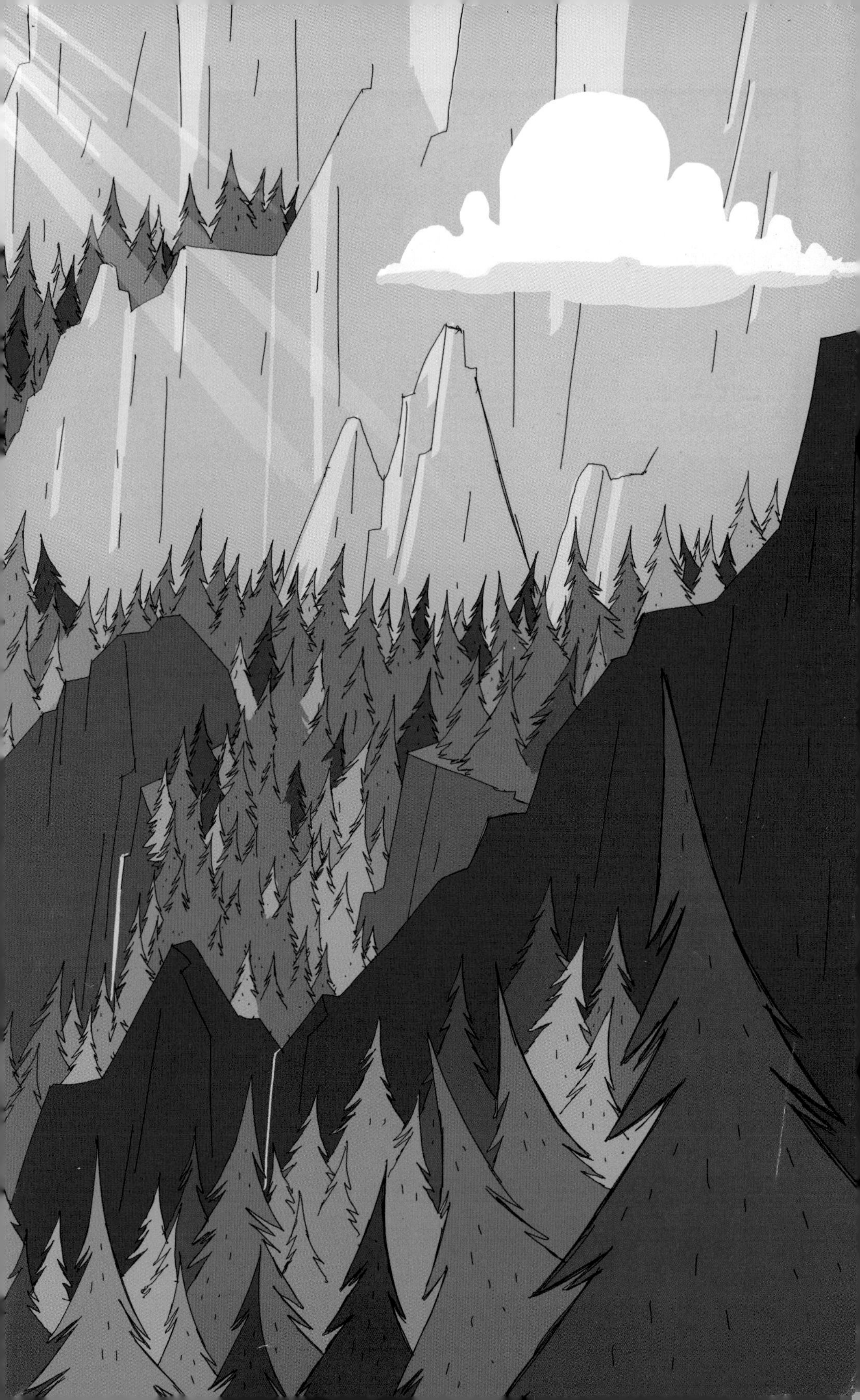

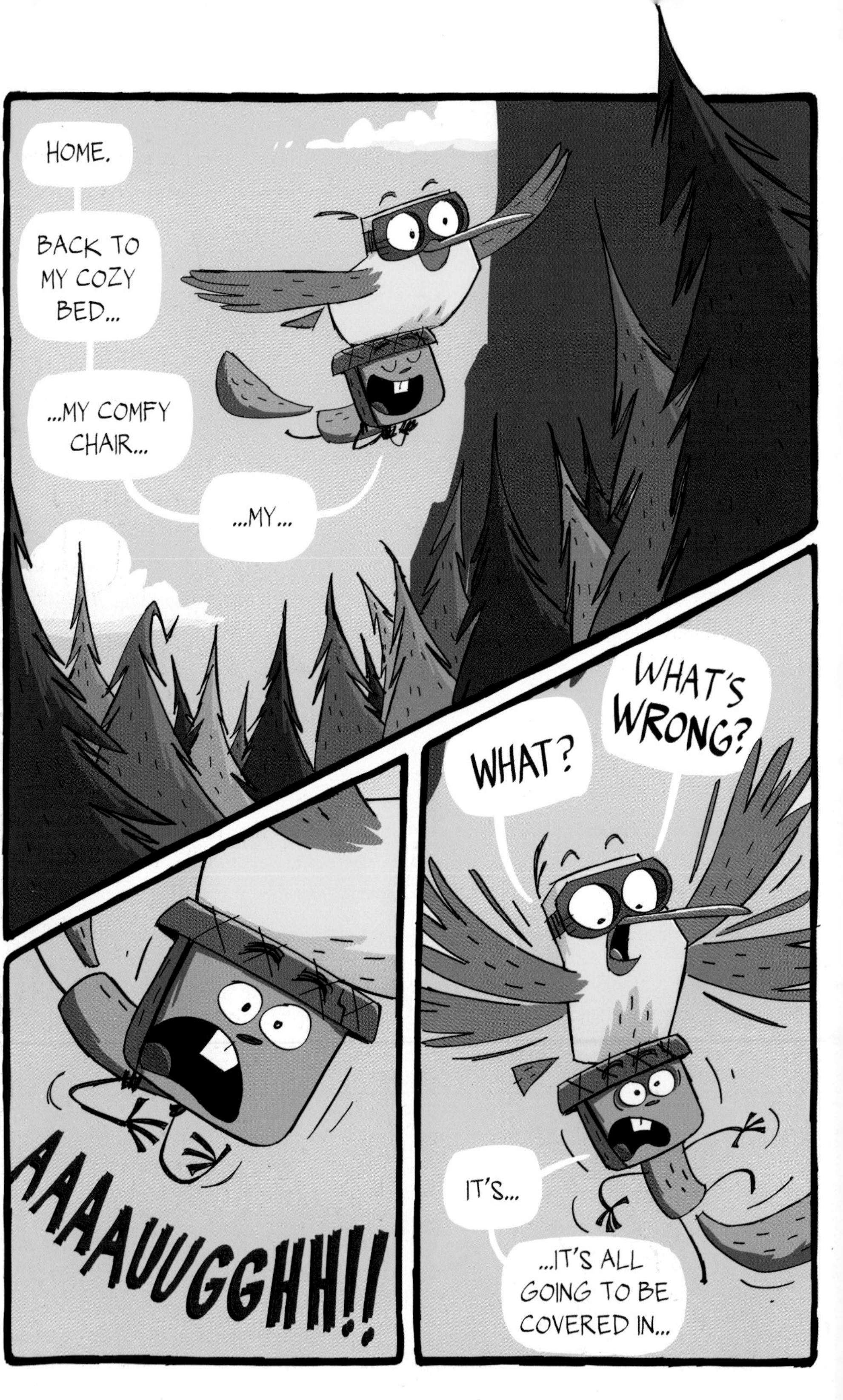
HOME.
BACK TO MY COZY BED...
...MY COMFY CHAIR...
...MY...
AAAAUUGGHH!!
WHAT?
WHAT'S WRONG?
IT'S...
...IT'S ALL GOING TO BE COVERED IN...

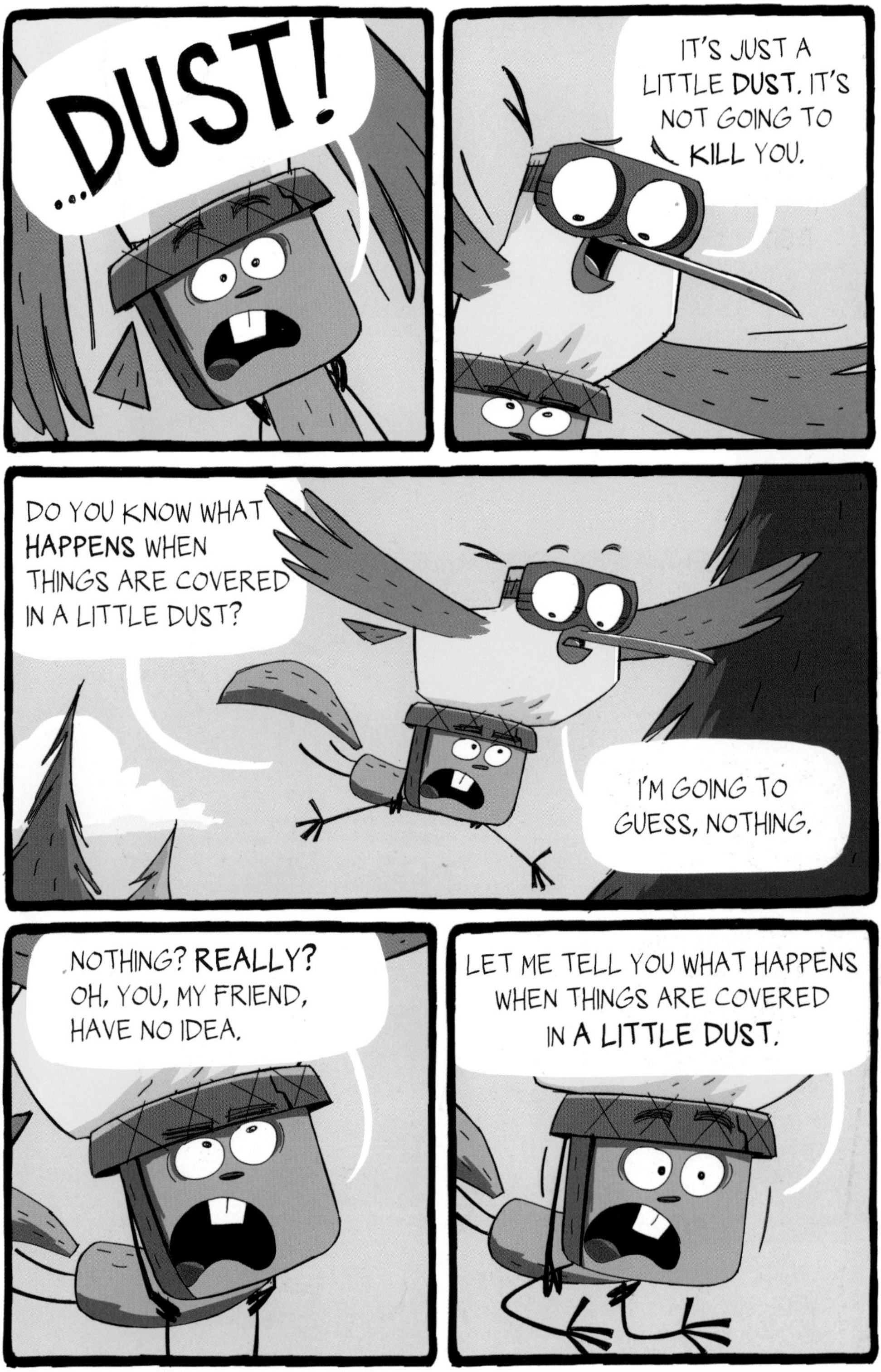
...DUST!
IT'S JUST A LITTLE DUST. IT'S NOT GOING TO KILL YOU.
DO YOU KNOW WHAT HAPPENS WHEN THINGS ARE COVERED IN A LITTLE DUST?
I'M GOING TO GUESS, NOTHING.
NOTHING? REALLY? OH, YOU, MY FRIEND, HAVE NO IDEA.
LET ME TELL YOU WHAT HAPPENS WHEN THINGS ARE COVERED IN A LITTLE DUST.

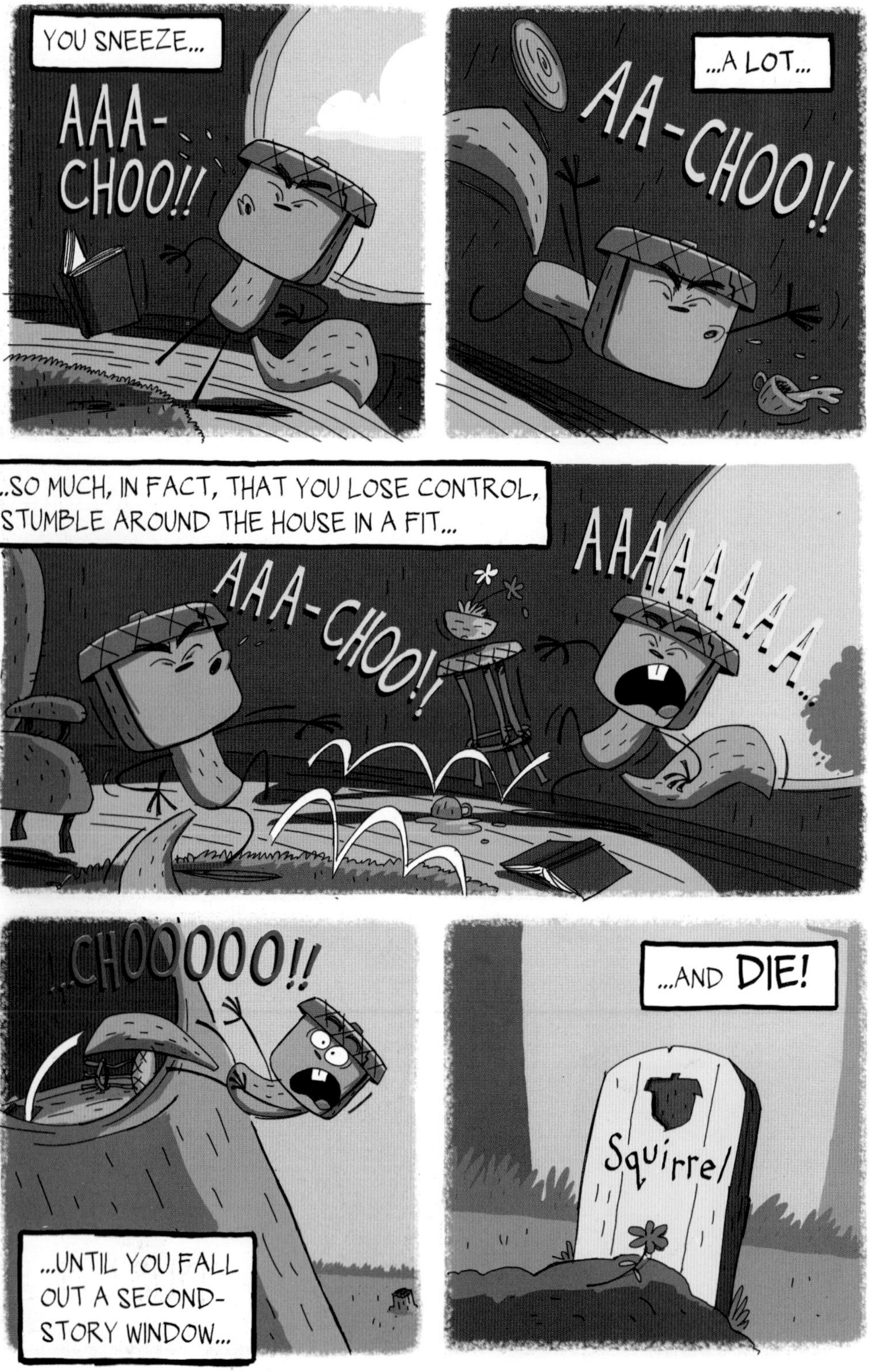
YOU SNEEZE...
AAA-CHOO!!
...A LOT...
AA-CHOO!!
...SO MUCH, IN FACT, THAT YOU LOSE CONTROL, STUMBLE AROUND THE HOUSE IN A FIT...
AAA-CHOO!!
AAAAAAAA...
...CHOOOOOO!!
...UNTIL YOU FALL OUT A SECOND-STORY WINDOW...
...AND DIE!
Squirrel

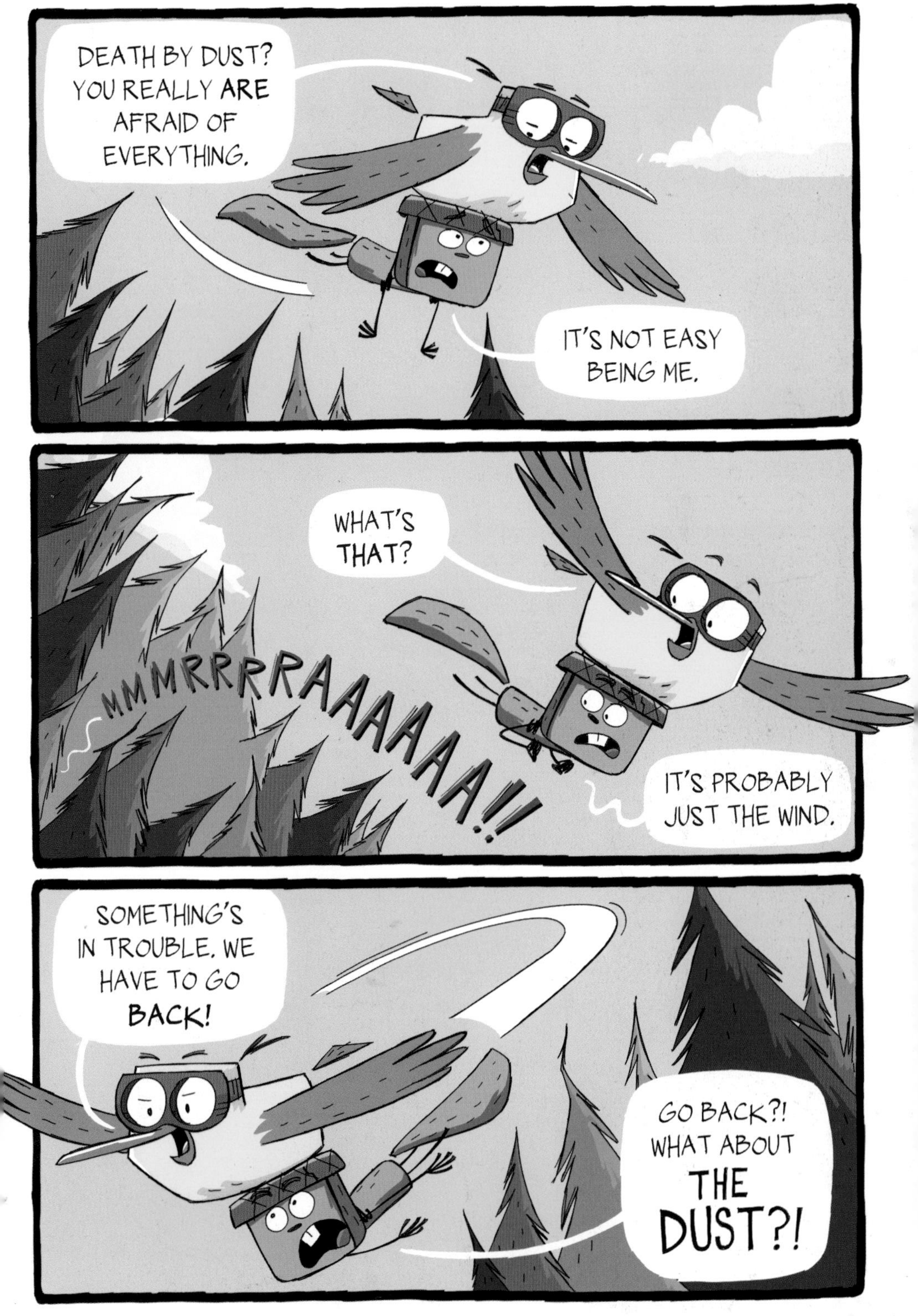
DEATH BY DUST? YOU REALLY ARE AFRAID OF EVERYTHING.
IT'S NOT EASY BEING ME.
WHAT'S THAT?
MMMRRRRRAAAAAAAA!!
IT'S PROBABLY JUST THE WIND.
SOMETHING'S IN TROUBLE. WE HAVE TO GO BACK!
GO BACK?! WHAT ABOUT THE DUST?!

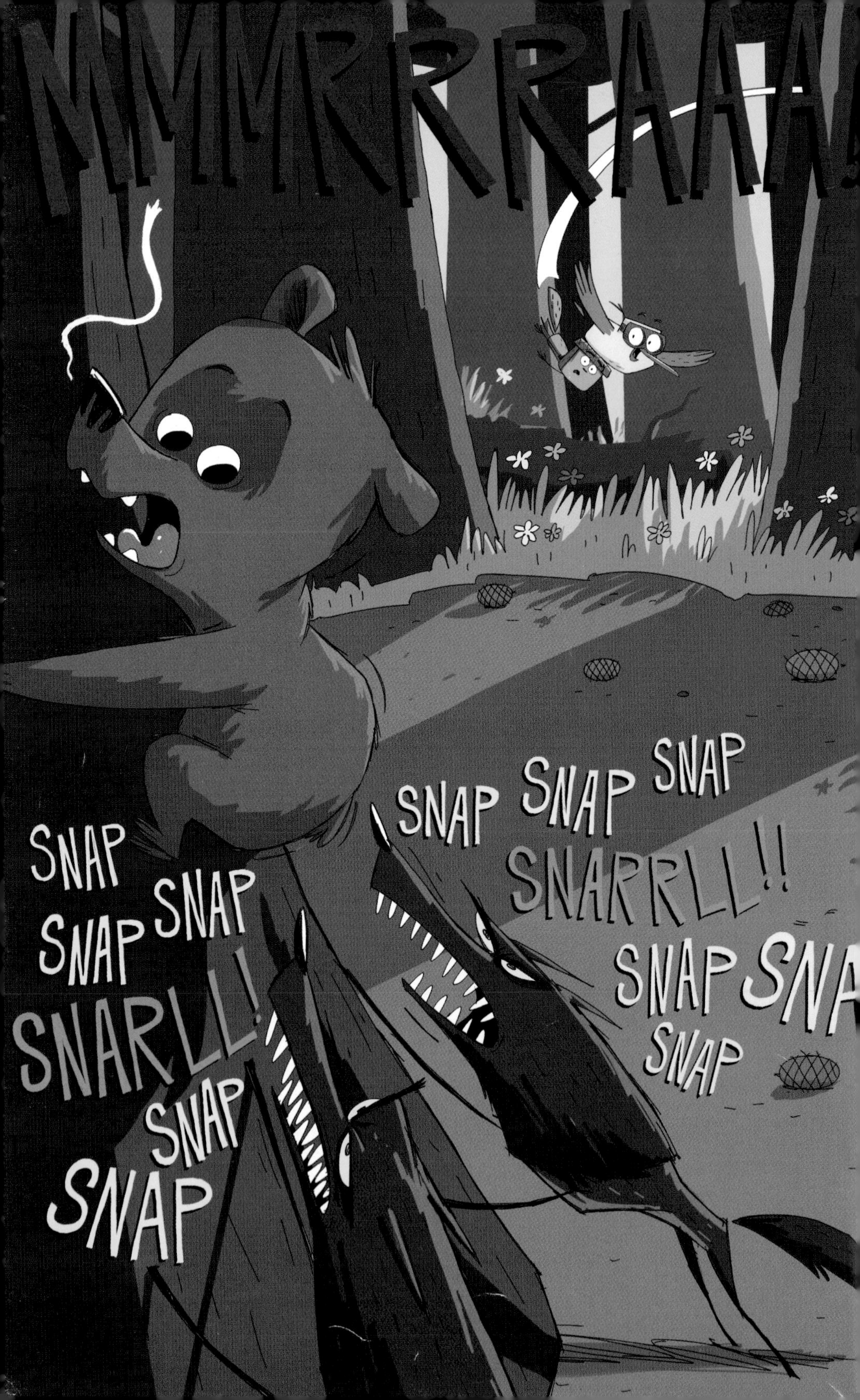
MMMRRRAAA!
SNAP
SNAP SNAP
SNARLL!
SNAP
SNAP
SNAP SNAP SNAP
SNARRLL!!
SNAP SNA
SNAP

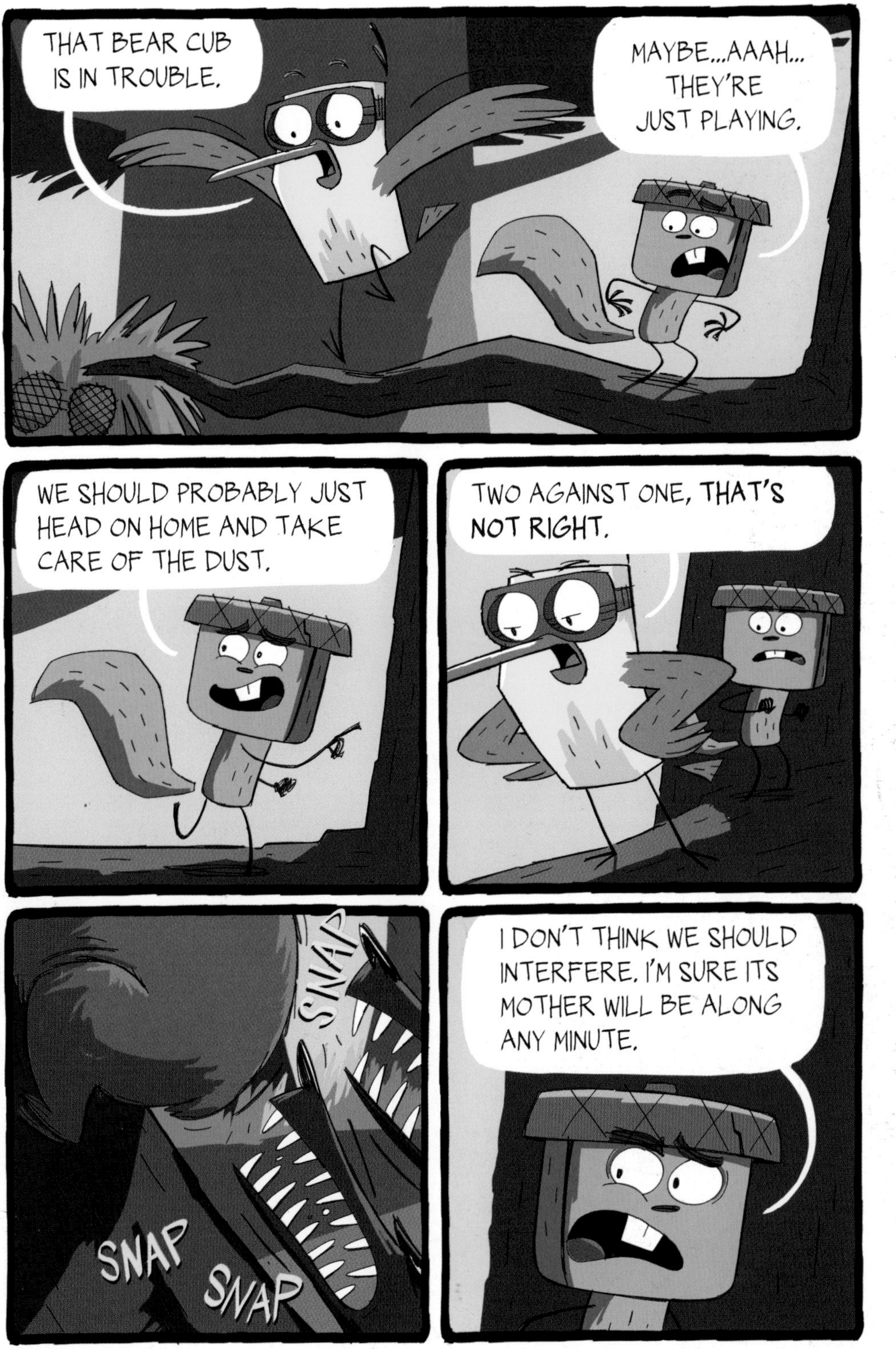
THAT BEAR CUB IS IN TROUBLE.
MAYBE...AAAH... THEY'RE JUST PLAYING.
WE SHOULD PROBABLY JUST HEAD ON HOME AND TAKE CARE OF THE DUST.
TWO AGAINST ONE, THAT'S NOT RIGHT.
SNAP
SNAP
SNAP
I DON'T THINK WE SHOULD INTERFERE. I'M SURE ITS MOTHER WILL BE ALONG ANY MINUTE.

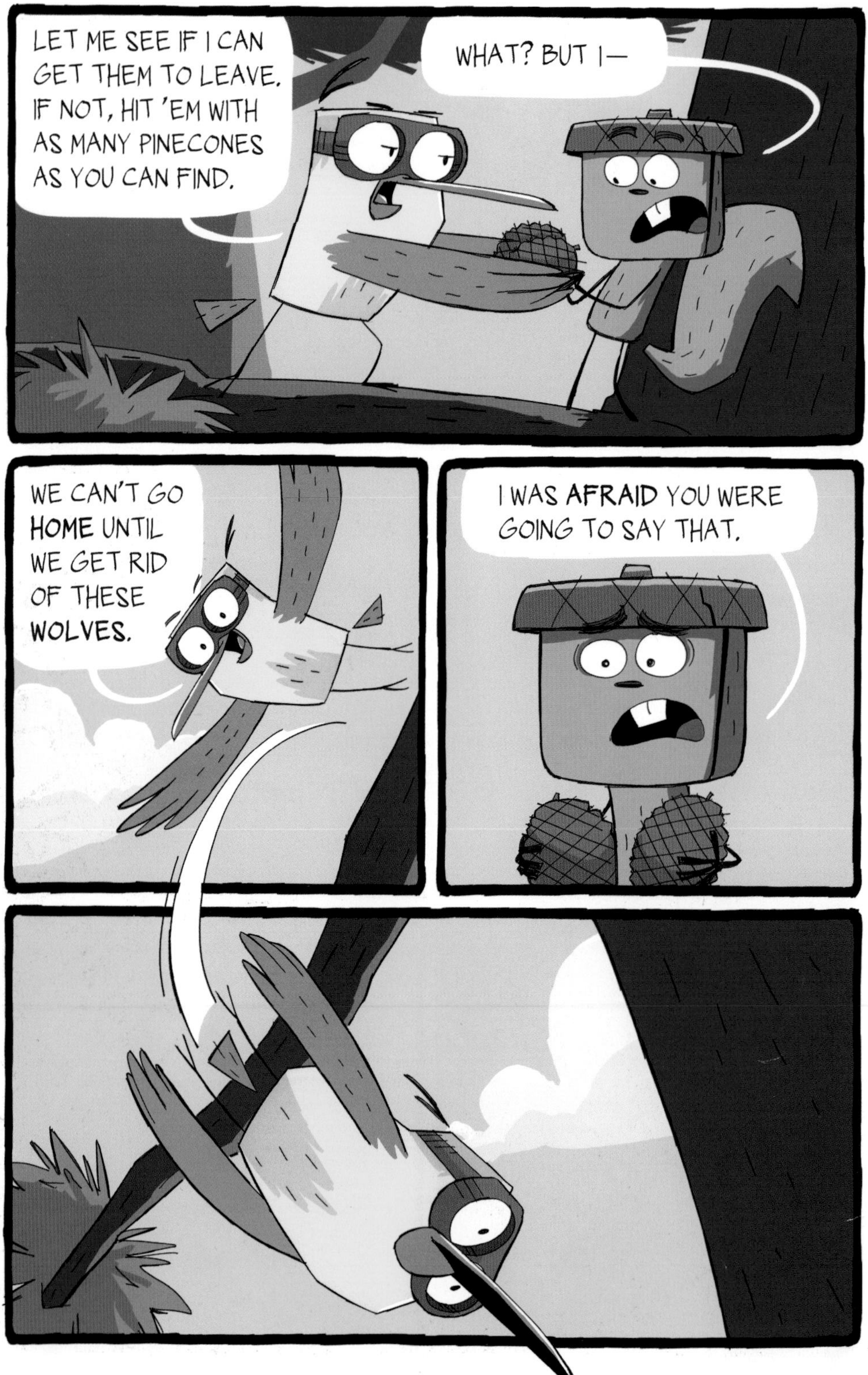
LET ME SEE IF I CAN GET THEM TO LEAVE. IF NOT, HIT 'EM WITH AS MANY PINECONES AS YOU CAN FIND.
WHAT? BUT I—
WE CAN'T GO **HOME** UNTIL WE GET RID OF THESE **WOLVES.**
I WAS **AFRAID** YOU WERE GOING TO SAY THAT.

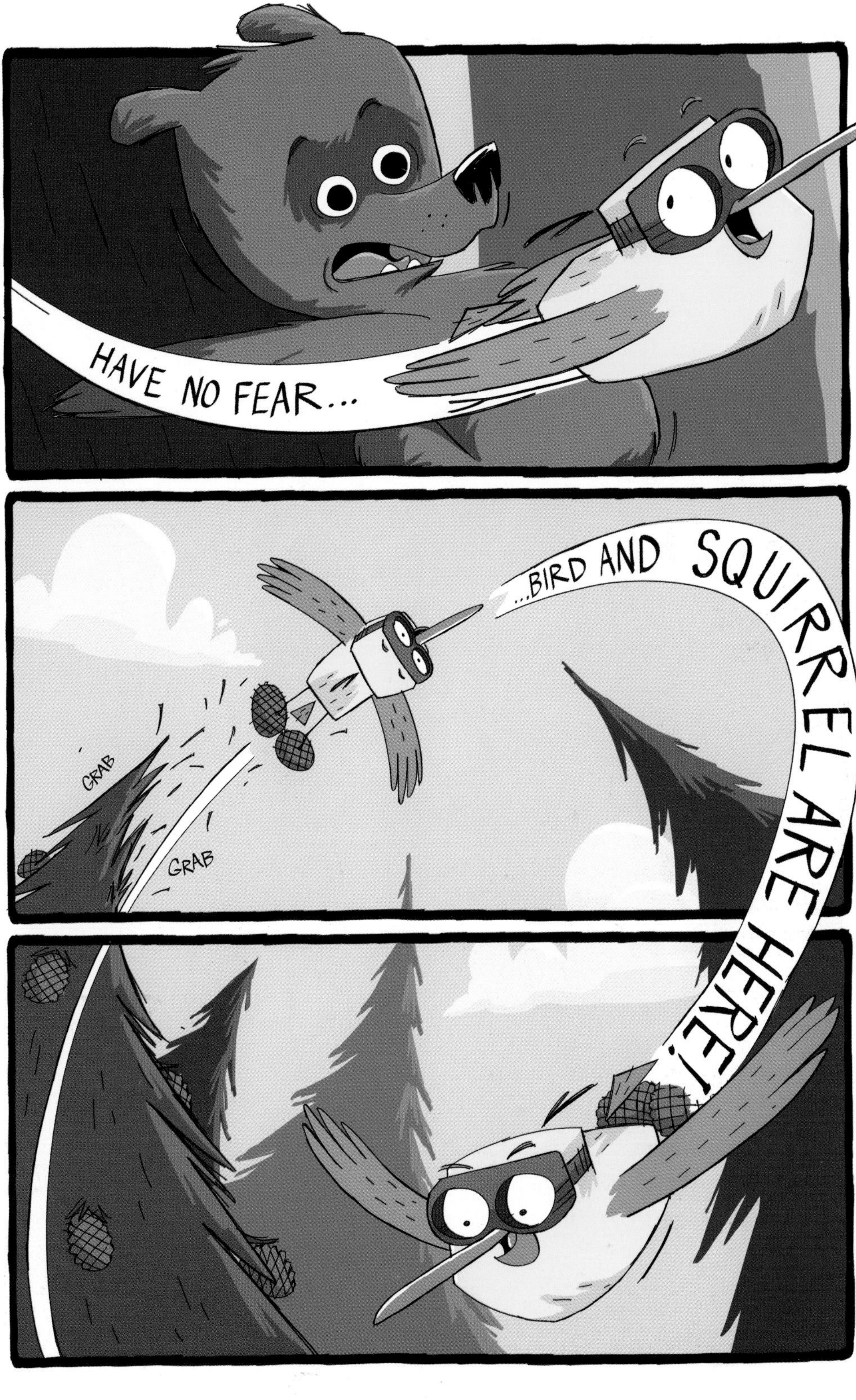
HAVE NO FEAR...
...BIRD AND SQUIRREL ARE HERE!
GRAB
GRAB

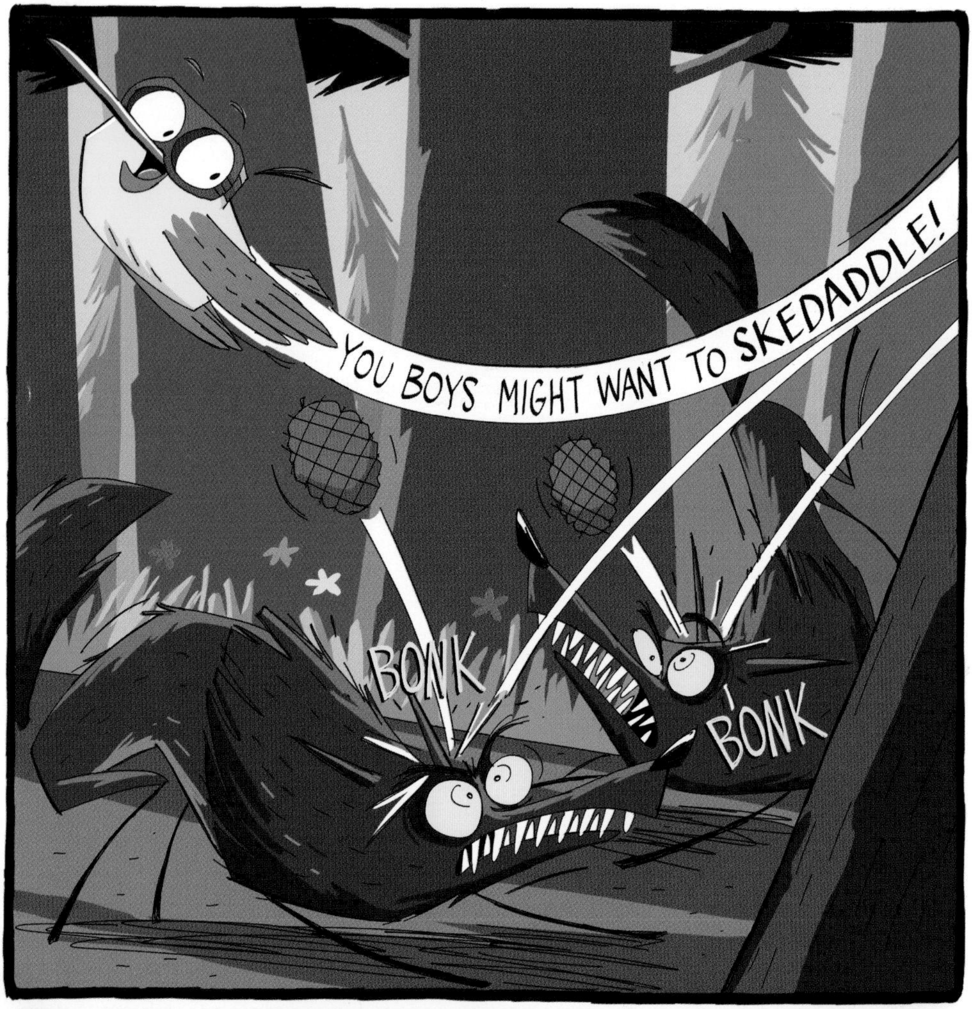
YOU BOYS MIGHT WANT TO SKEDADDLE!
BONK
BONK

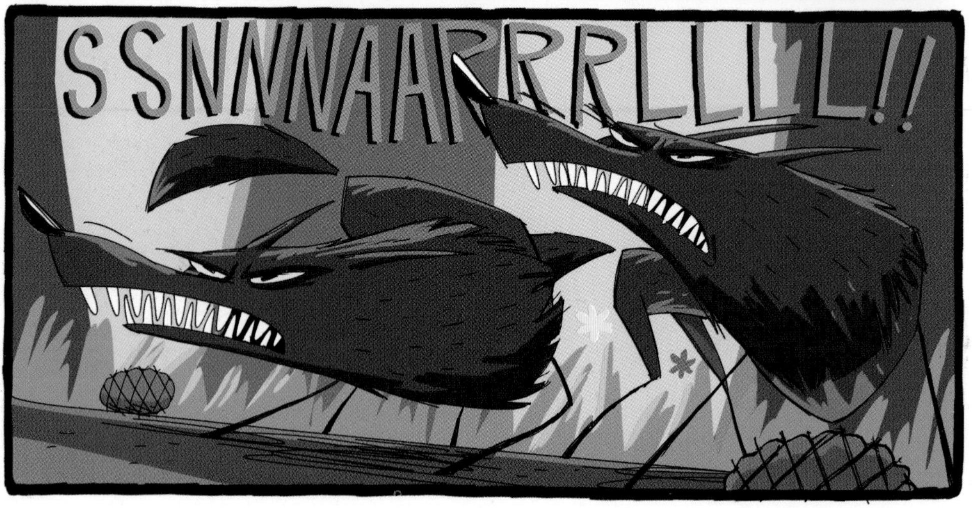
SSNNNAARRRLLLLL!!

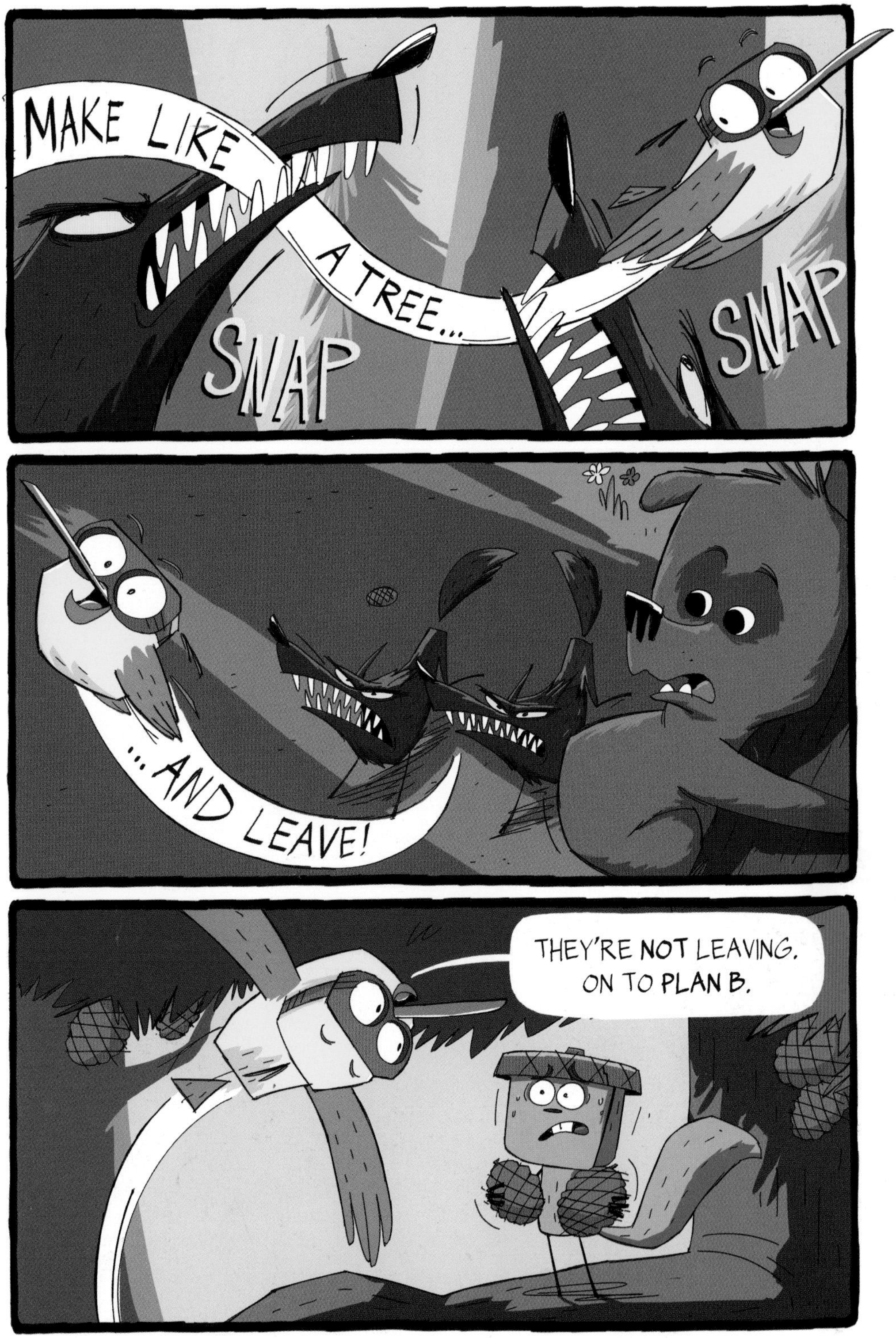
MAKE LIKE A TREE...
SNAP
SNAP
...AND LEAVE!
THEY'RE NOT LEAVING. ON TO PLAN B.

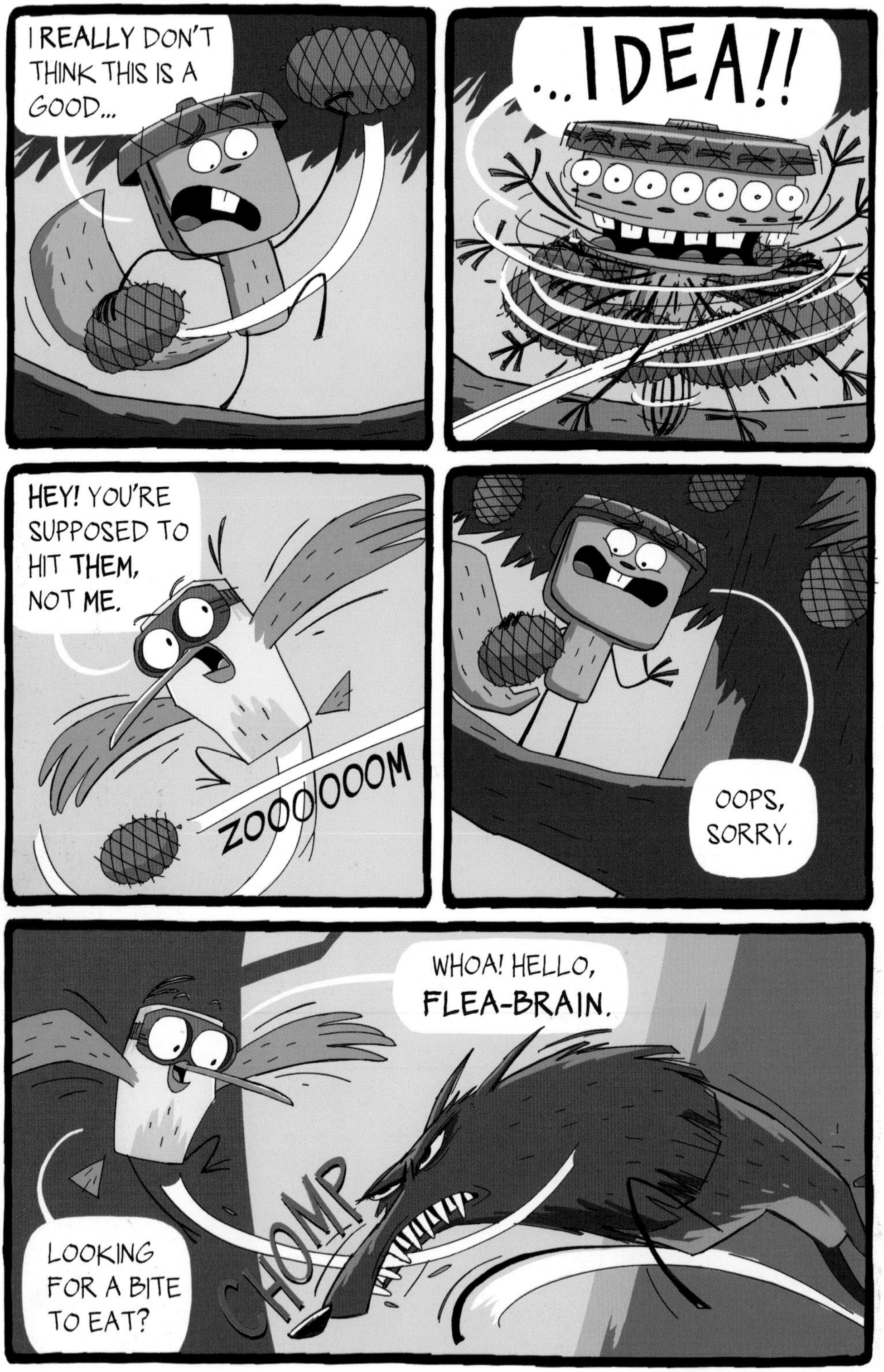
I REALLY DON'T THINK THIS IS A GOOD...
...IDEA!!
HEY! YOU'RE SUPPOSED TO HIT THEM, NOT ME.
ZOOOOOOM
OOPS, SORRY.
WHOA! HELLO, FLEA-BRAIN.
LOOKING FOR A BITE TO EAT?
CHOMP

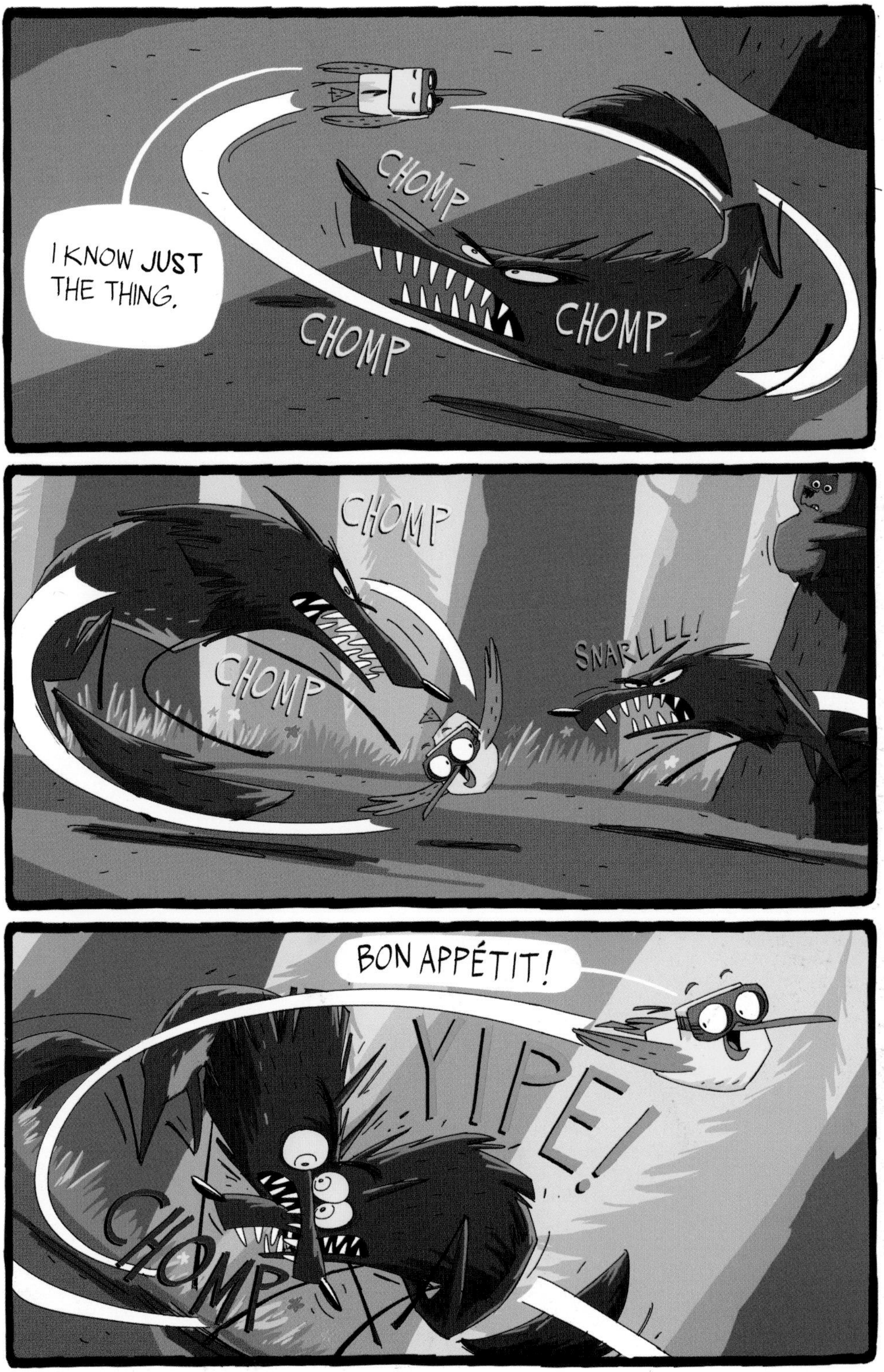
I KNOW JUST THE THING.
CHOMP
CHOMP
CHOMP
CHOMP
CHOMP
SNARLLLL!
BON APPÉTIT!
YIPE!
CHOMP

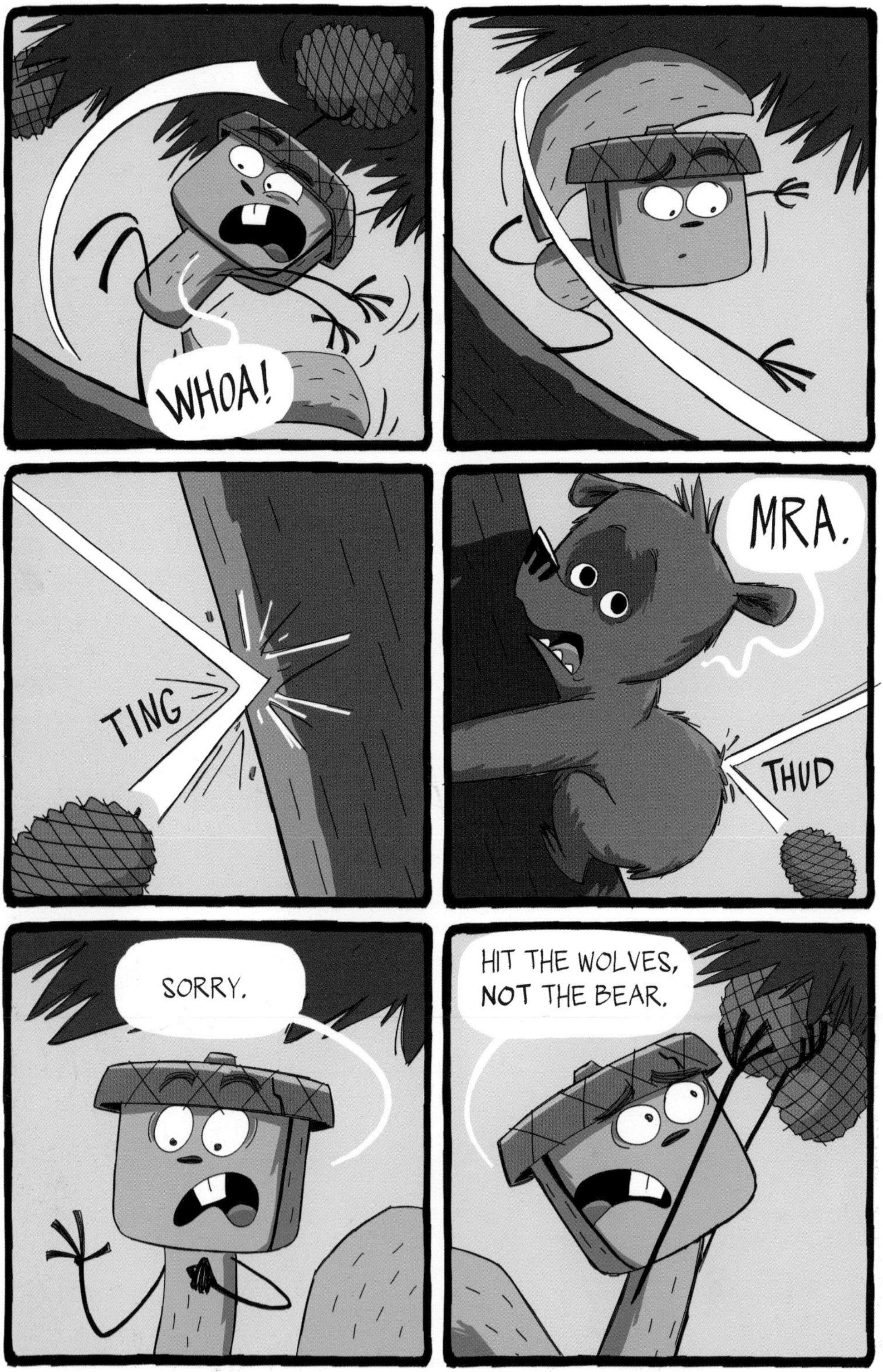
WHOA!
TING
MRA.
THUD
SORRY.
HIT THE WOLVES,
NOT THE BEAR.

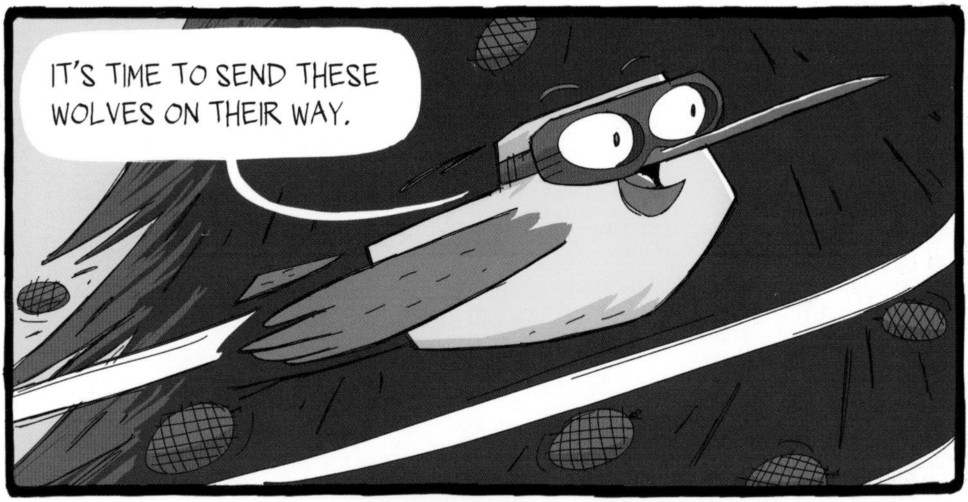
IT'S TIME TO SEND THESE WOLVES ON THEIR WAY.

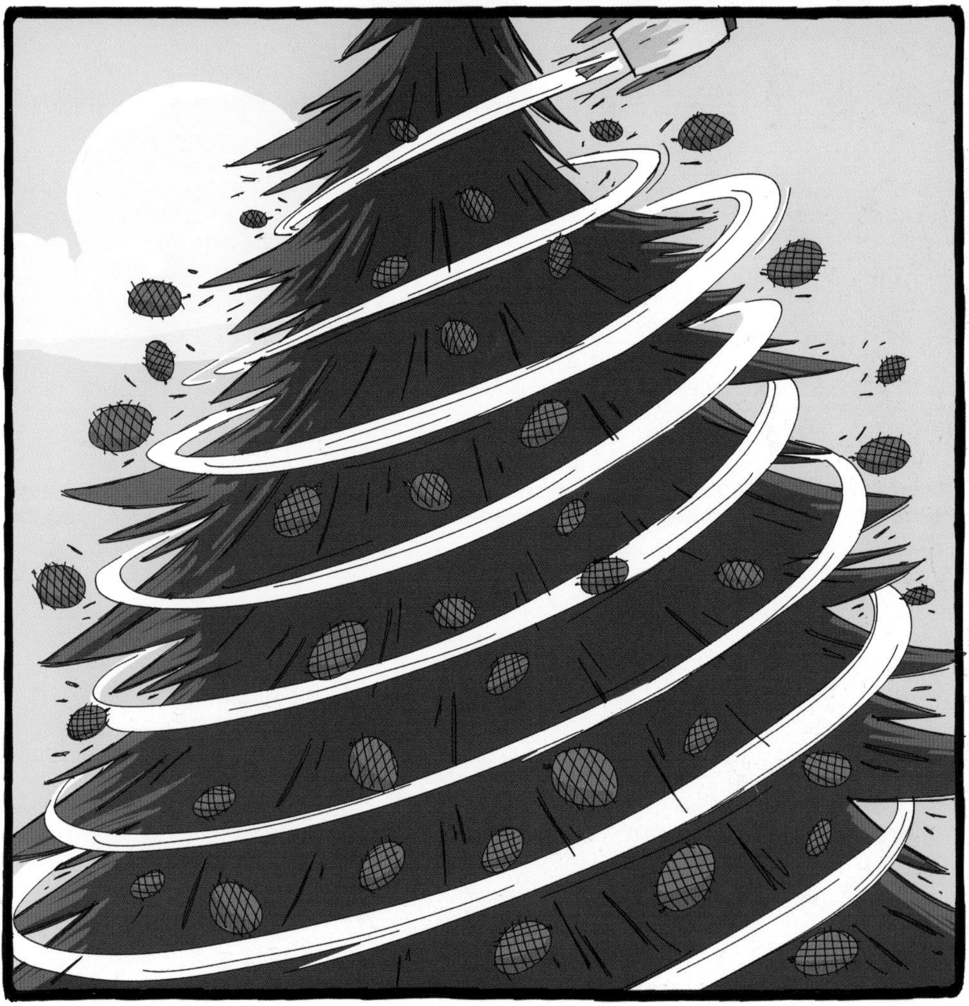

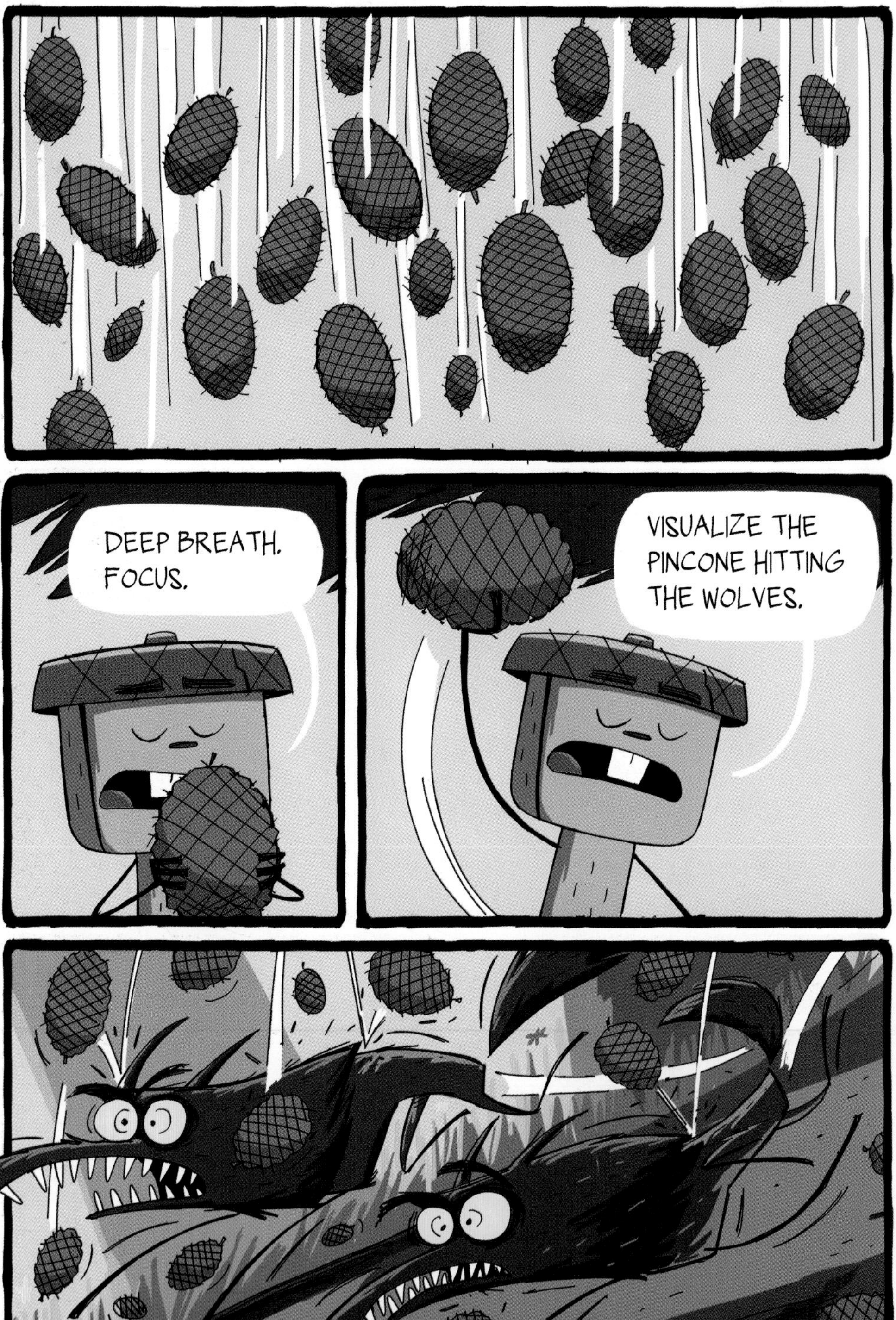
DEEP BREATH. FOCUS.
VISUALIZE THE PINCONE HITTING THE WOLVES.

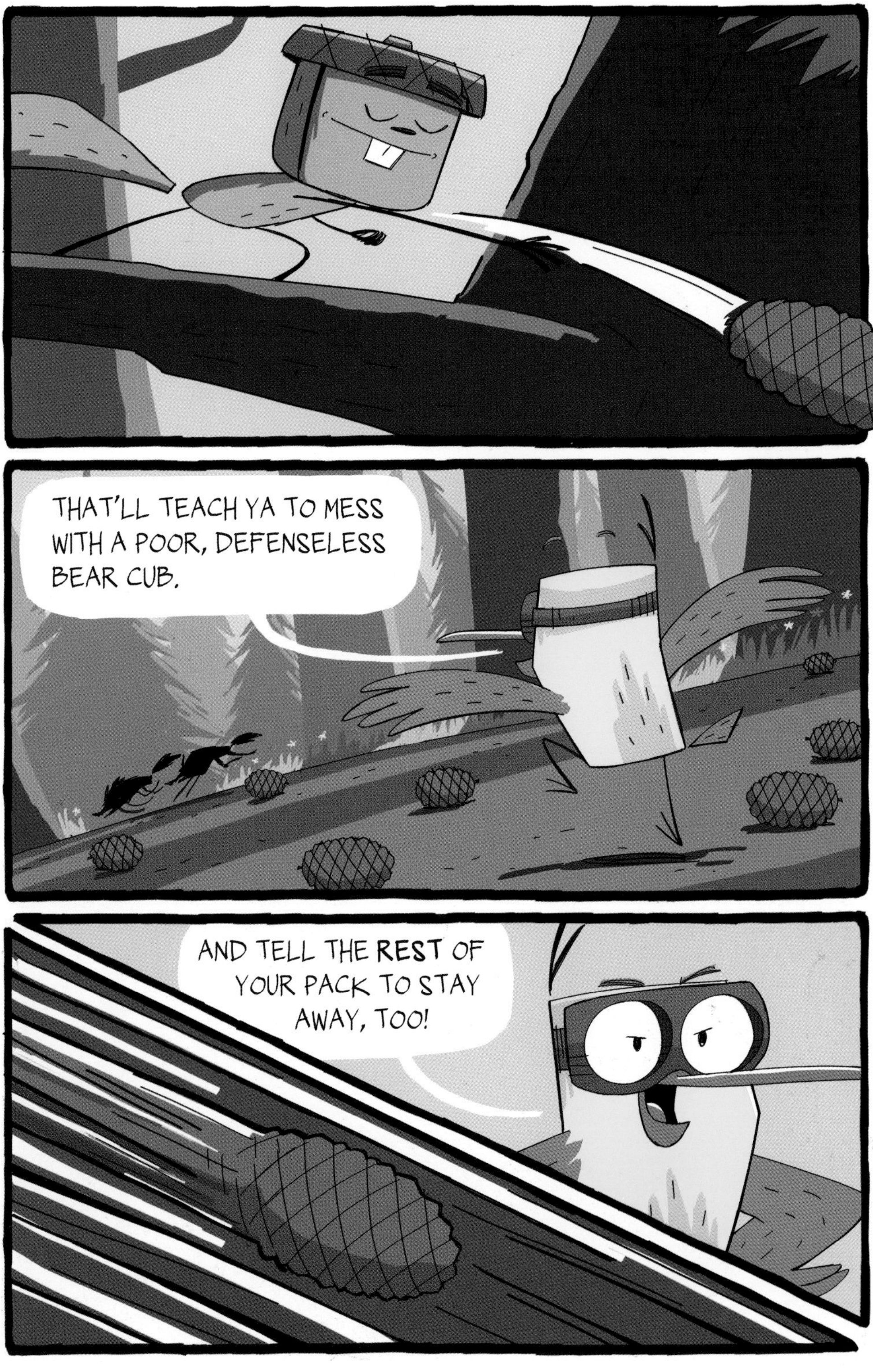
THAT'LL TEACH YA TO MESS WITH A POOR, DEFENSELESS BEAR CUB.
AND TELL THE **REST** OF YOUR PACK TO STAY AWAY, TOO!

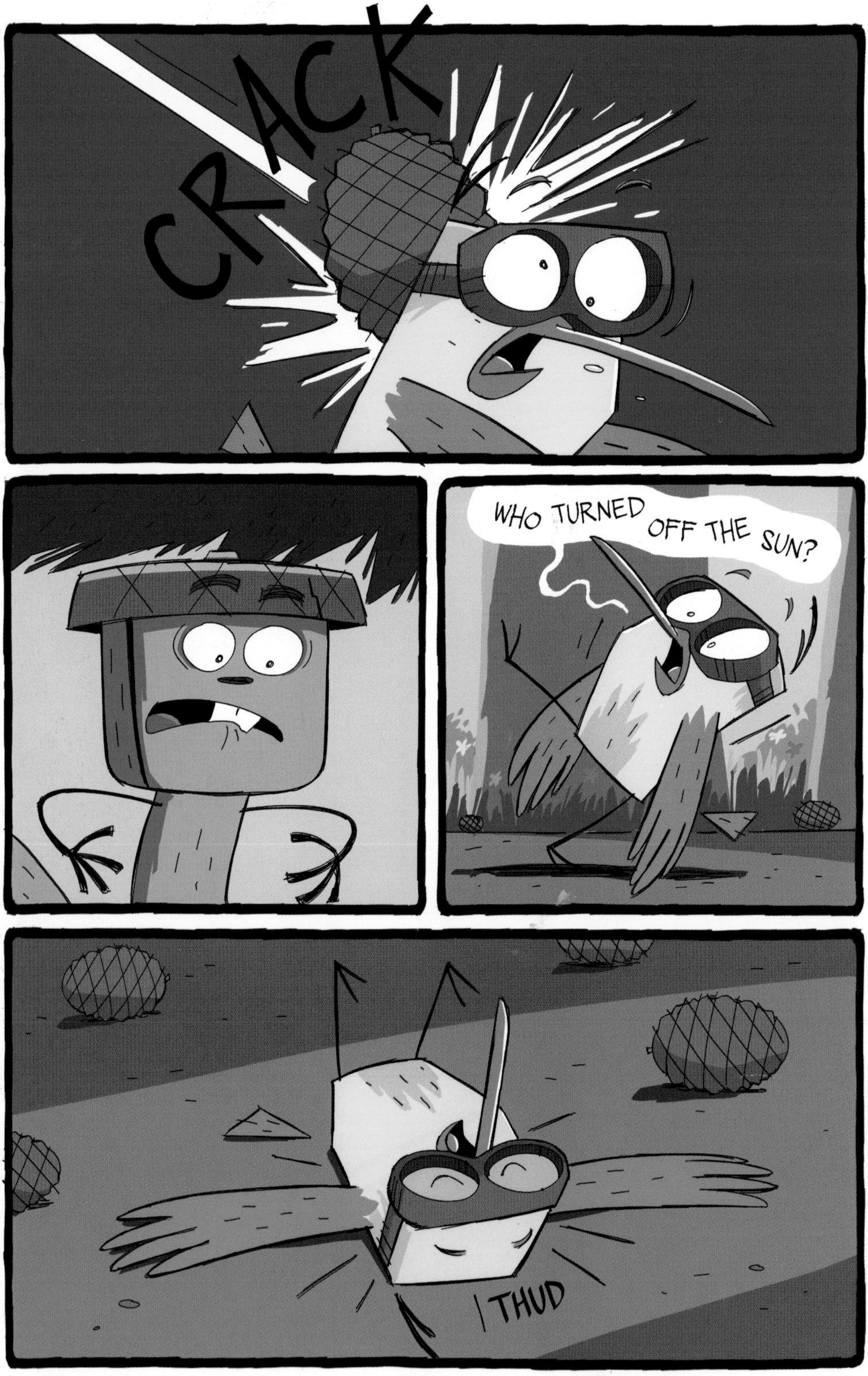
CRACK
WHO TURNED OFF THE SUN?
THUD

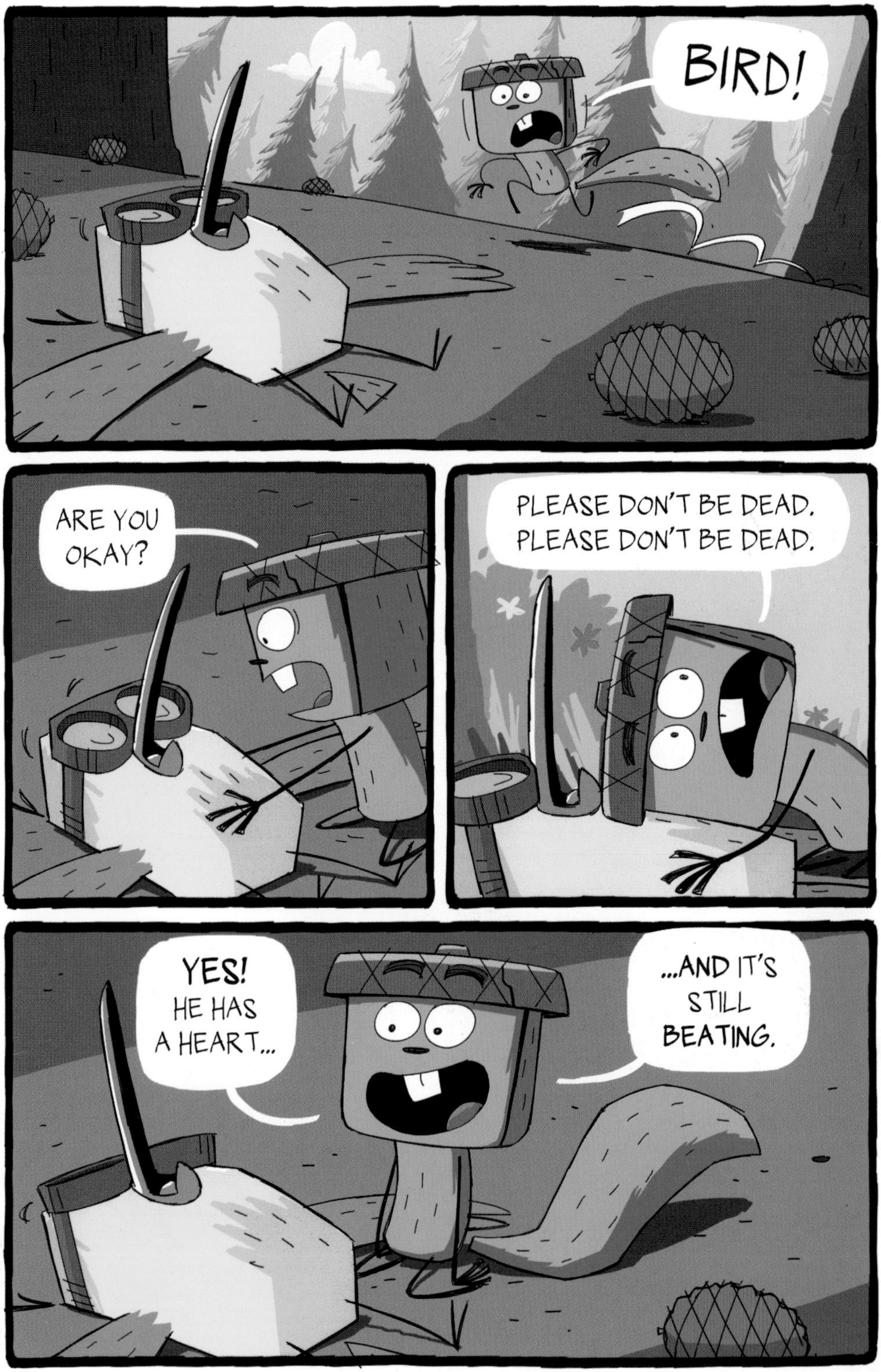
BIRD!
ARE YOU OKAY?
PLEASE DON'T BE DEAD. PLEASE DON'T BE DEAD.
YES! HE HAS A HEART...
...AND IT'S STILL BEATING.

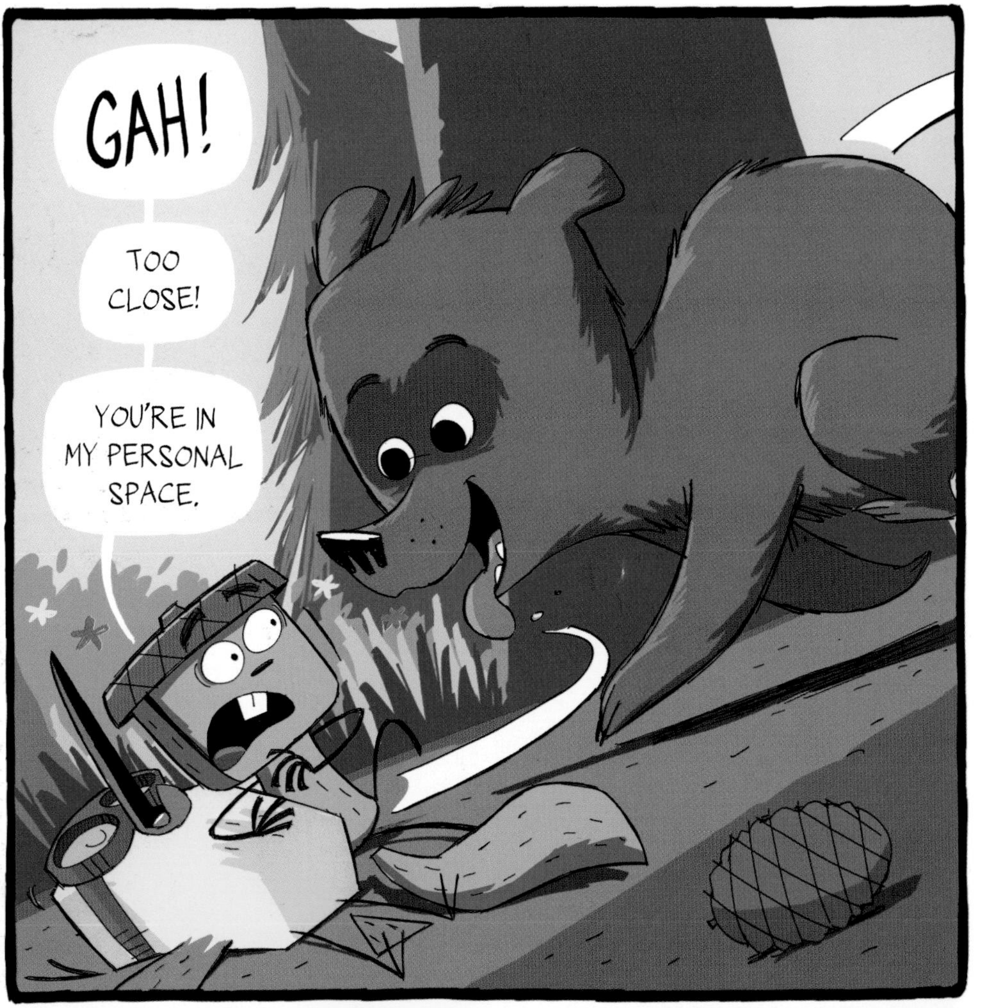
GAH!
TOO CLOSE!
YOU'RE IN MY PERSONAL SPACE.

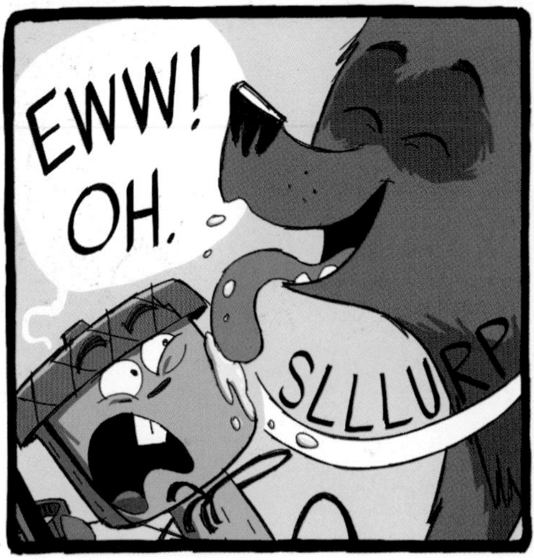
EWW! OH.
SLLLURP

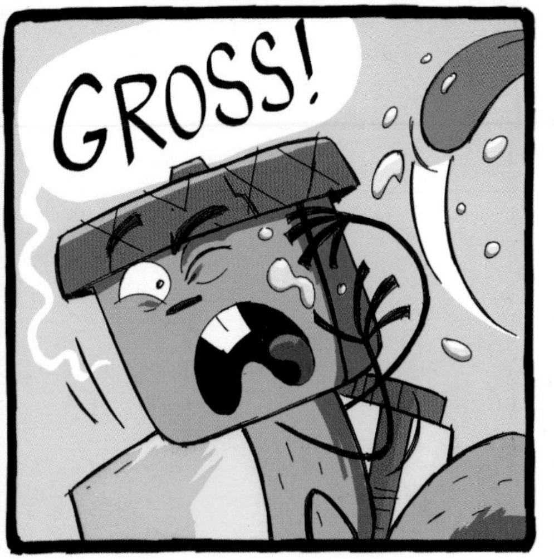
GROSS!

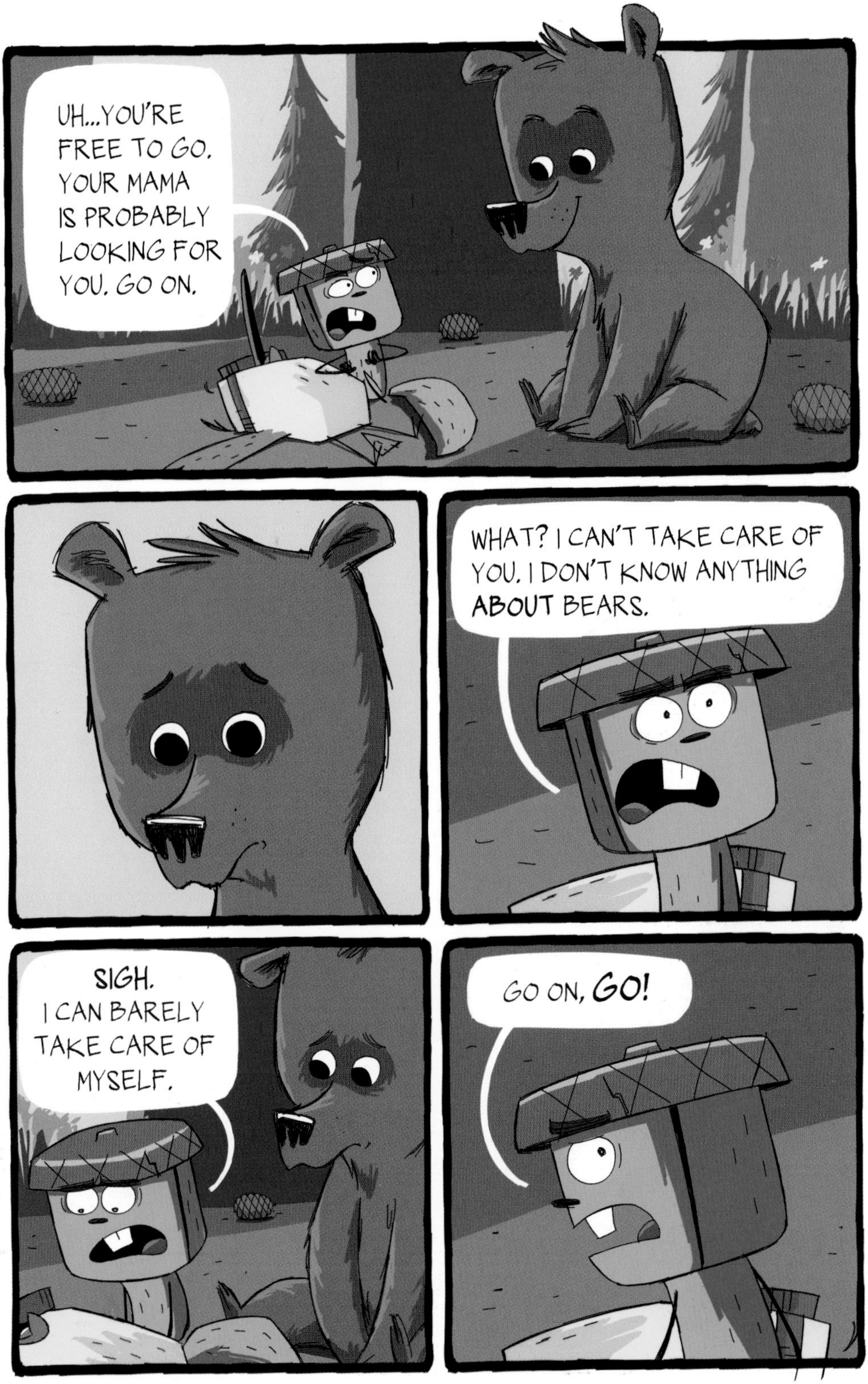

UH...YOU'RE FREE TO GO. YOUR MAMA IS PROBABLY LOOKING FOR YOU. GO ON.
WHAT? I CAN'T TAKE CARE OF YOU. I DON'T KNOW ANYTHING ABOUT BEARS.
SIGH. I CAN BARELY TAKE CARE OF MYSELF.
GO ON, GO!

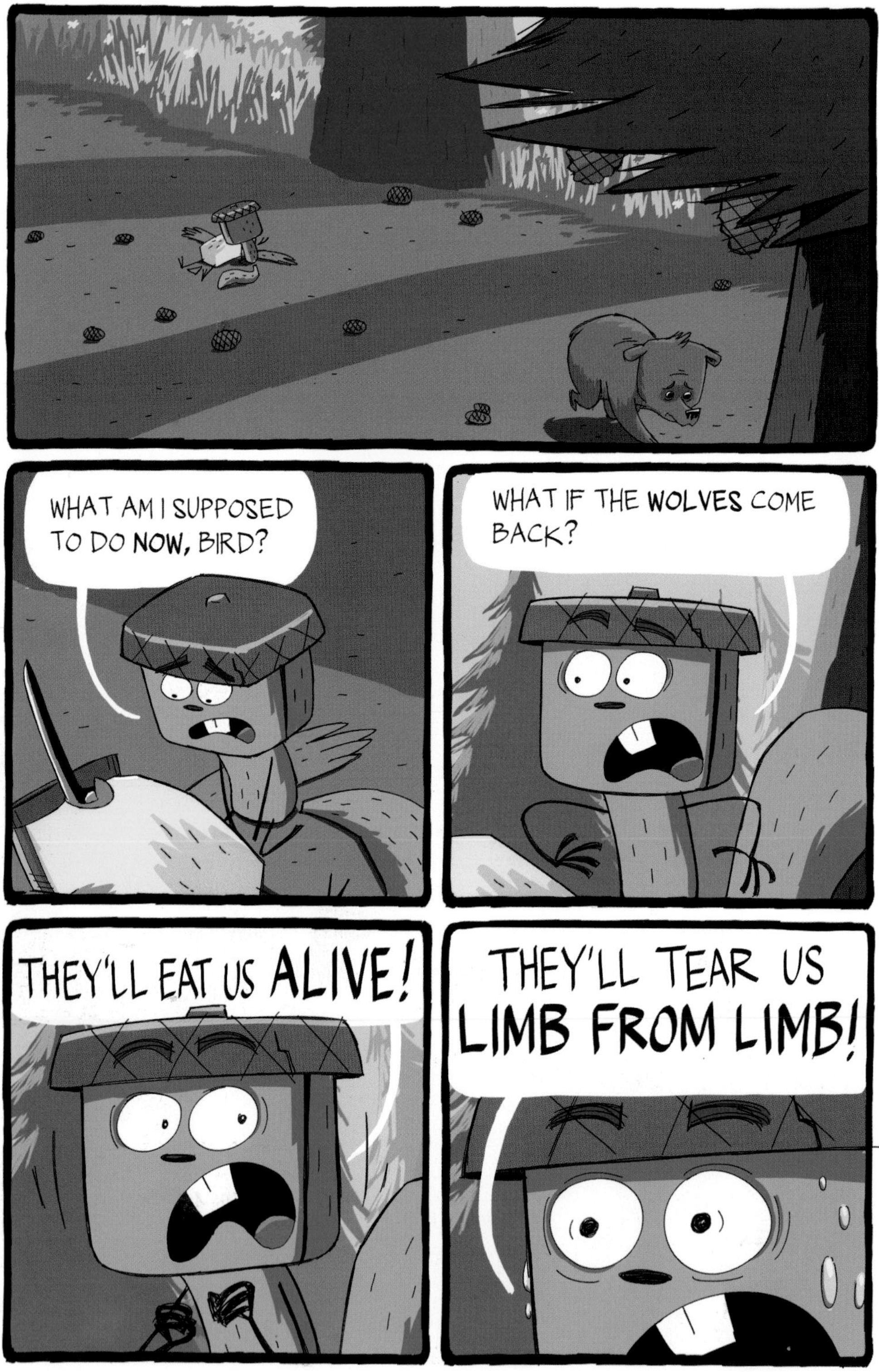
WHAT AM I SUPPOSED TO DO NOW, BIRD?
WHAT IF THE WOLVES COME BACK?
THEY'LL EAT US ALIVE!
THEY'LL TEAR US LIMB FROM LIMB!

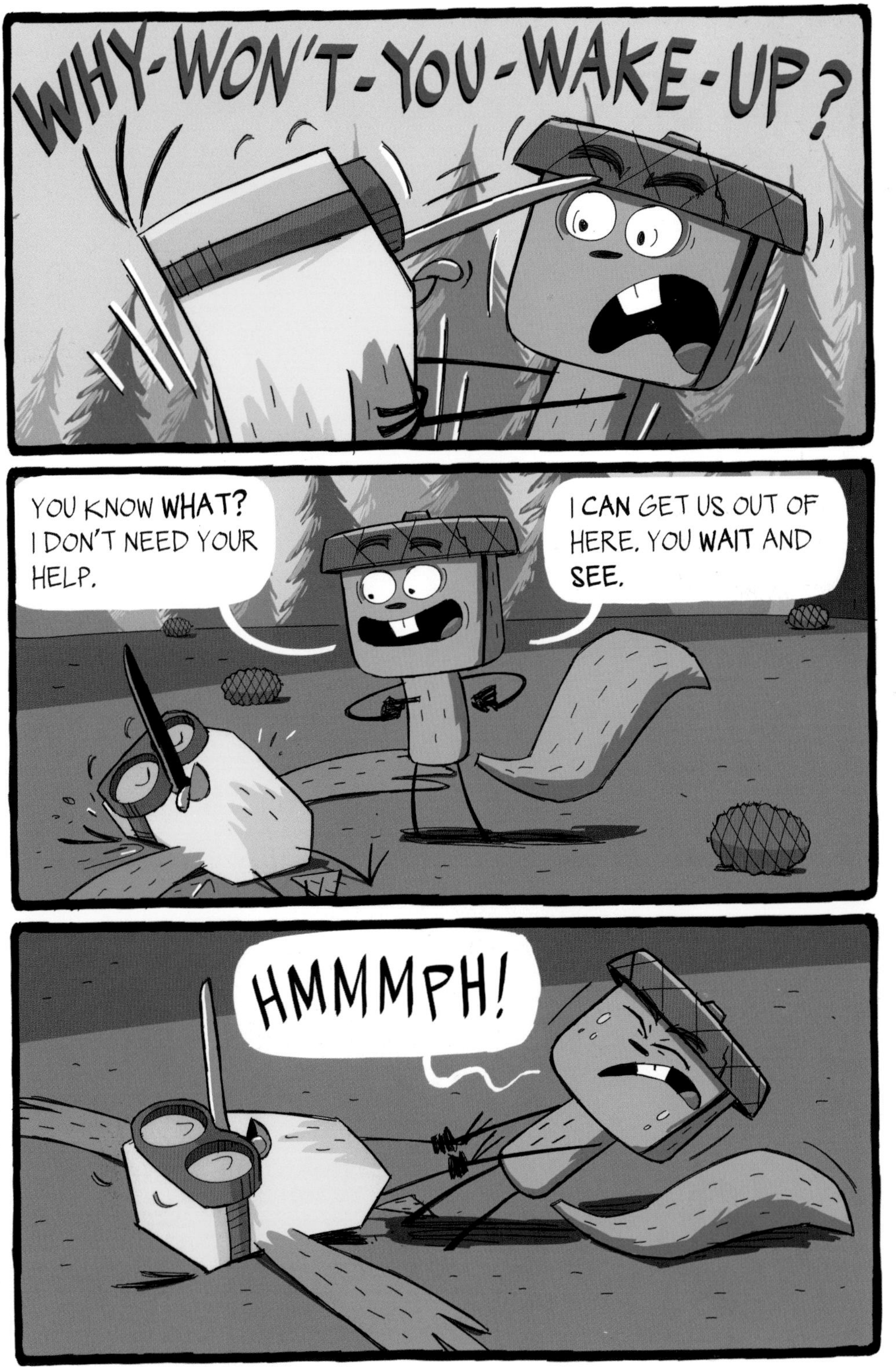
WHY-WON'T-YOU-WAKE-UP?
YOU KNOW WHAT? I DON'T NEED YOUR HELP.
I CAN GET US OUT OF HERE. YOU WAIT AND SEE.
HMMMPH!

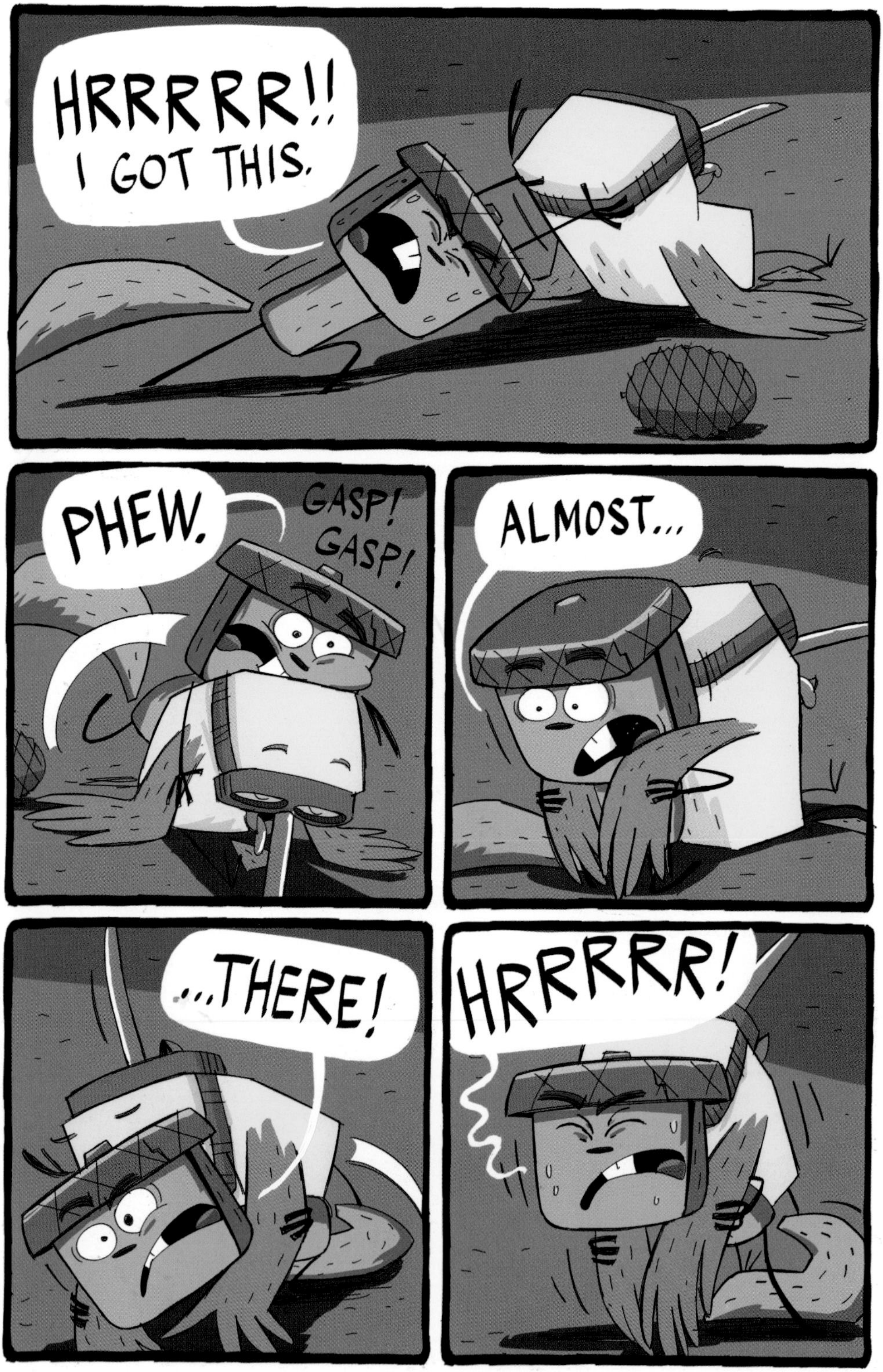
HRRRRR!!
I GOT THIS.
PHEW.
GASP! GASP!
ALMOST...
...THERE!
HRRRRR!

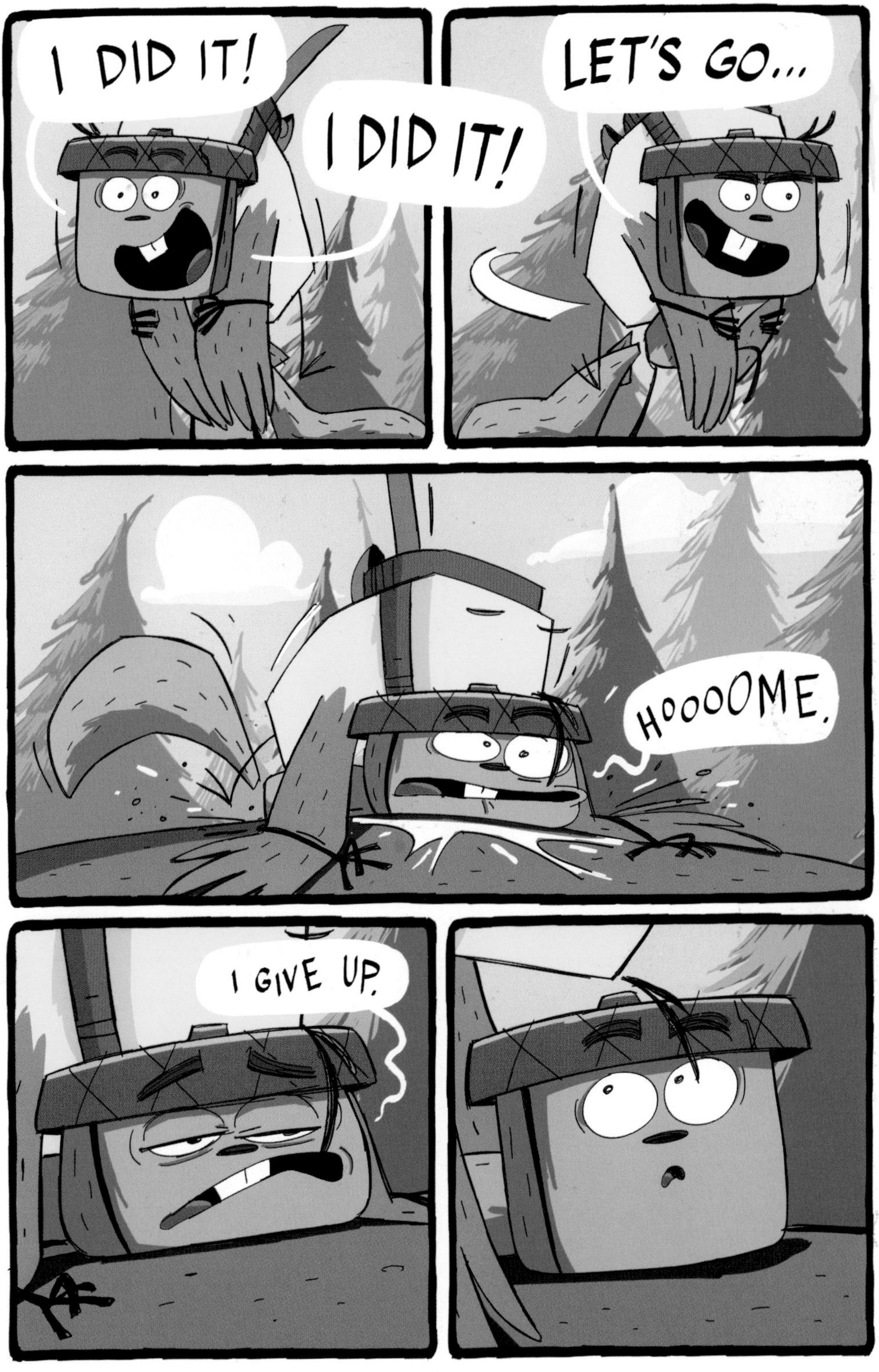
I DID IT!
I DID IT!
LET'S GO...
HOOOOME.
I GIVE UP.

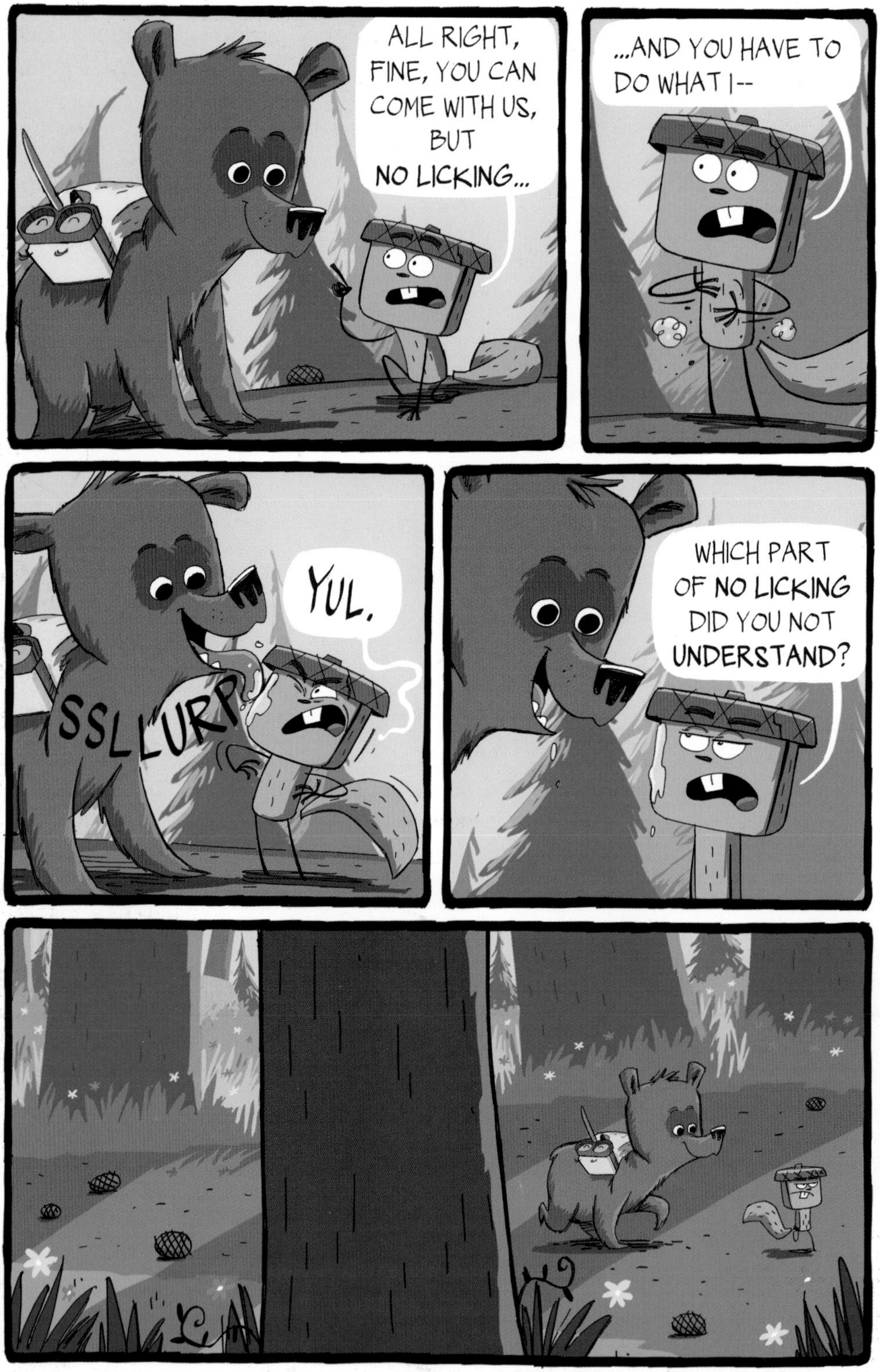
ALL RIGHT, FINE, YOU CAN COME WITH US, BUT NO LICKING...
...AND YOU HAVE TO DO WHAT I--
SSLLURP
YUL.
WHICH PART OF NO LICKING DID YOU NOT UNDERSTAND?

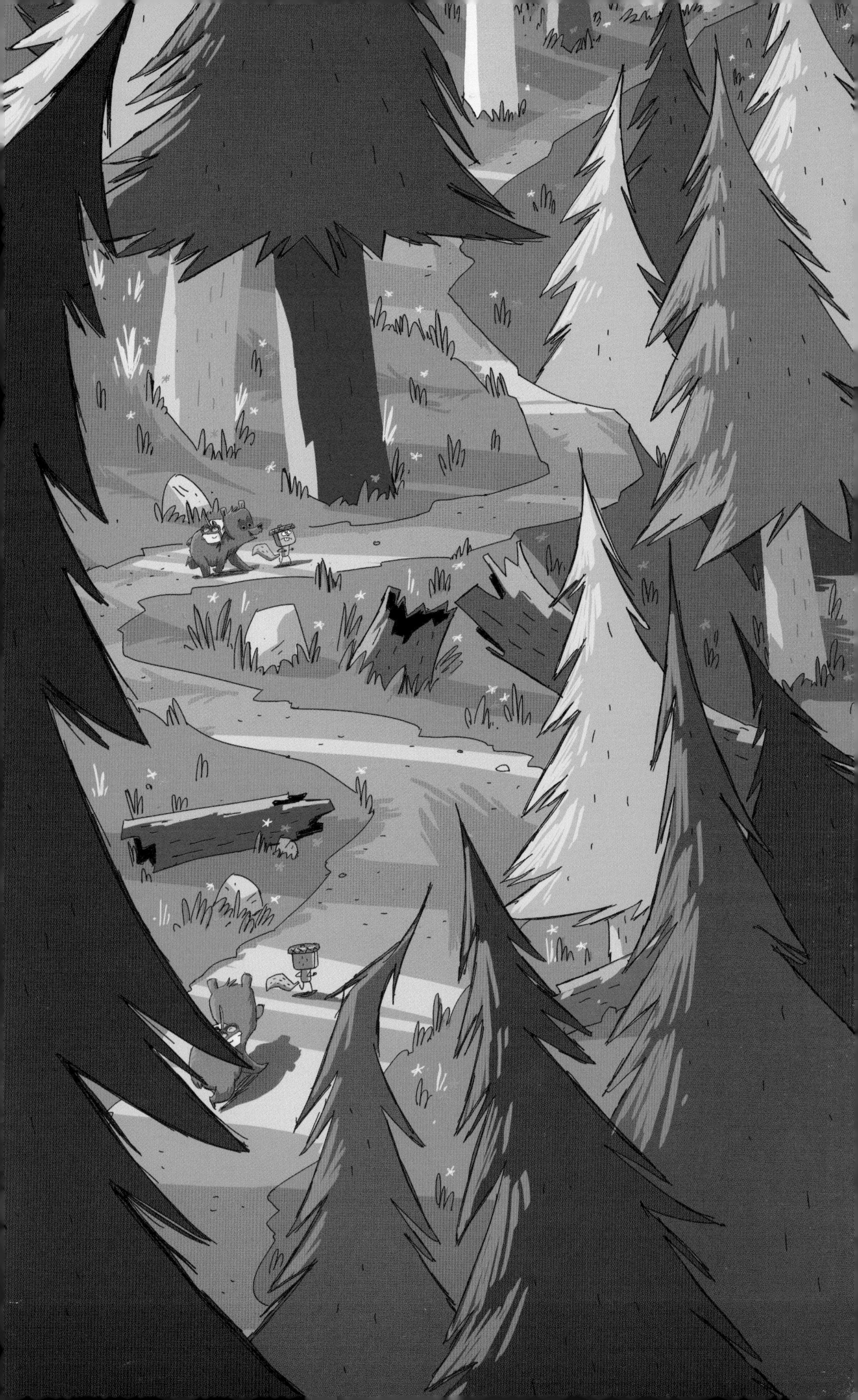

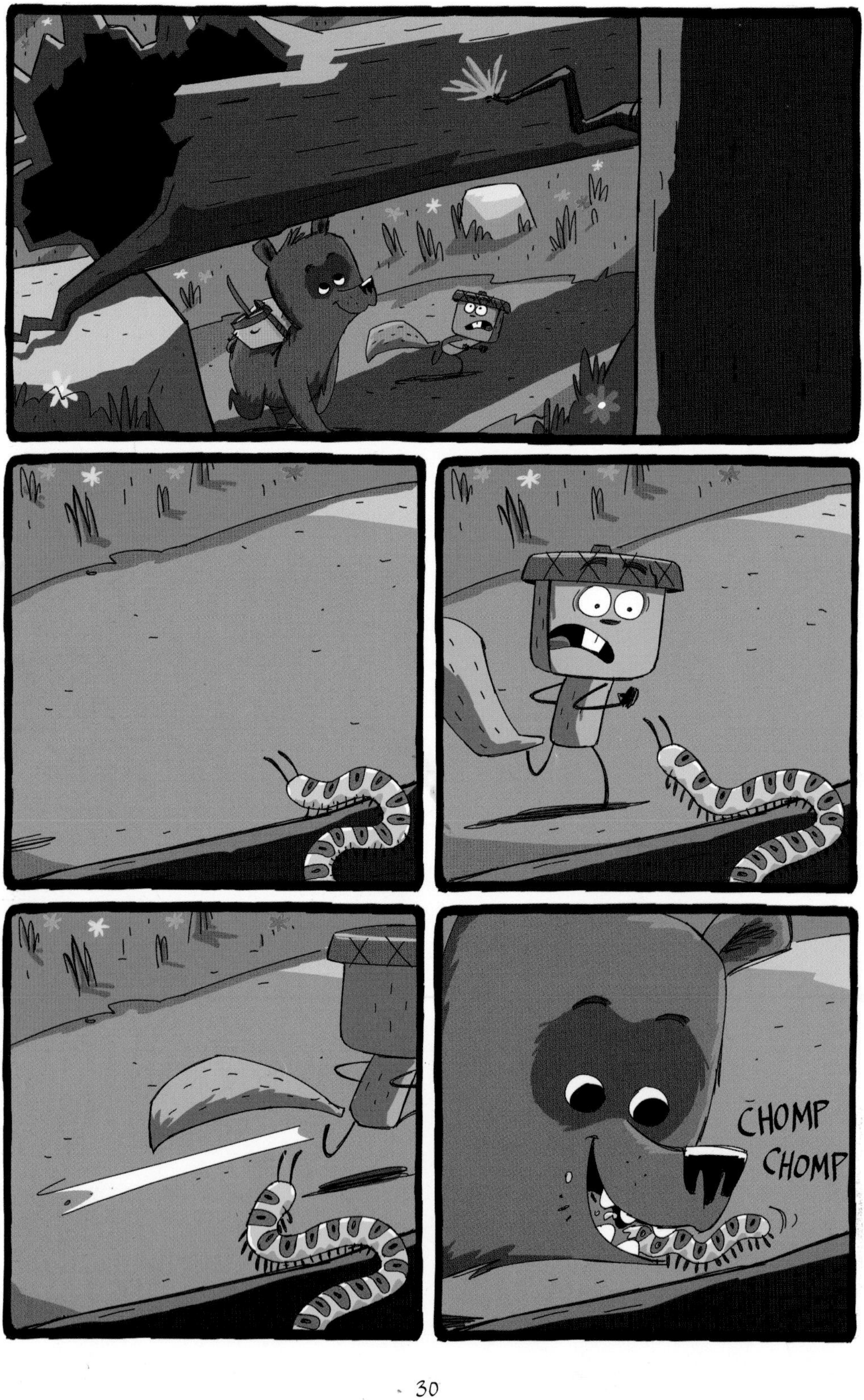
CHOMP
CHOMP

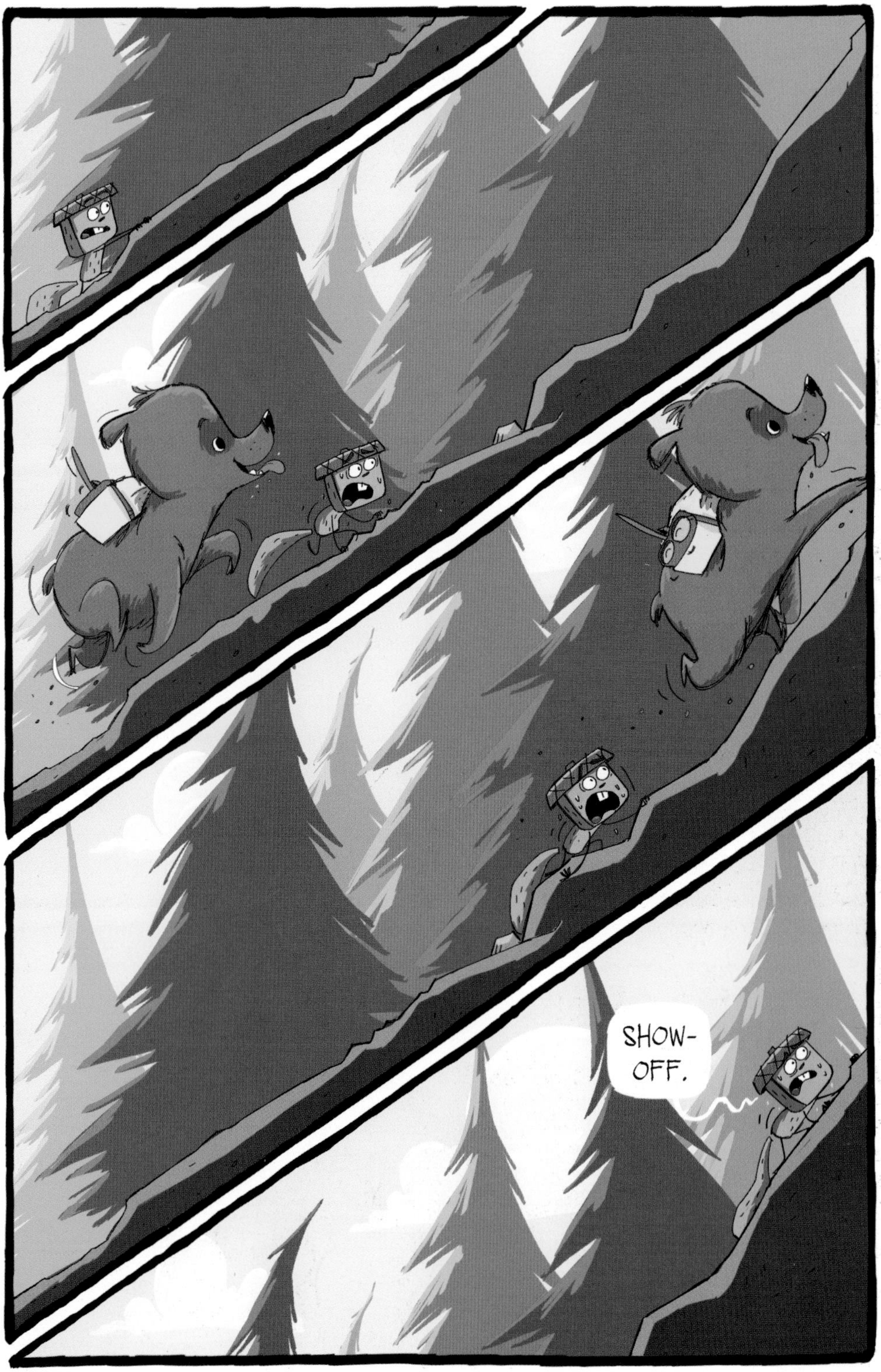
SHOW-
OFF.

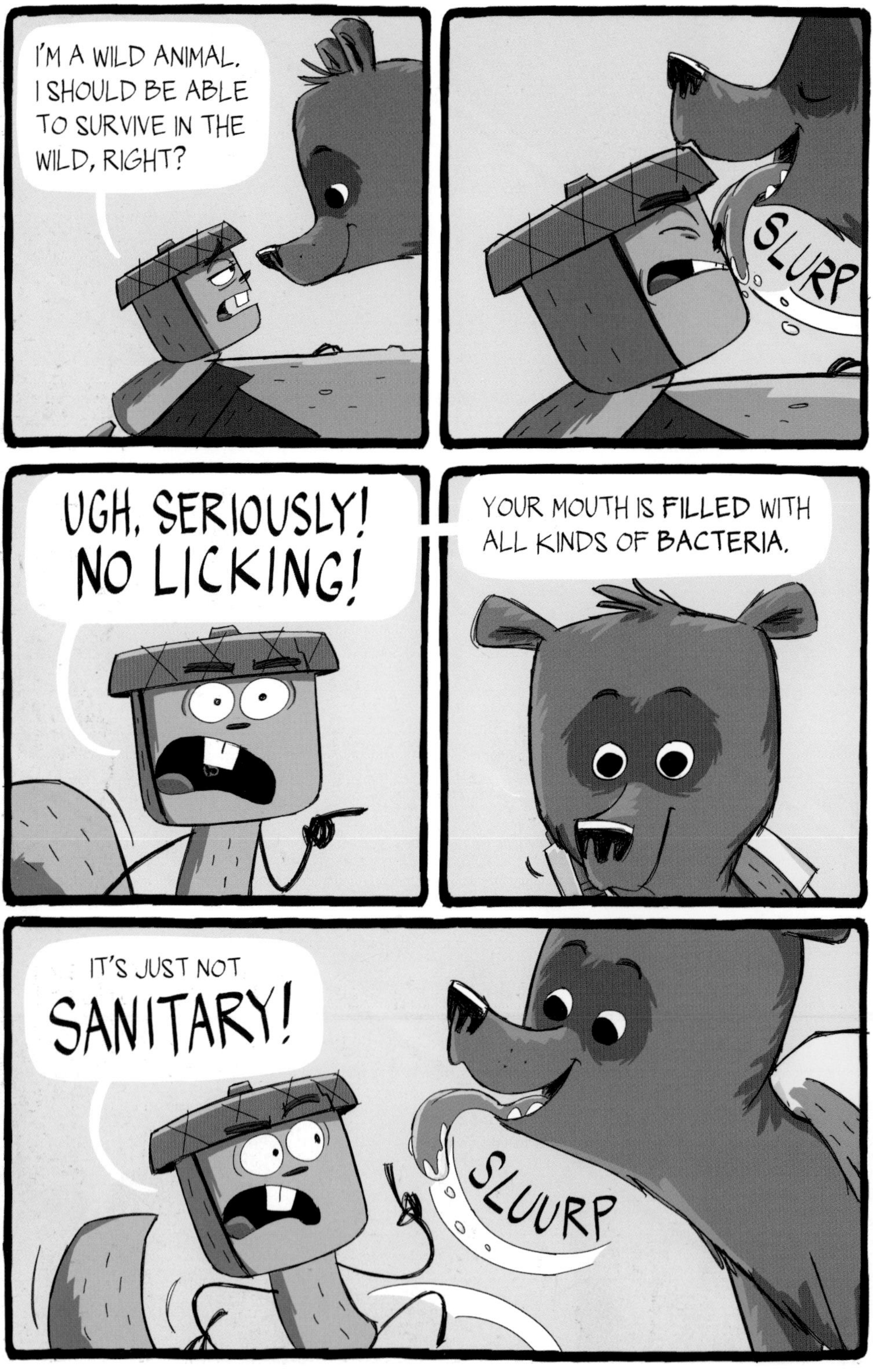
I'M A WILD ANIMAL. I SHOULD BE ABLE TO SURVIVE IN THE WILD, RIGHT?
SLURP
UGH, SERIOUSLY! NO LICKING!
YOUR MOUTH IS FILLED WITH ALL KINDS OF BACTERIA.
IT'S JUST NOT SANITARY!
SLUURP

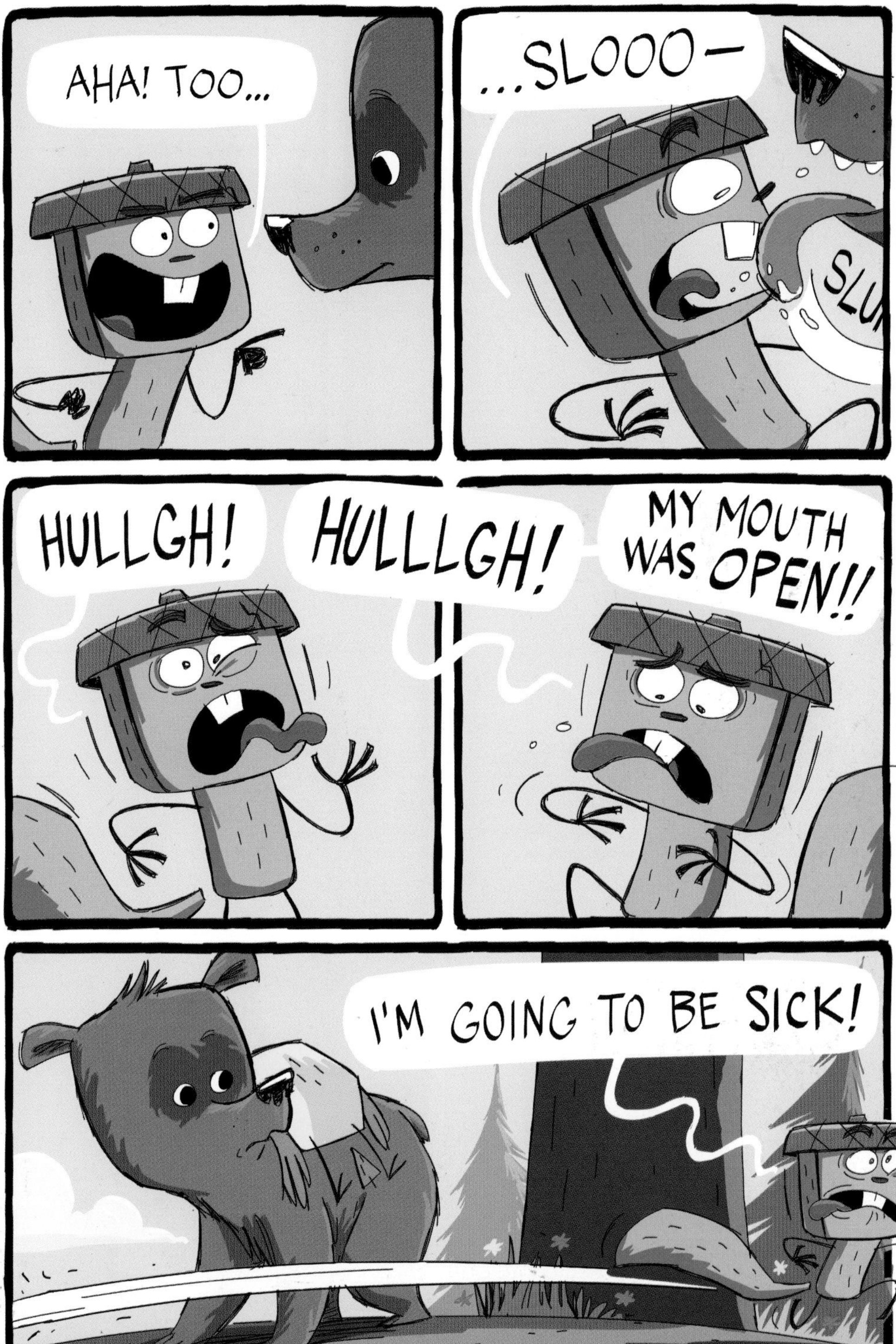
AHA! TOO...
...SLOOO–
SLU
HULLGH!
HULLLGH!
MY MOUTH WAS OPEN!!
I'M GOING TO BE SICK!

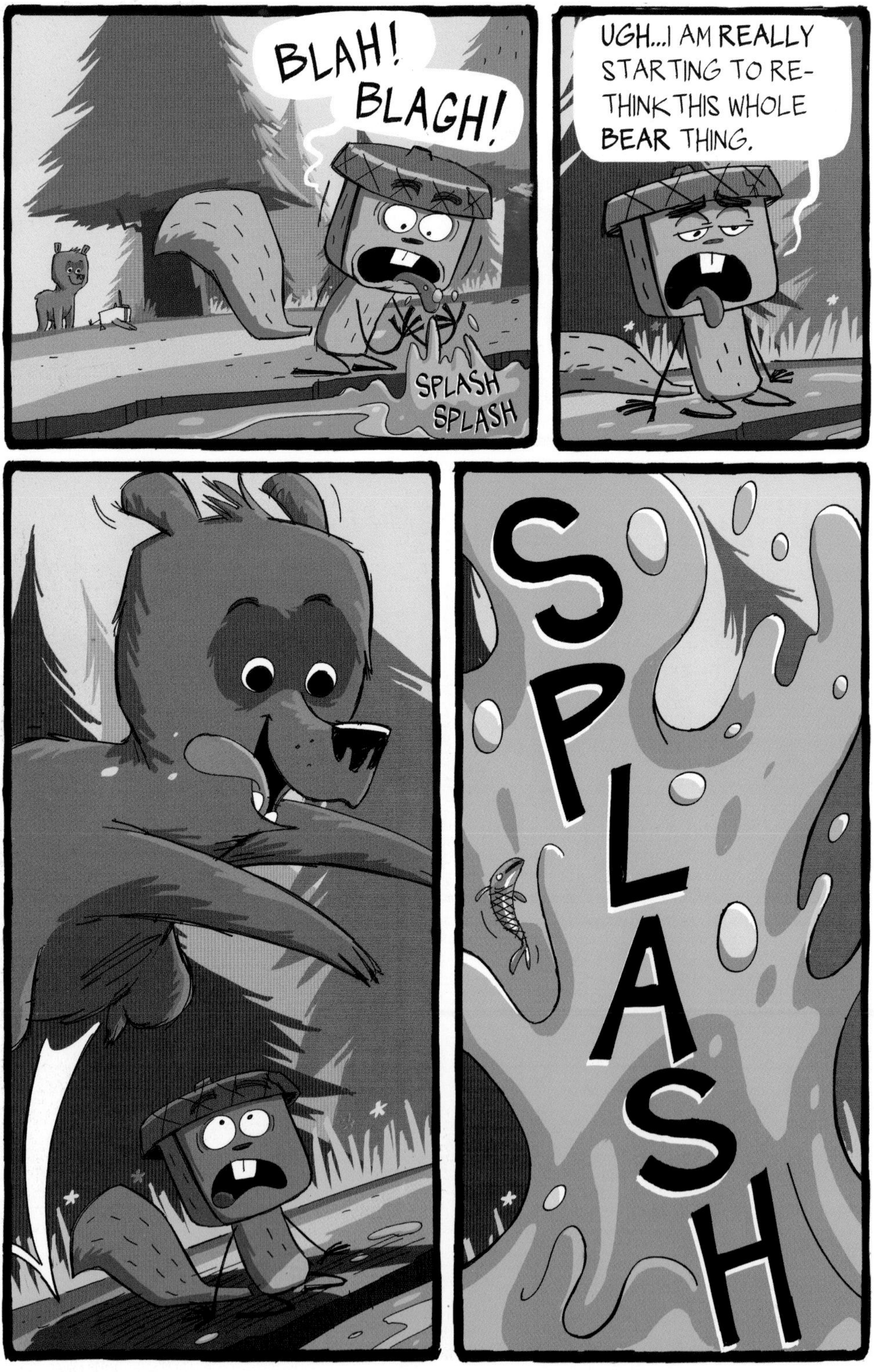
BLAH! BLAGH!
SPLASH SPLASH
UGH...I AM REALLY STARTING TO RE-THINK THIS WHOLE BEAR THING.
SPLASH

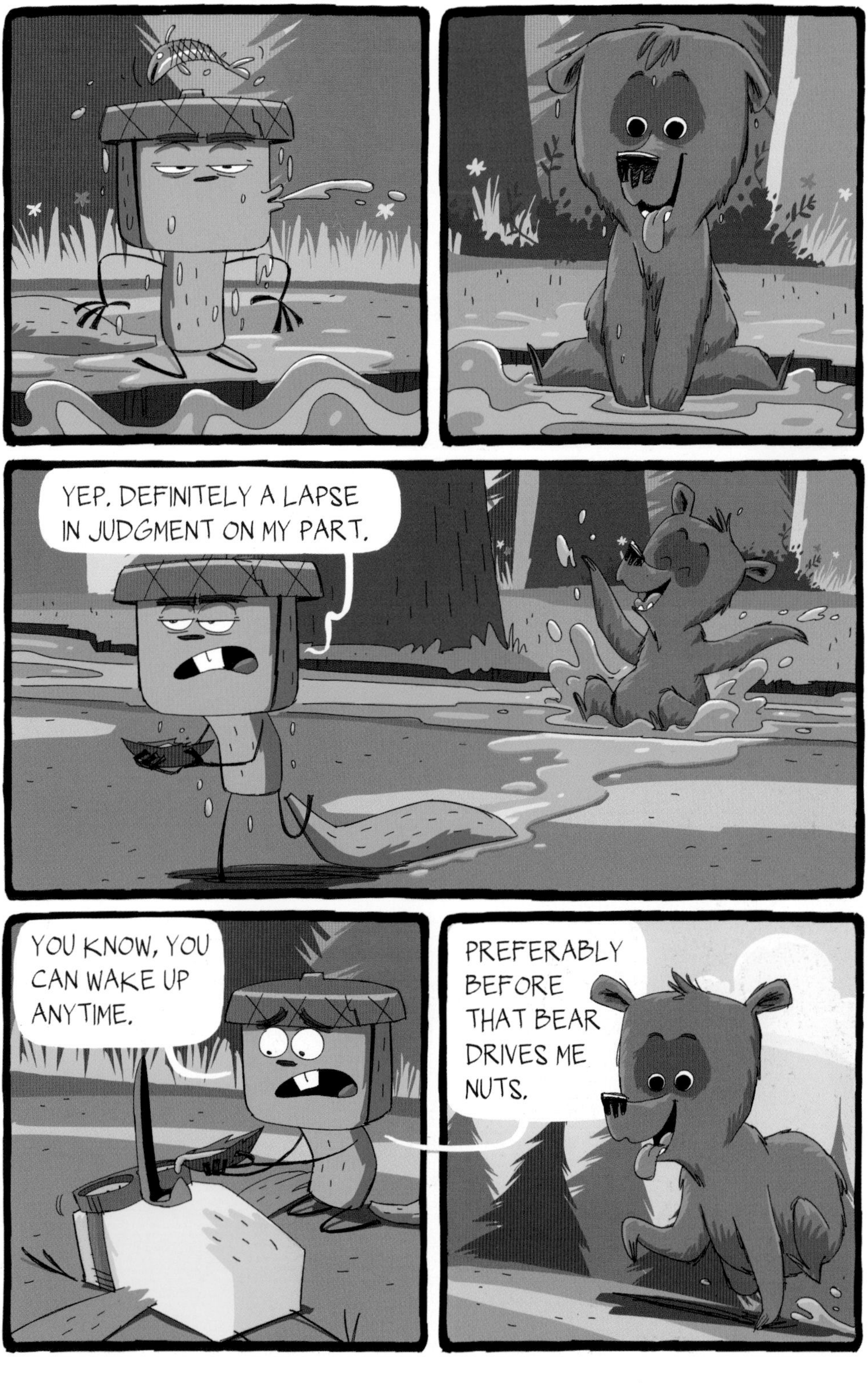
YEP. DEFINITELY A LAPSE IN JUDGMENT ON MY PART.
YOU KNOW, YOU CAN WAKE UP ANYTIME.
PREFERABLY BEFORE THAT BEAR DRIVES ME NUTS.

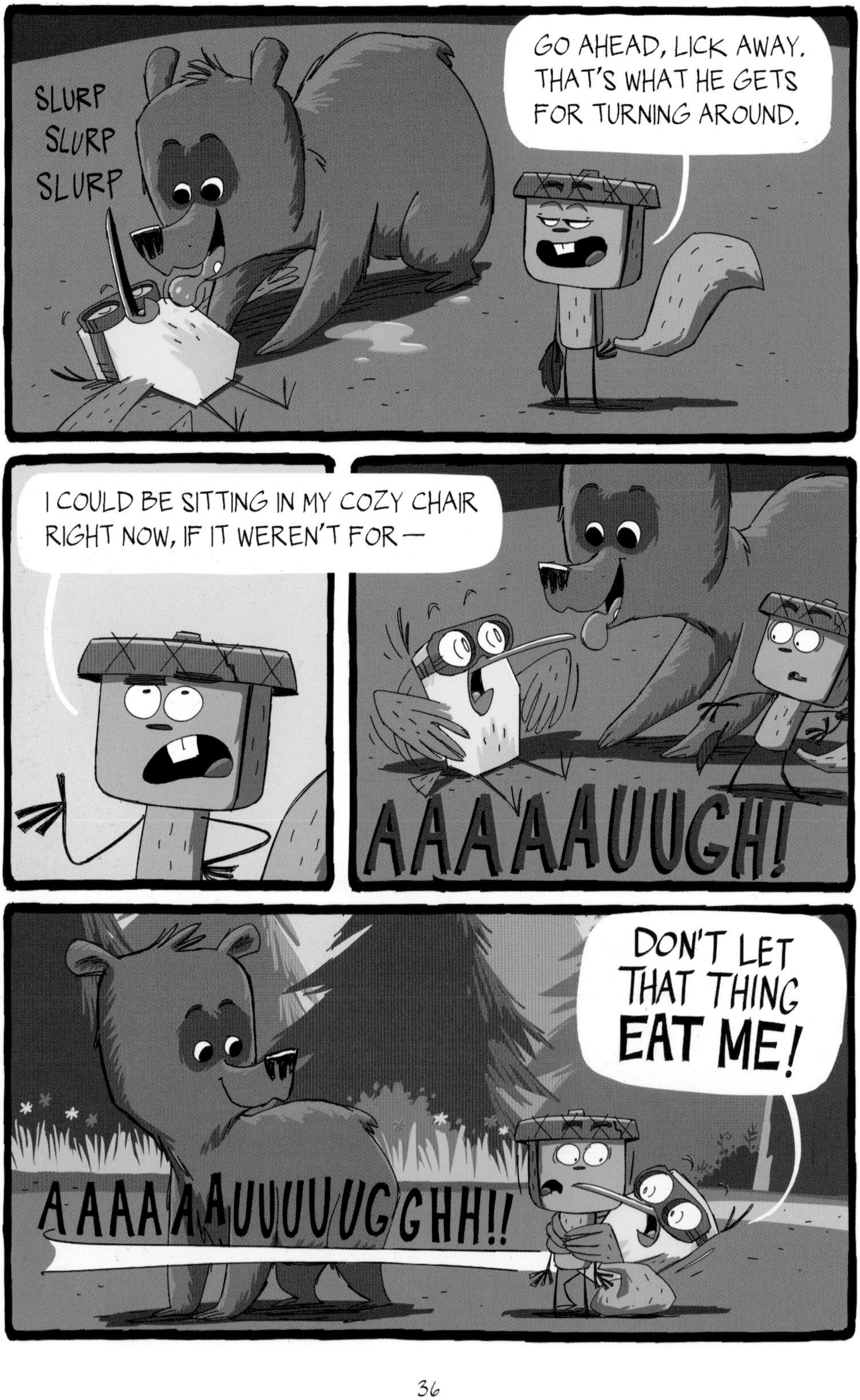
SLURP
SLURP
SLURP
GO AHEAD, LICK AWAY. THAT'S WHAT HE GETS FOR TURNING AROUND.
I COULD BE SITTING IN MY COZY CHAIR RIGHT NOW, IF IT WEREN'T FOR—
AAAAAAUUGH!
AAAAAAUUUUUGGHH!!
DON'T LET THAT THING EAT ME!

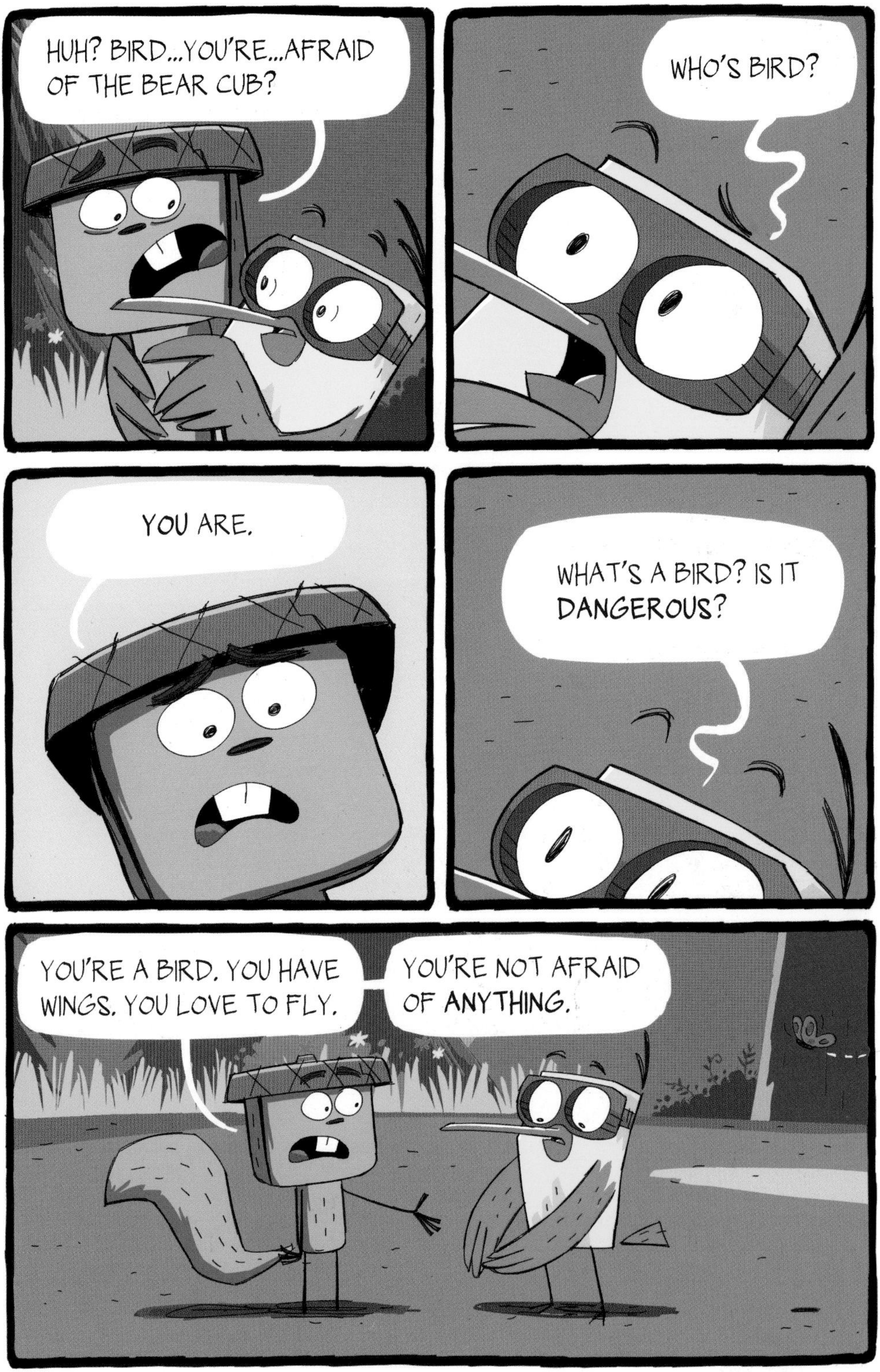
HUH? BIRD...YOU'RE...AFRAID OF THE BEAR CUB?
WHO'S BIRD?
YOU ARE.
WHAT'S A BIRD? IS IT DANGEROUS?
YOU'RE A BIRD. YOU HAVE WINGS. YOU LOVE TO FLY.
YOU'RE NOT AFRAID OF ANYTHING.

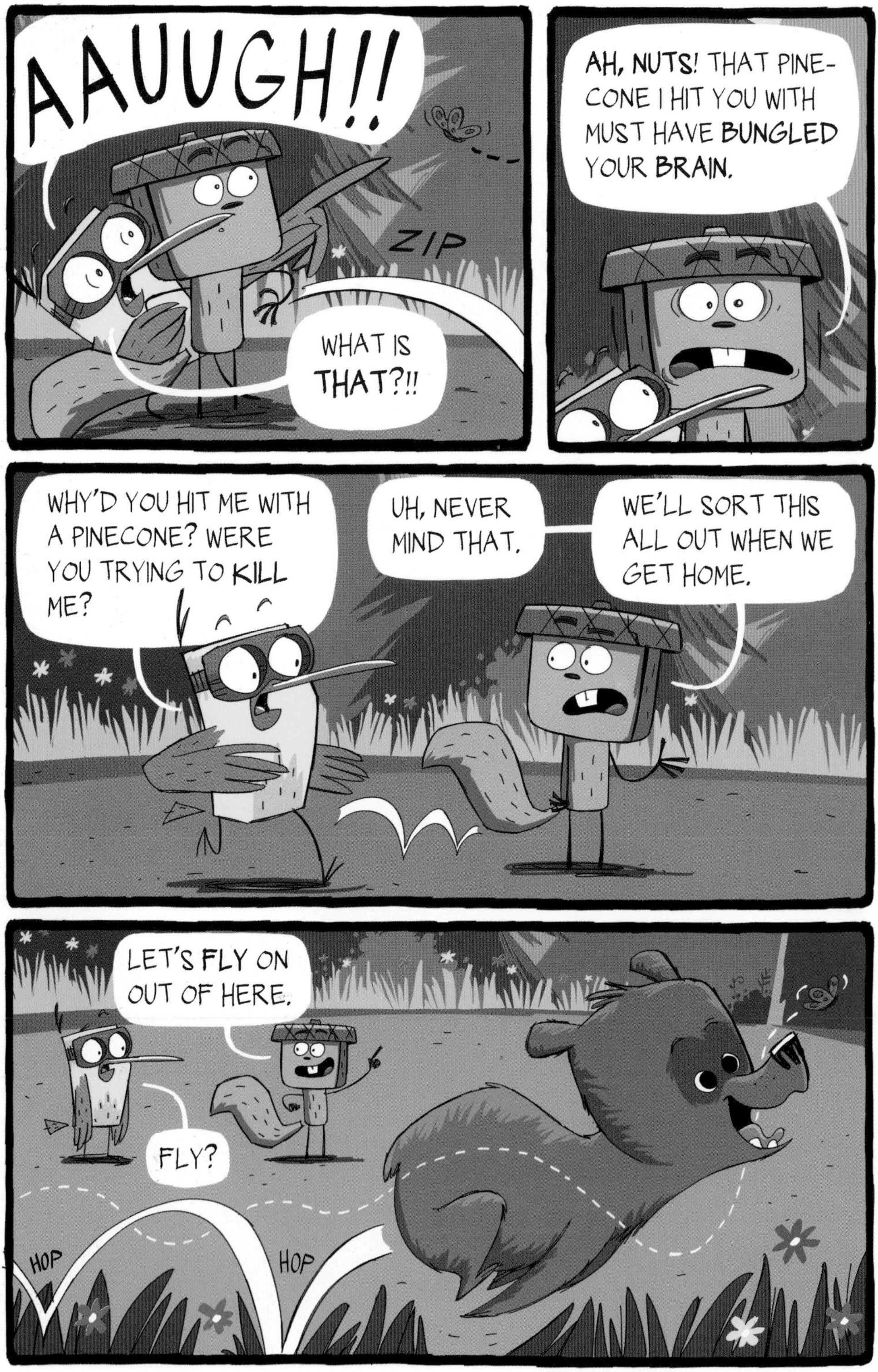
AAUUGH!!
ZIP
WHAT IS THAT?!!
AH, NUTS! THAT PINE-CONE I HIT YOU WITH MUST HAVE BUNGLED YOUR BRAIN.
WHY'D YOU HIT ME WITH A PINECONE? WERE YOU TRYING TO KILL ME?
UH, NEVER MIND THAT.
WE'LL SORT THIS ALL OUT WHEN WE GET HOME.
LET'S FLY ON OUT OF HERE.
FLY?
HOP
HOP

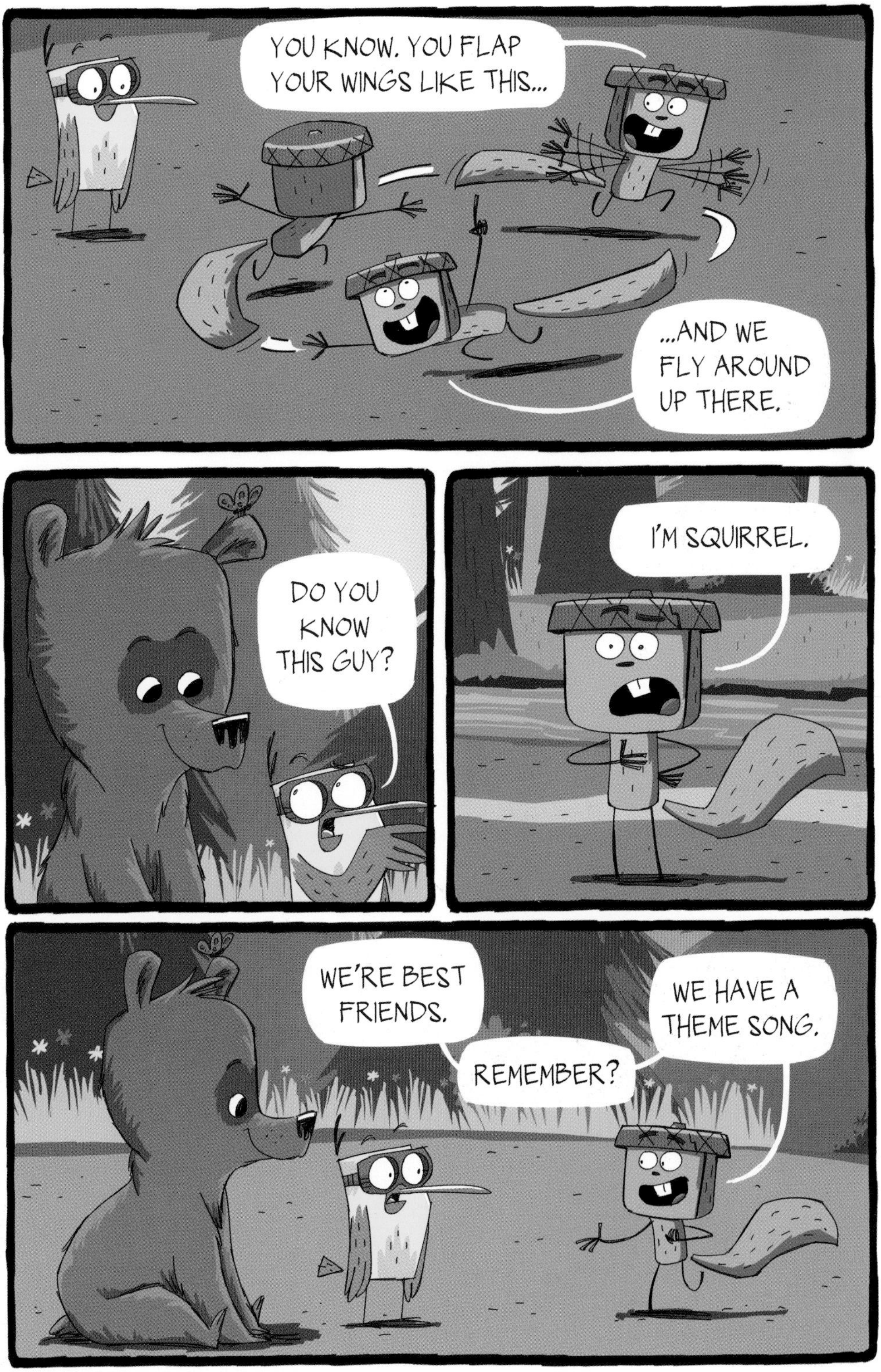
YOU KNOW. YOU FLAP YOUR WINGS LIKE THIS...
...AND WE FLY AROUND UP THERE.
DO YOU KNOW THIS GUY?
I'M SQUIRREL.
WE'RE BEST FRIENDS.
REMEMBER?
WE HAVE A THEME SONG.

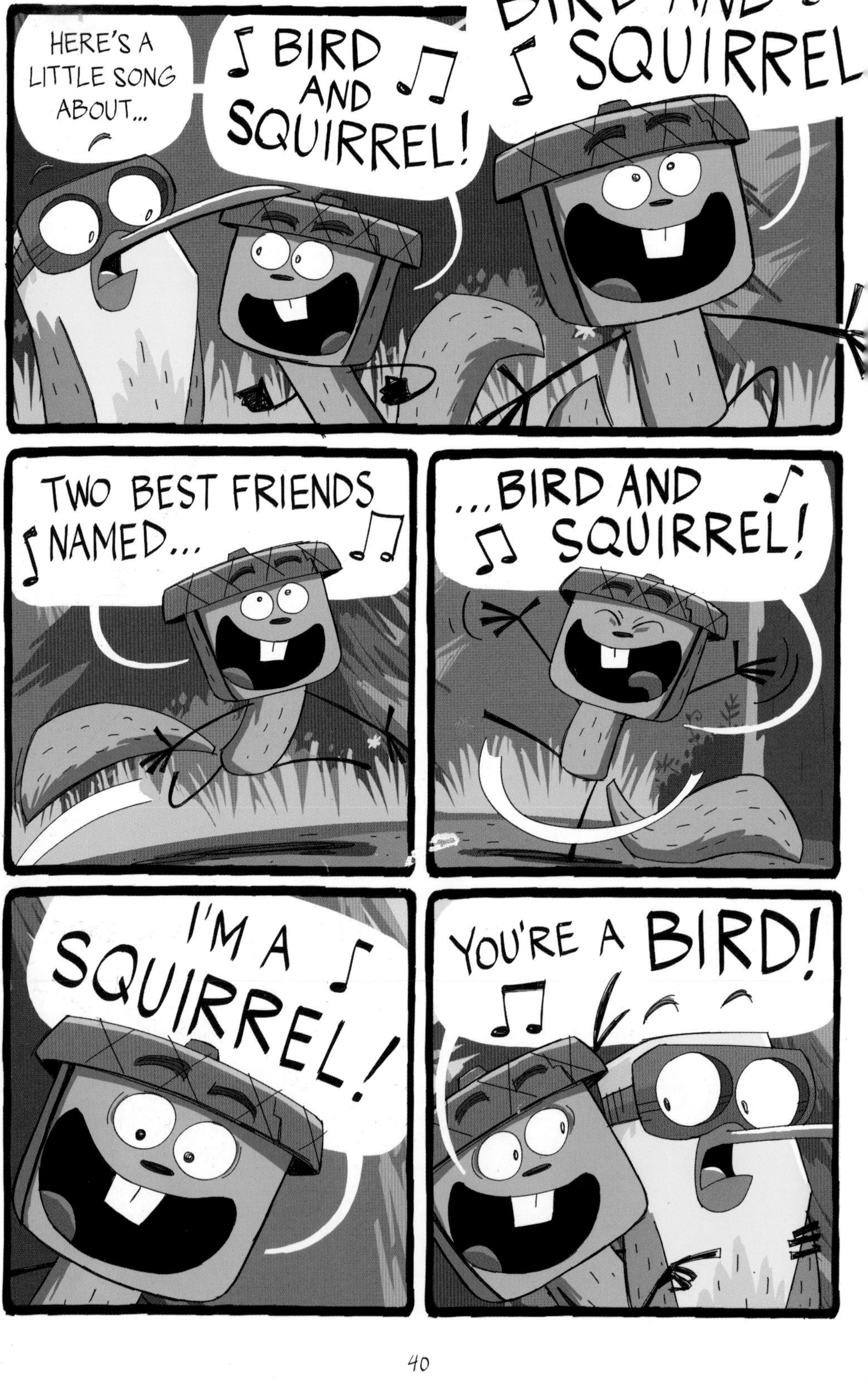
HERE'S A LITTLE SONG ABOUT...
BIRD AND SQUIRREL!
BIRD AND SQUIRREL
TWO BEST FRIENDS NAMED...
...BIRD AND SQUIRREL!
I'M A SQUIRREL!
YOU'RE A BIRD!

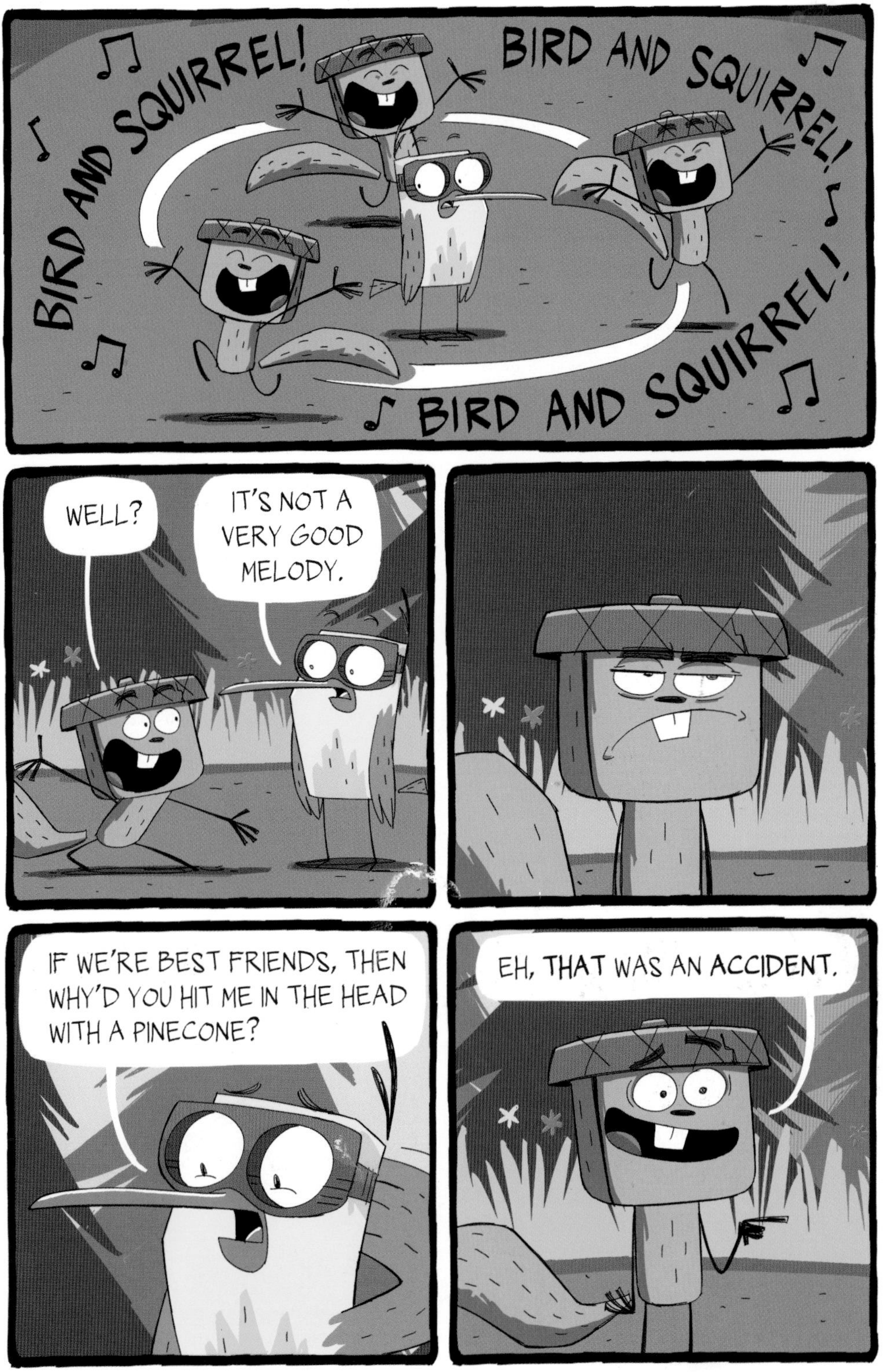
BIRD AND SQUIRREL!
BIRD AND SQUIRREL!
BIRD AND SQUIRREL!
BIRD AND SQUIRREL
WELL?
IT'S NOT A VERY GOOD MELODY.
IF WE'RE BEST FRIENDS, THEN WHY'D YOU HIT ME IN THE HEAD WITH A PINECONE?
EH, THAT WAS AN ACCIDENT.

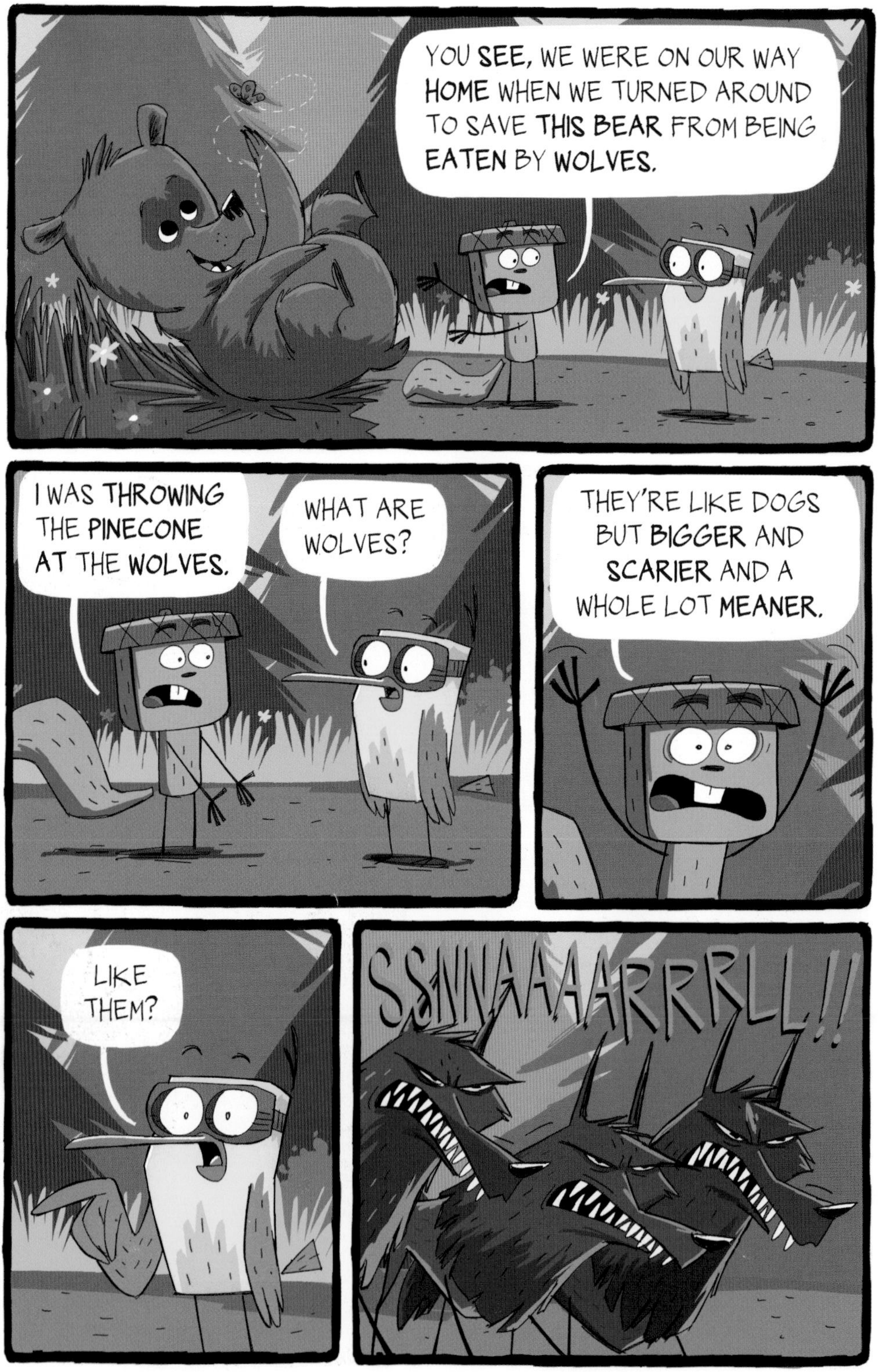
YOU SEE, WE WERE ON OUR WAY HOME WHEN WE TURNED AROUND TO SAVE THIS BEAR FROM BEING EATEN BY WOLVES.
I WAS THROWING THE PINECONE AT THE WOLVES.
WHAT ARE WOLVES?
THEY'RE LIKE DOGS BUT BIGGER AND SCARIER AND A WHOLE LOT MEANER.
LIKE THEM?
SSNNAAAARRRLL!!

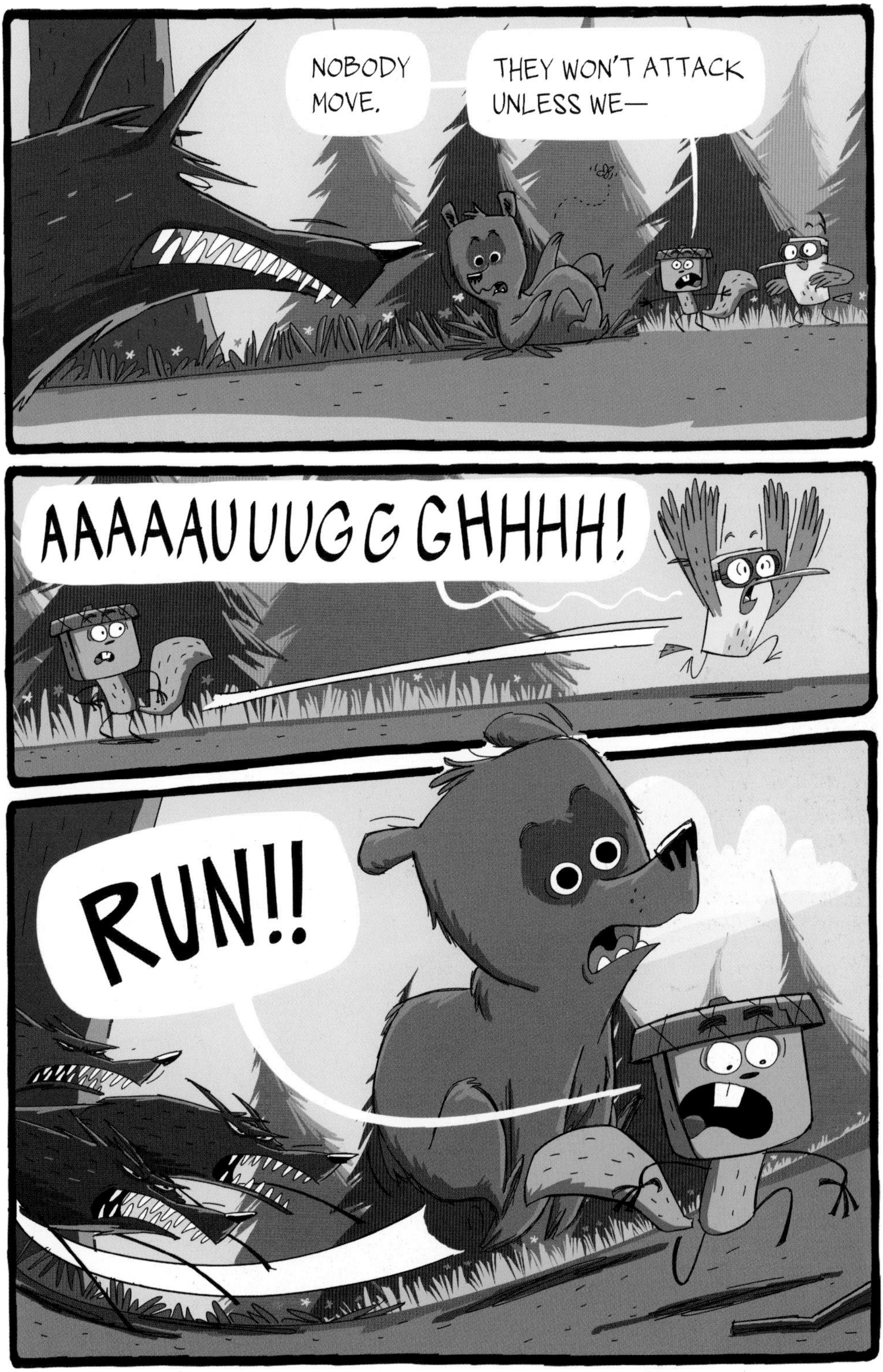
NOBODY MOVE.
THEY WON'T ATTACK UNLESS WE—
AAAAAUUUGGGHHHH!
RUN!!

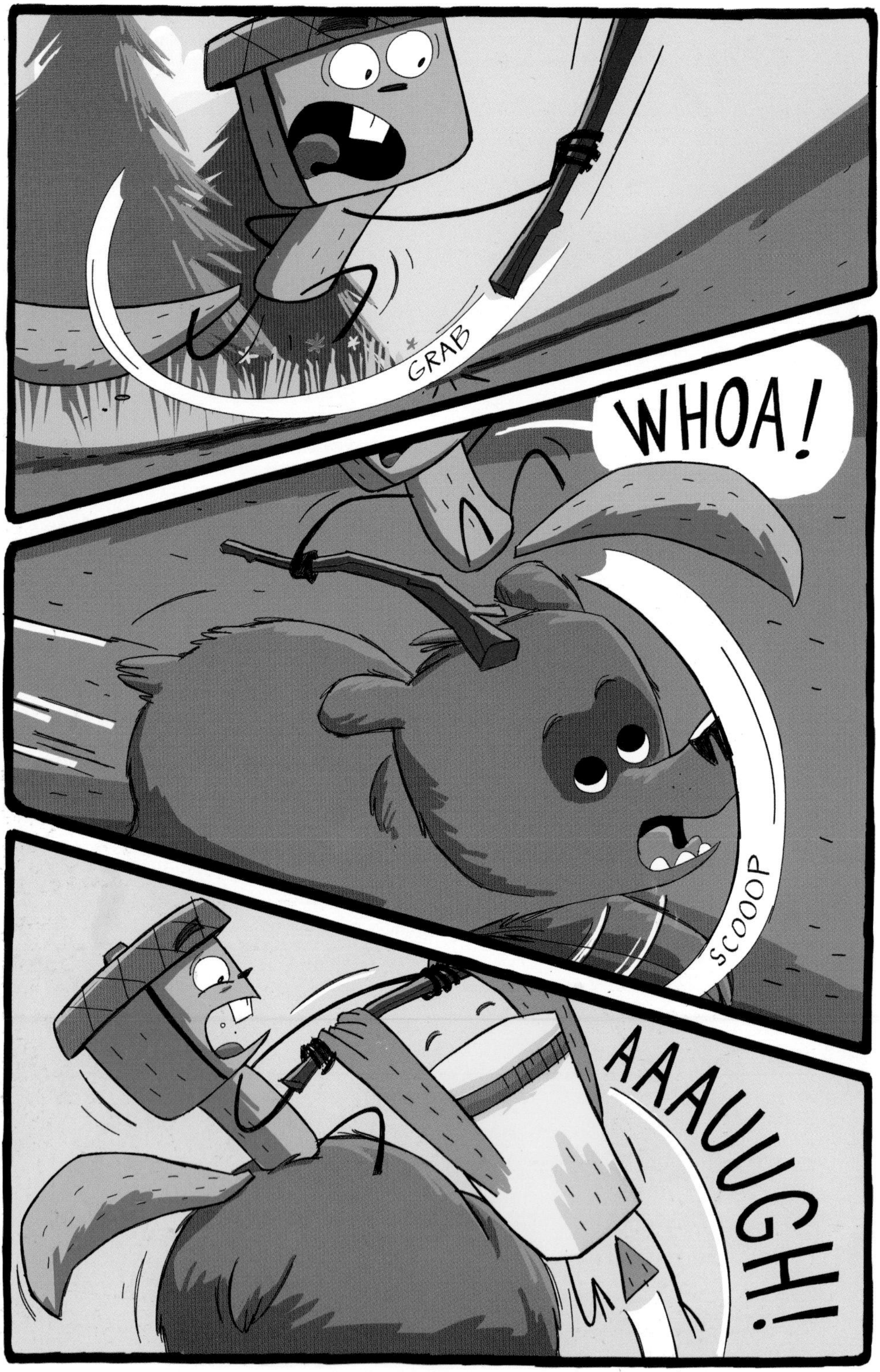
GRAB
WHOA!
SCOOOP
AAAUUGH!

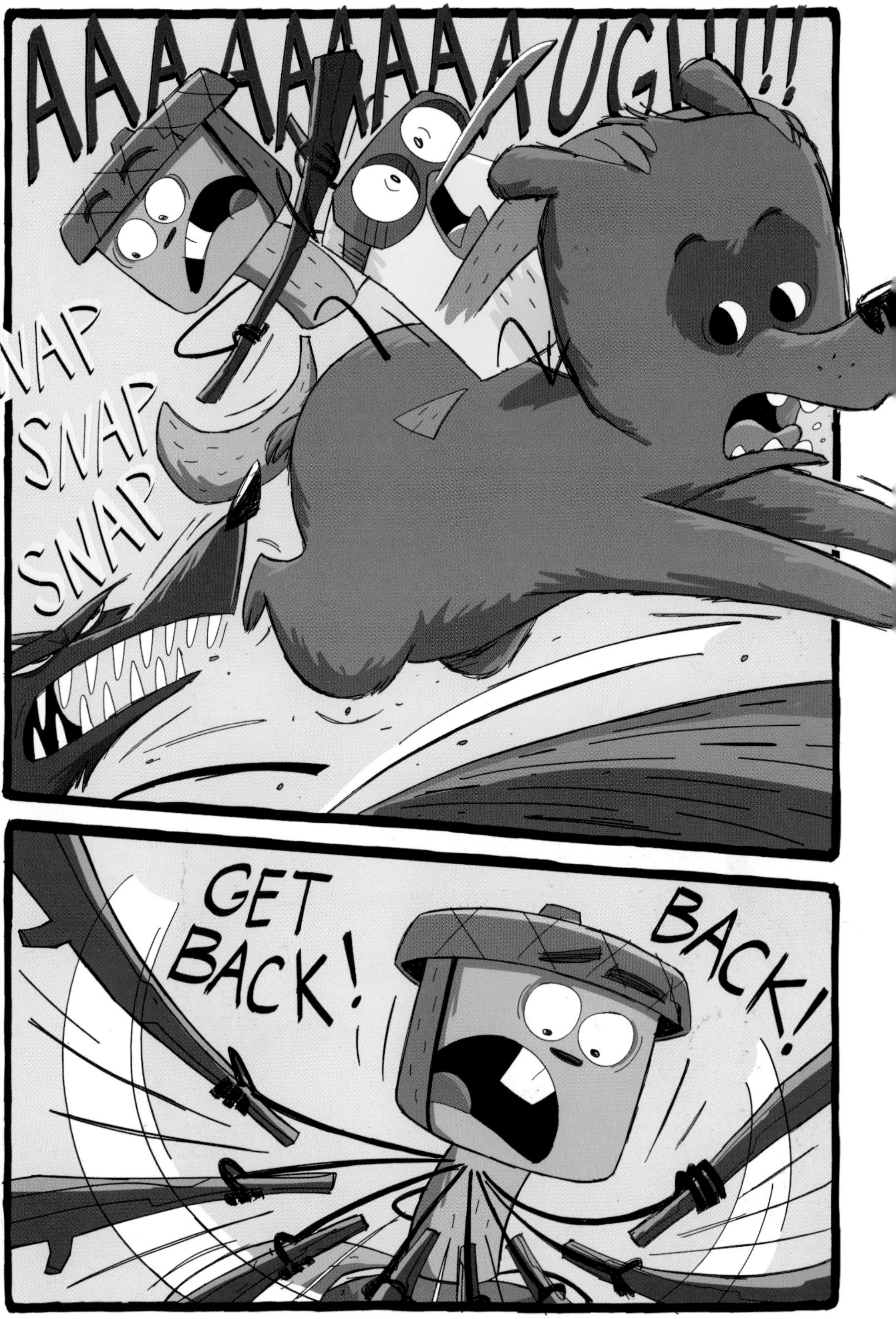
AAAAAAAAAUGH!!!
SNAP
SNAP
SNAP
GET BACK!
BACK!

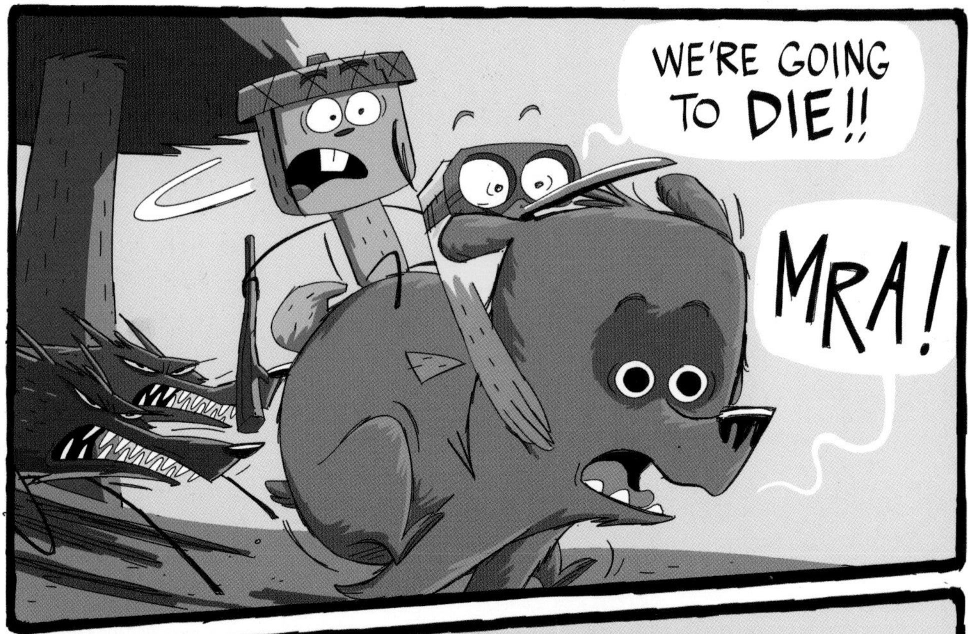
WE'RE GOING TO DIE!!
MRA!

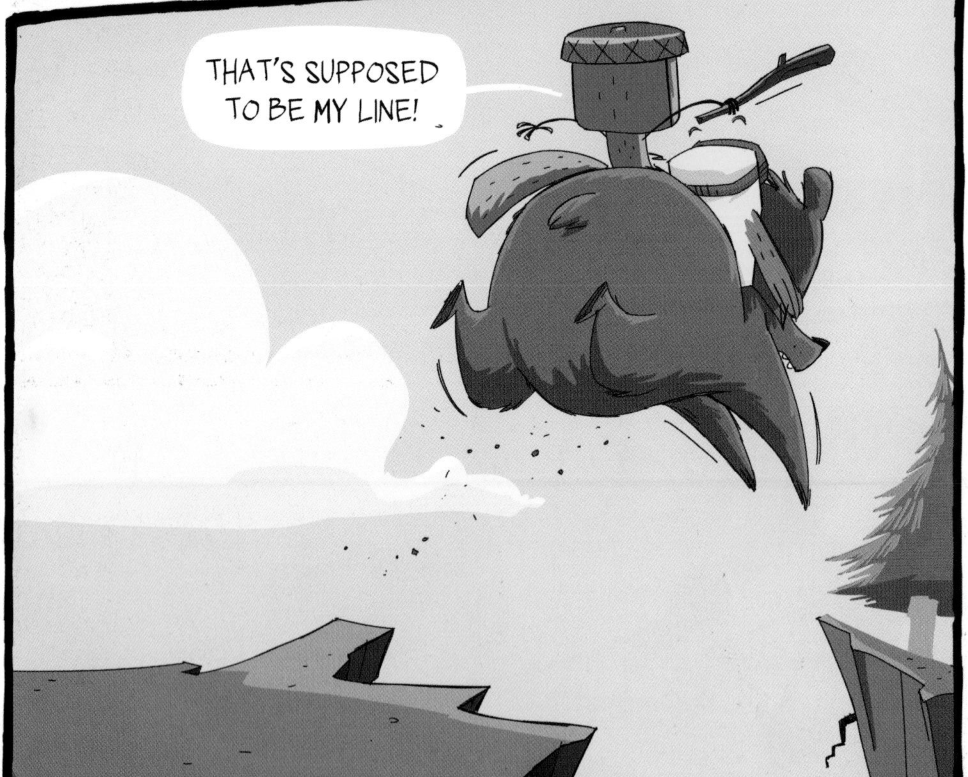
THAT'S SUPPOSED TO BE MY LINE!

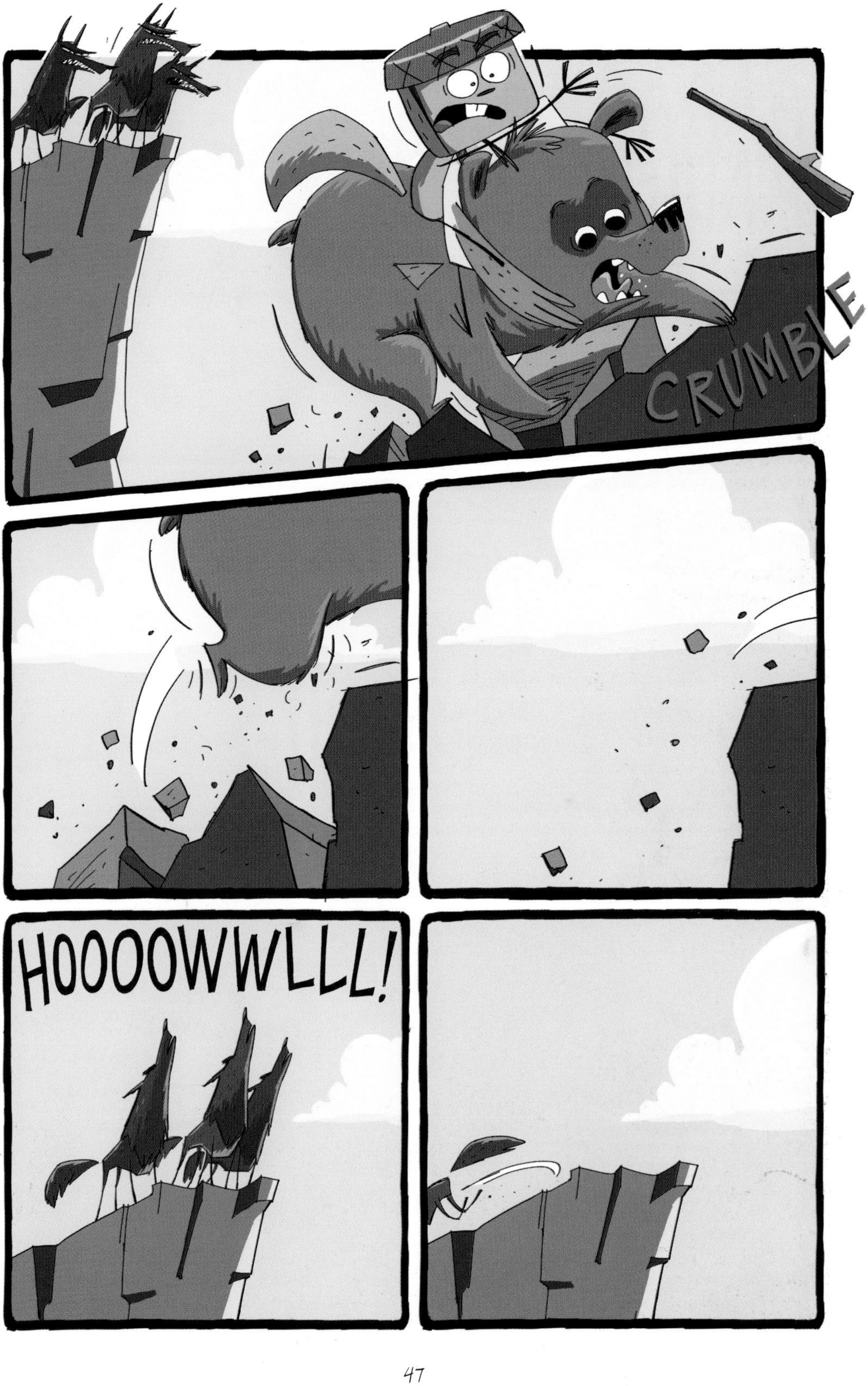
CRUMBLE
HOOOOWWLLL!

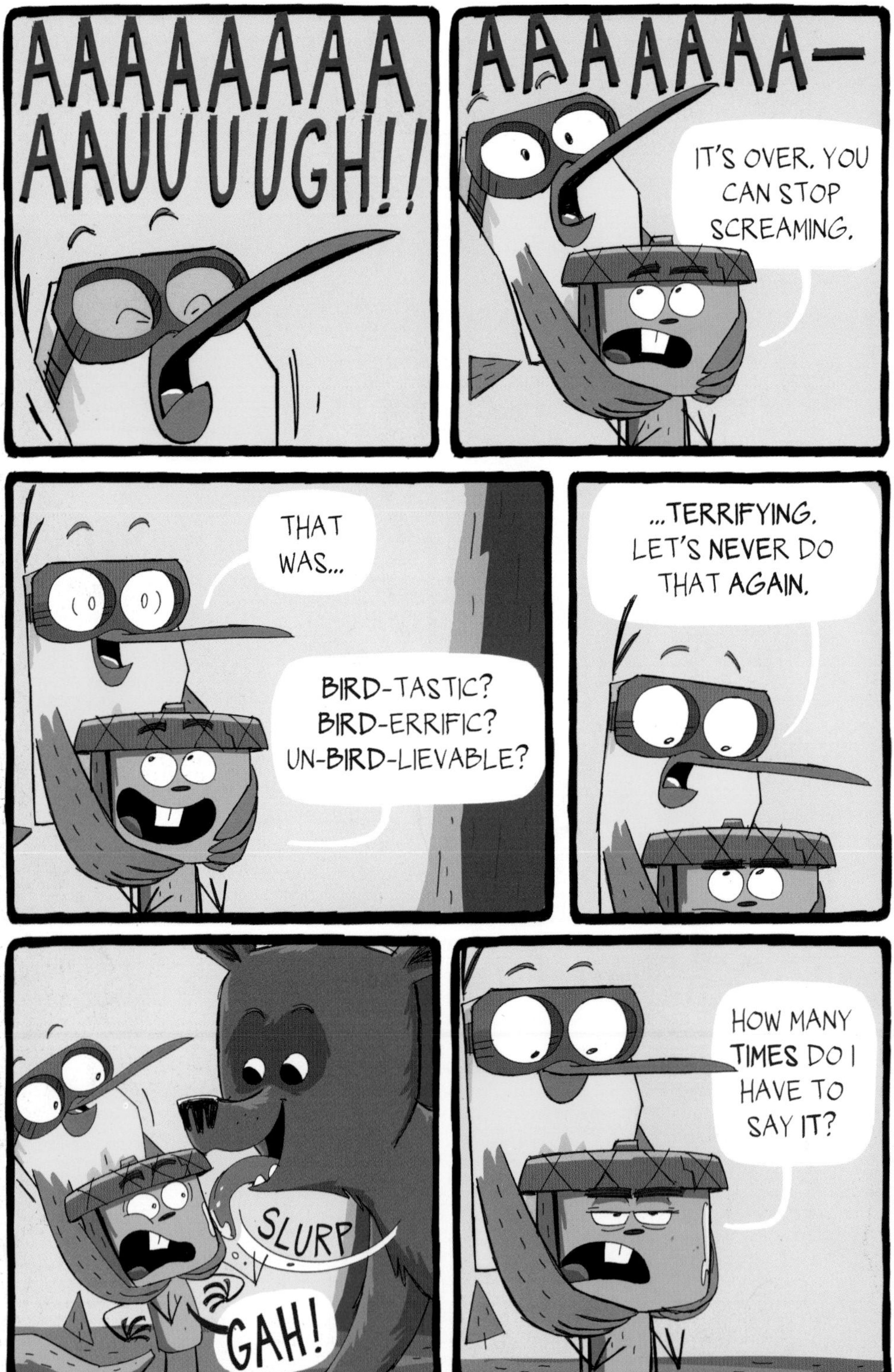
AAAAAAAA AAUUUUGH!!
AAAAAAA—
IT'S OVER. YOU CAN STOP SCREAMING.
THAT WAS...
BIRD-TASTIC? BIRD-ERRIFIC? UN-BIRD-LIEVABLE?
...TERRIFYING. LET'S NEVER DO THAT AGAIN.
SLURP
GAH!
HOW MANY TIMES DO I HAVE TO SAY IT?

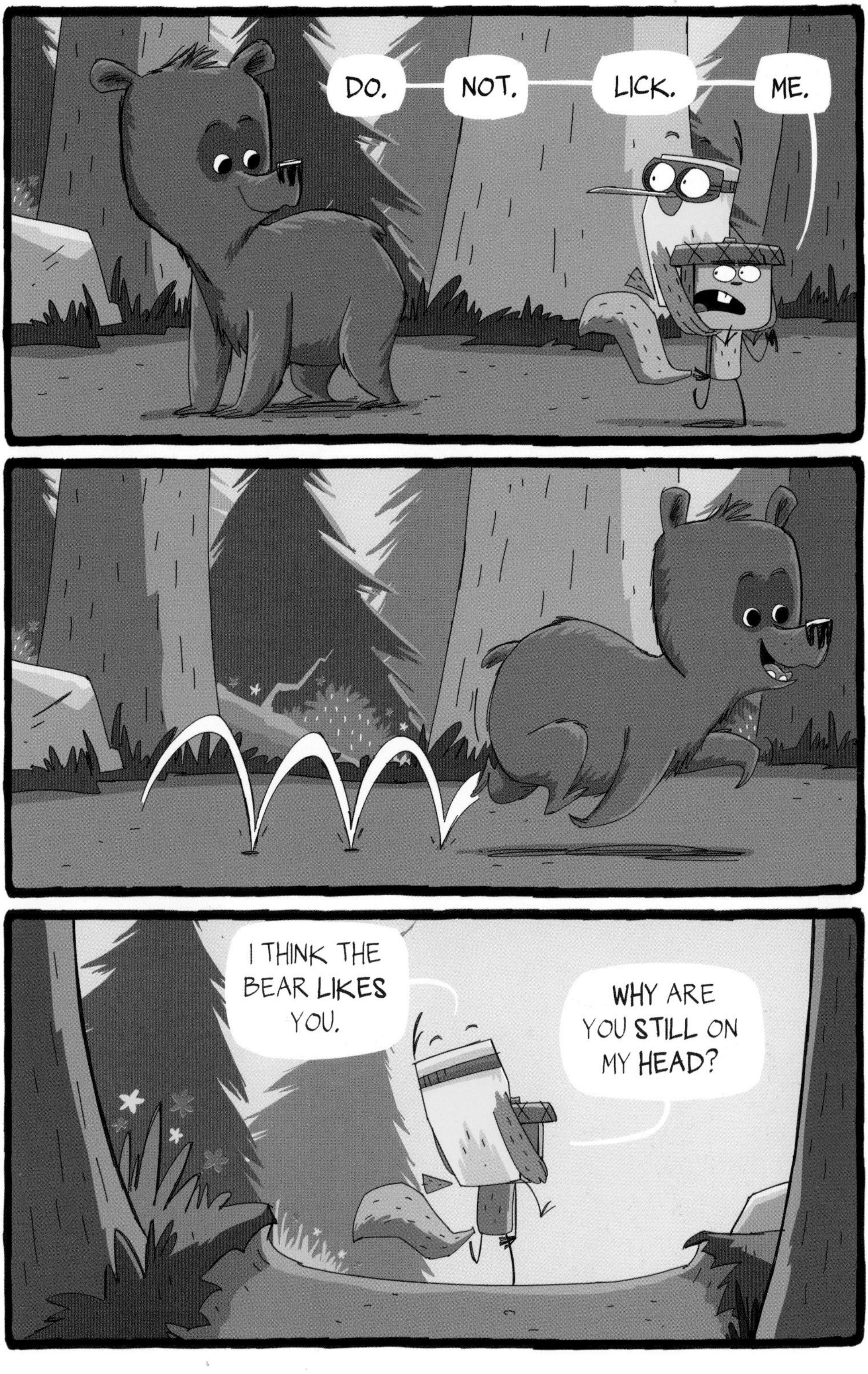
DO.
NOT.
LICK.
ME.
I THINK THE BEAR LIKES YOU.
WHY ARE YOU STILL ON MY HEAD?

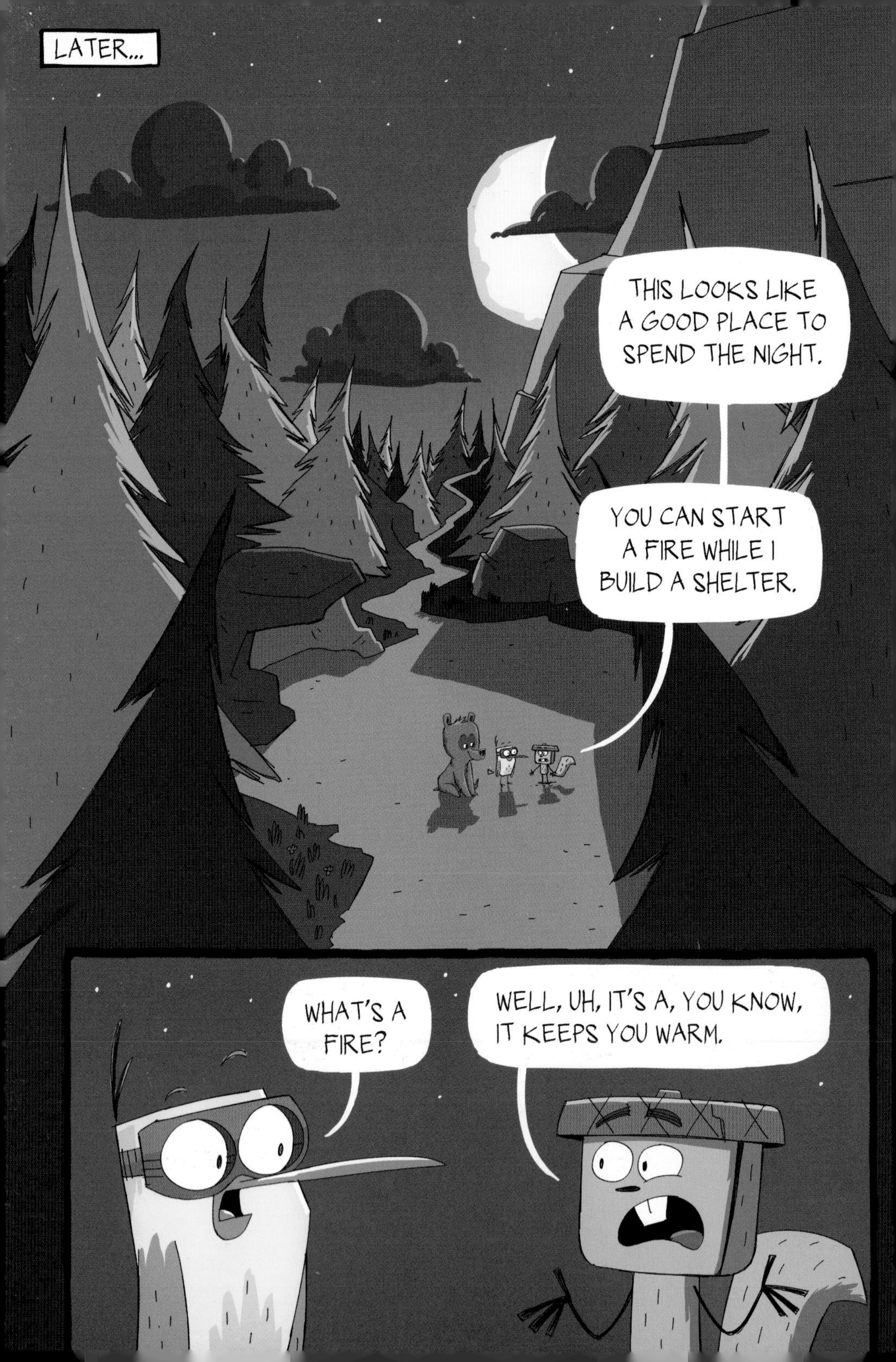
LATER...
THIS LOOKS LIKE A GOOD PLACE TO SPEND THE NIGHT.
YOU CAN START A FIRE WHILE I BUILD A SHELTER.
WHAT'S A FIRE?
WELL, UH, IT'S A, YOU KNOW, IT KEEPS YOU WARM.

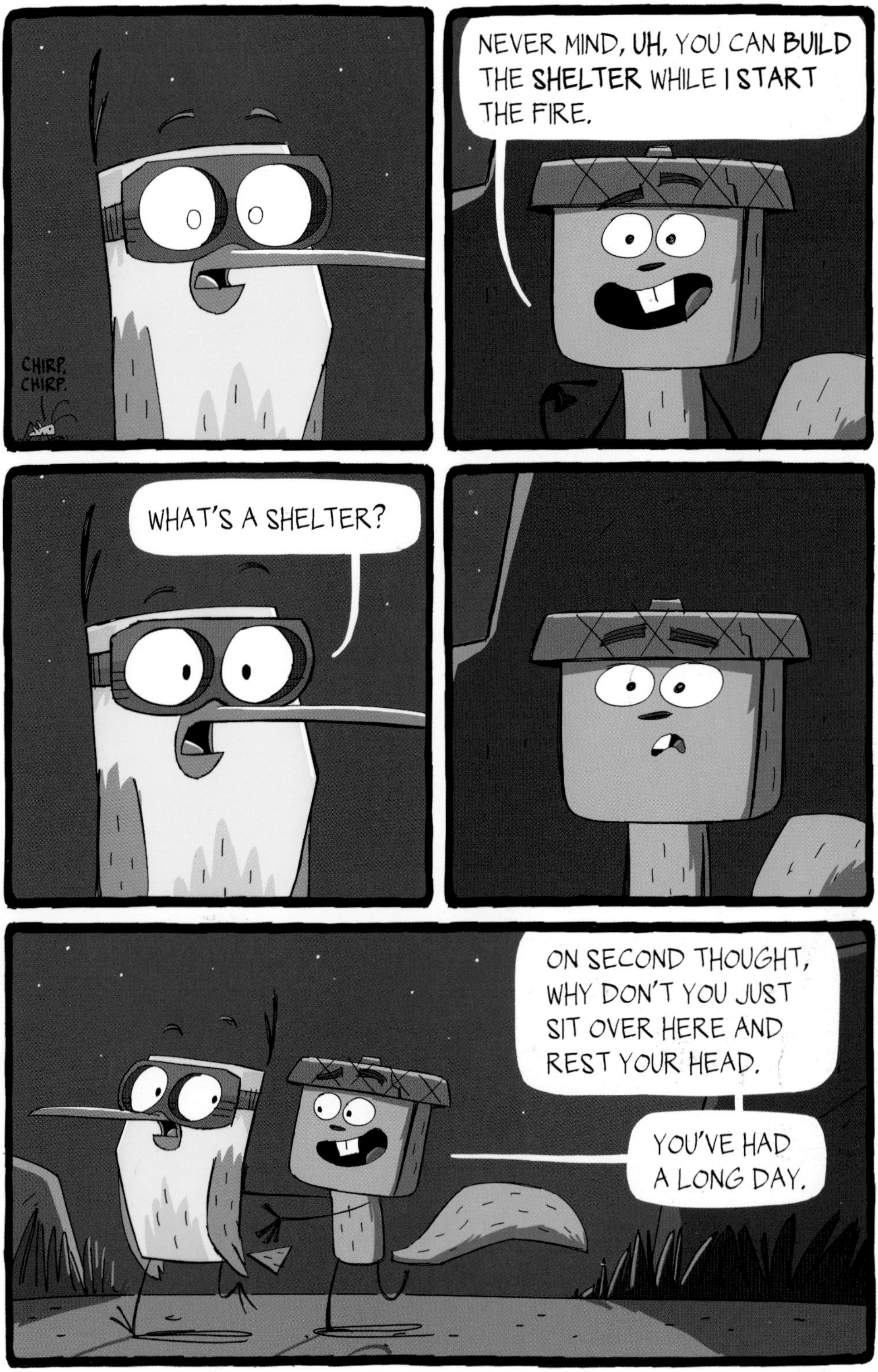
CHIRP. CHIRP.
NEVER MIND, UH, YOU CAN BUILD THE SHELTER WHILE I START THE FIRE.
WHAT'S A SHELTER?
ON SECOND THOUGHT, WHY DON'T YOU JUST SIT OVER HERE AND REST YOUR HEAD.
YOU'VE HAD A LONG DAY.

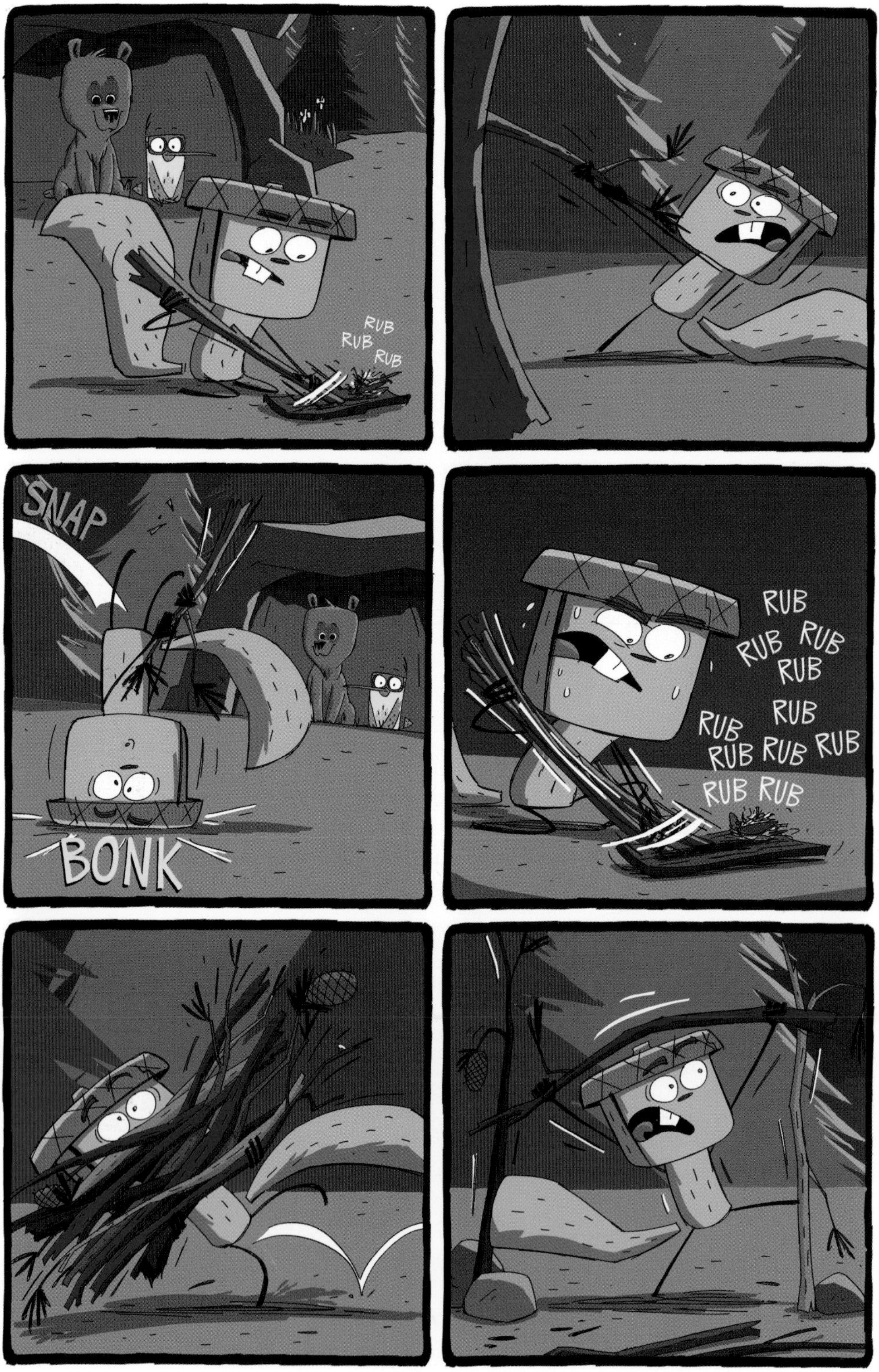
RUB
RUB
RUB
SNAP
BONK
RUB
RUB RUB
RUB
RUB
RUB
RUB RUB RUB
RUB RUB

53

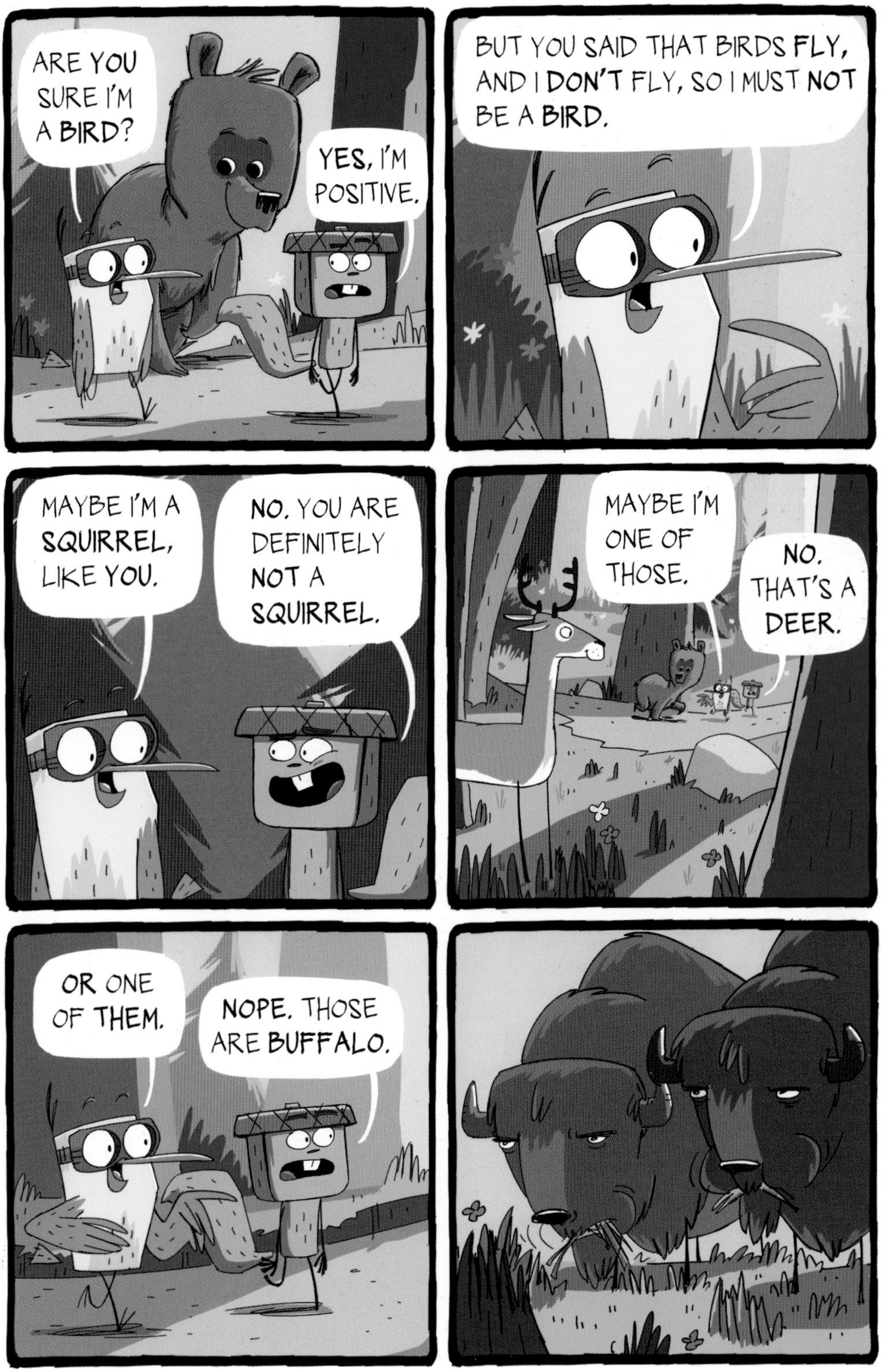
ARE YOU SURE I'M A BIRD?
YES, I'M POSITIVE.
BUT YOU SAID THAT BIRDS FLY, AND I DON'T FLY, SO I MUST NOT BE A BIRD.
MAYBE I'M A SQUIRREL, LIKE YOU.
NO. YOU ARE DEFINITELY NOT A SQUIRREL.
MAYBE I'M ONE OF THOSE.
NO. THAT'S A DEER.
OR ONE OF THEM.
NOPE. THOSE ARE BUFFALO.

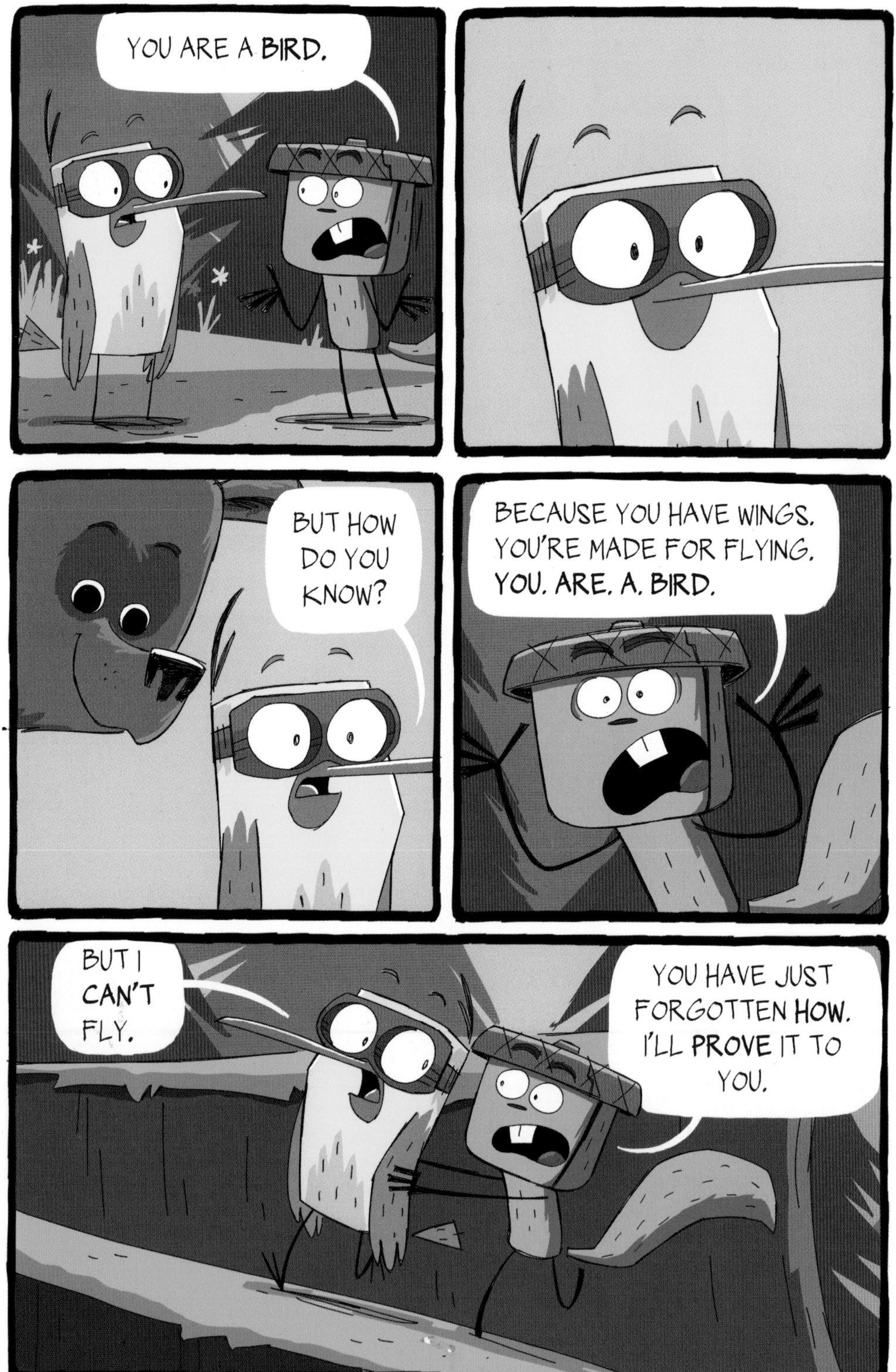
YOU ARE A **BIRD.**
BUT HOW DO YOU KNOW?
BECAUSE YOU HAVE WINGS. YOU'RE MADE FOR FLYING. **YOU. ARE. A. BIRD.**
BUT I **CAN'T** FLY.
YOU HAVE JUST FORGOTTEN **HOW.** I'LL **PROVE** IT TO YOU.

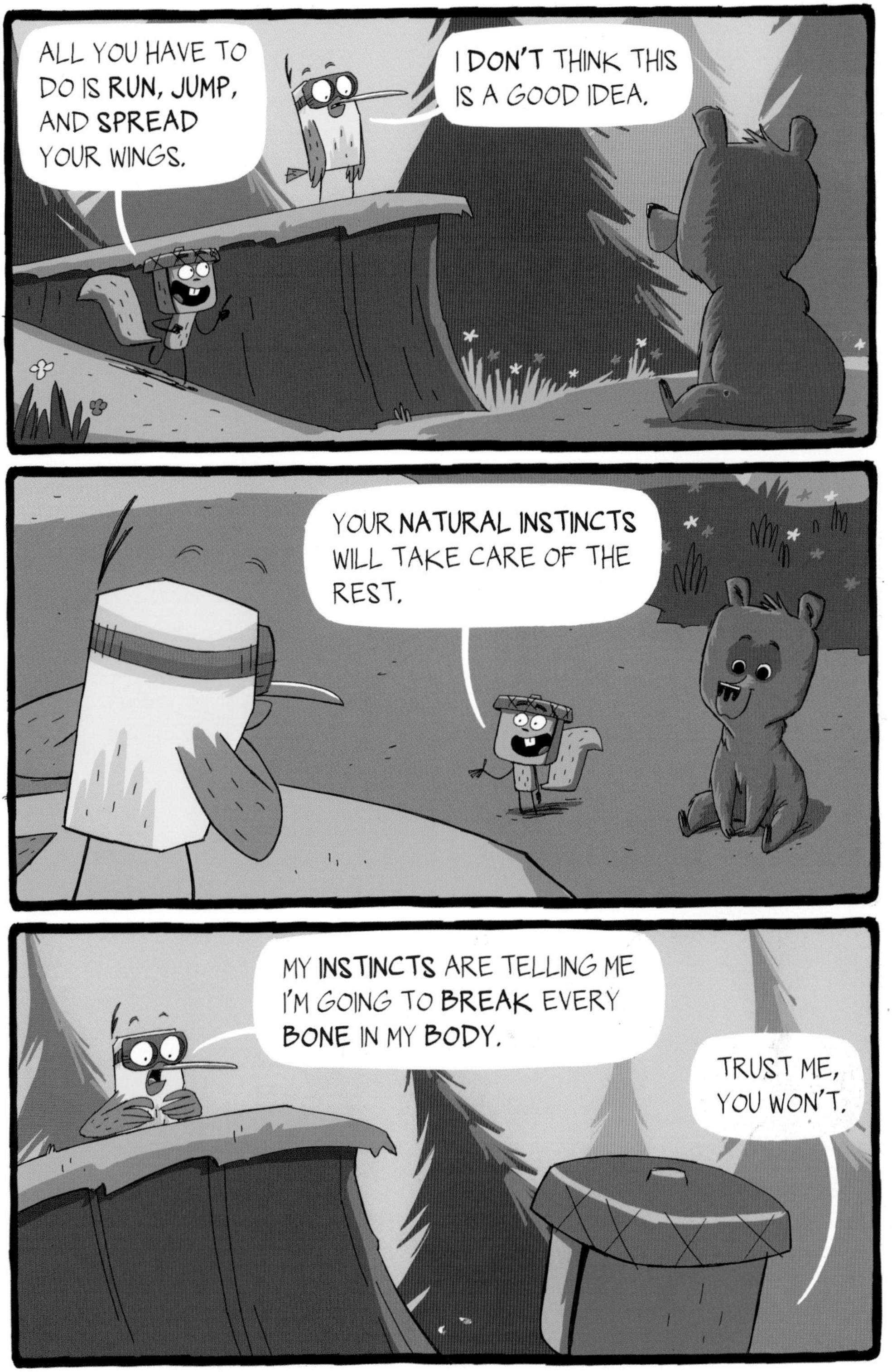
ALL YOU HAVE TO DO IS RUN, JUMP, AND SPREAD YOUR WINGS.
I DON'T THINK THIS IS A GOOD IDEA.
YOUR NATURAL INSTINCTS WILL TAKE CARE OF THE REST.
MY INSTINCTS ARE TELLING ME I'M GOING TO BREAK EVERY BONE IN MY BODY.
TRUST ME, YOU WON'T.

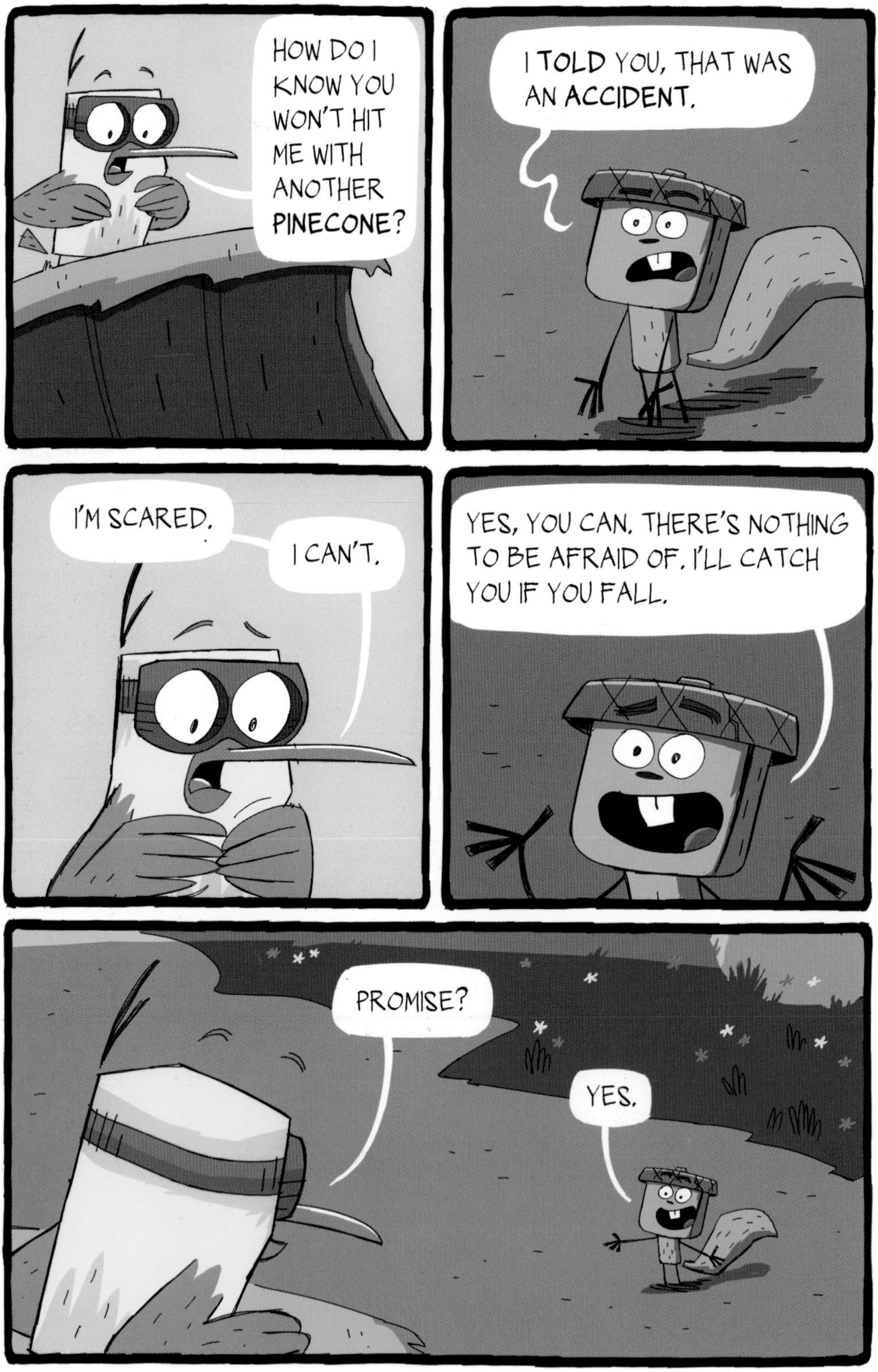
HOW DO I KNOW YOU WON'T HIT ME WITH ANOTHER **PINECONE**?
I **TOLD** YOU, THAT WAS AN **ACCIDENT**.
I'M SCARED.
I CAN'T.
YES, YOU CAN. THERE'S NOTHING TO BE AFRAID OF. I'LL CATCH YOU IF YOU FALL.
PROMISE?
YES.

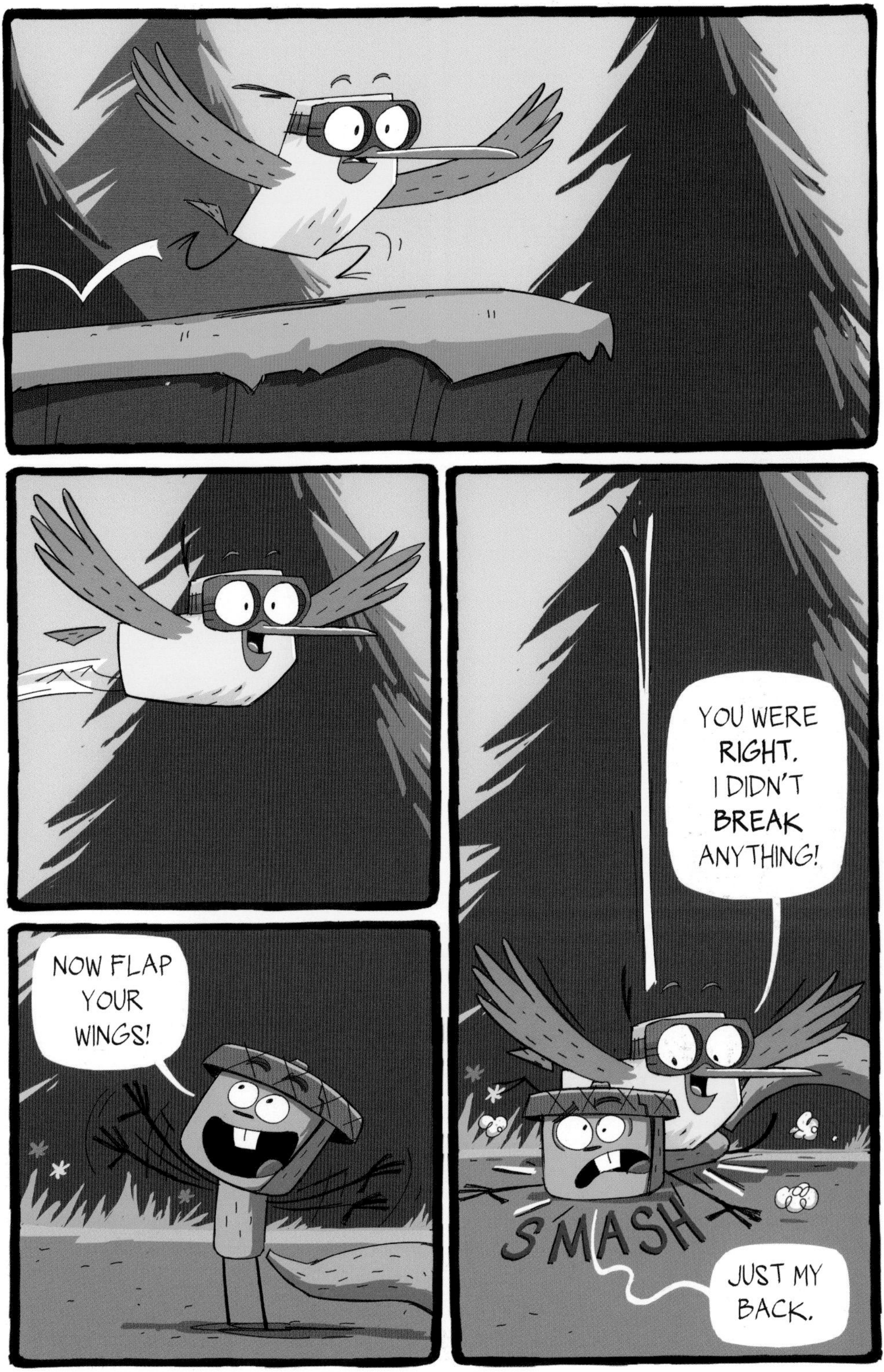

NOW FLAP YOUR WINGS!
YOU WERE RIGHT. I DIDN'T BREAK ANYTHING!
SMASH
JUST MY BACK.

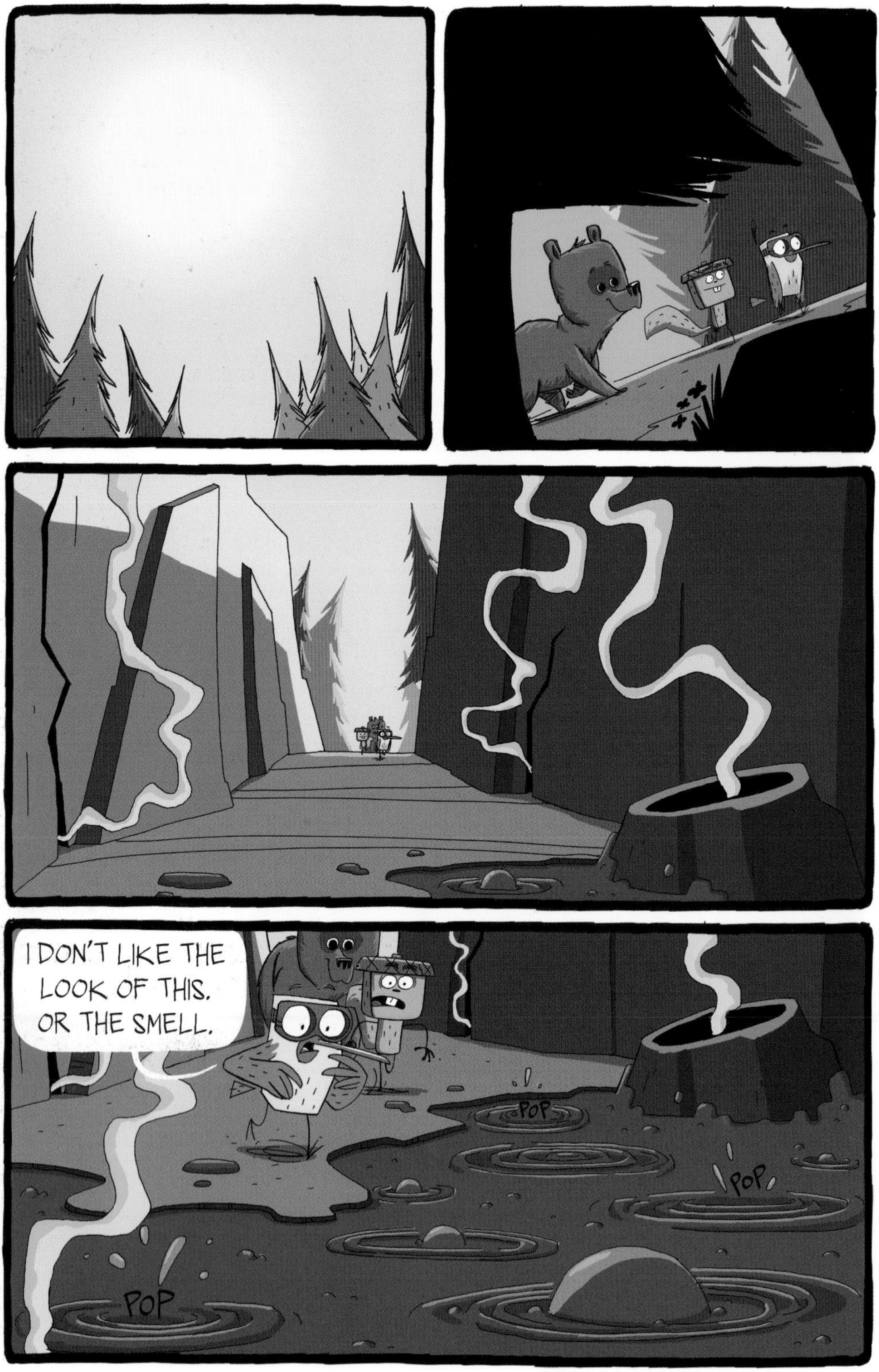
I DON'T LIKE THE
LOOK OF THIS.
OR THE SMELL.
POP
POP
POP

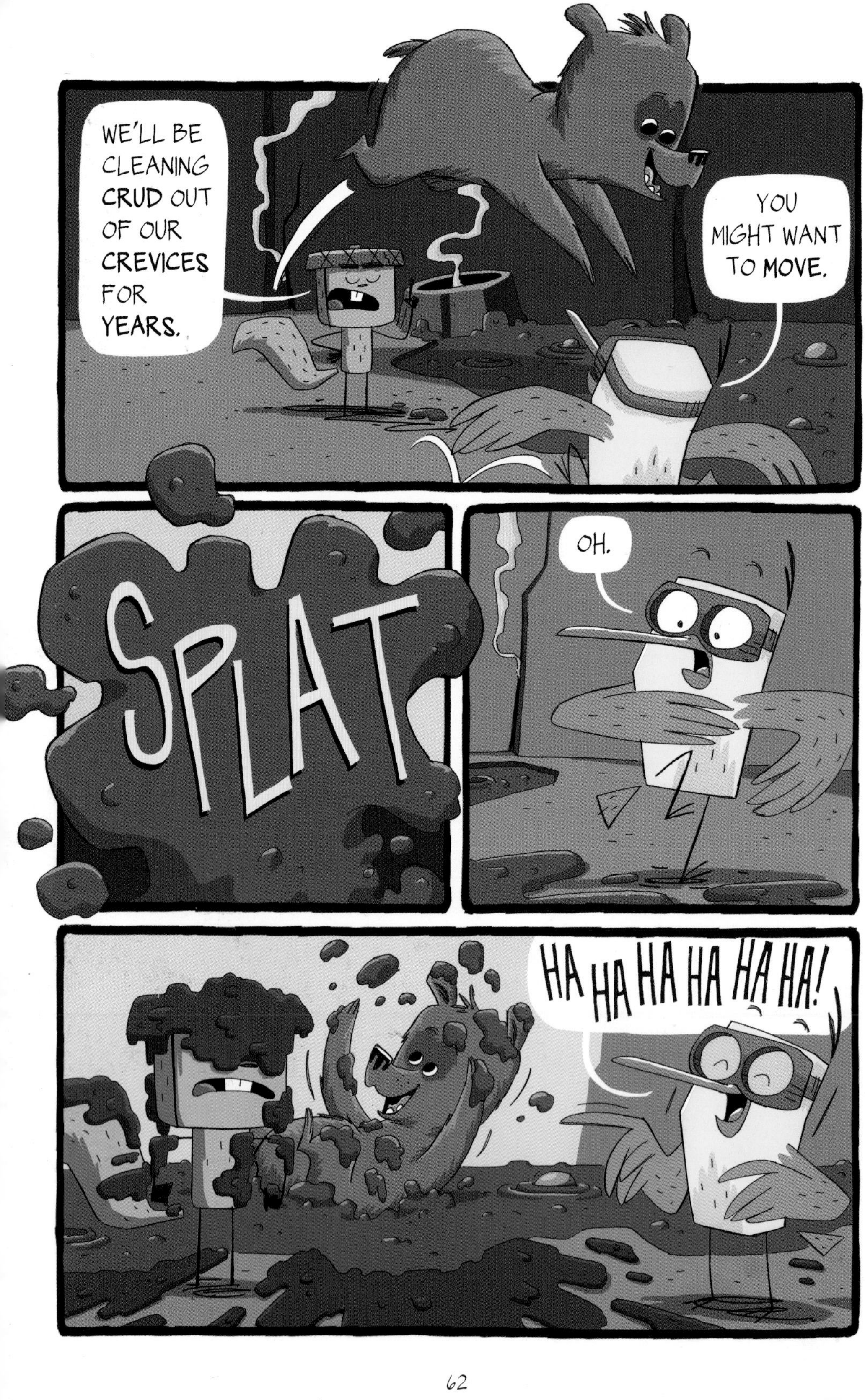
WE'LL BE CLEANING CRUD OUT OF OUR CREVICES FOR YEARS.
YOU MIGHT WANT TO MOVE.
SPLAT
OH.
HA HA HA HA HA HA!

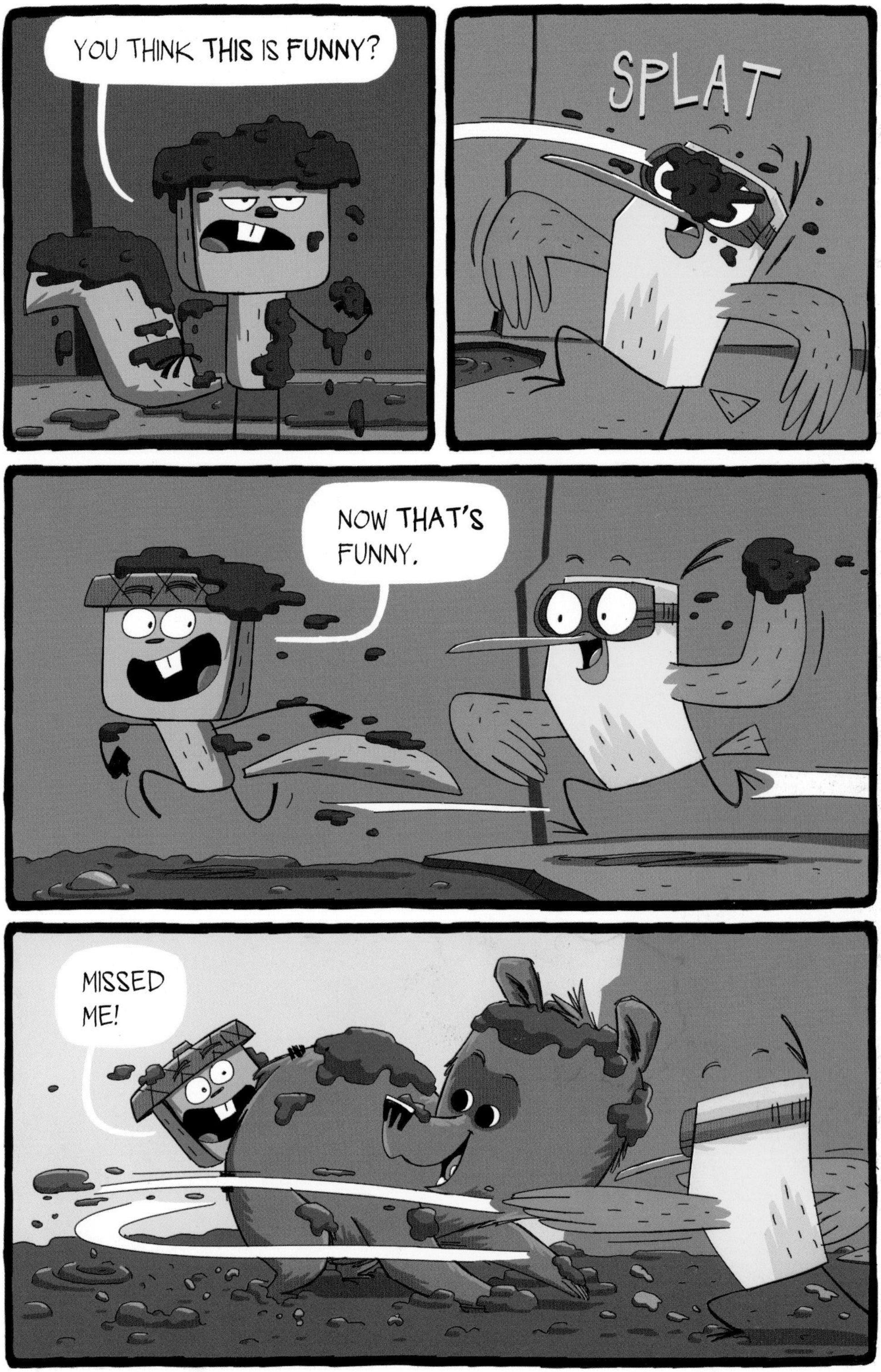
YOU THINK THIS IS FUNNY?
SPLAT
NOW THAT'S FUNNY.
MISSED ME!

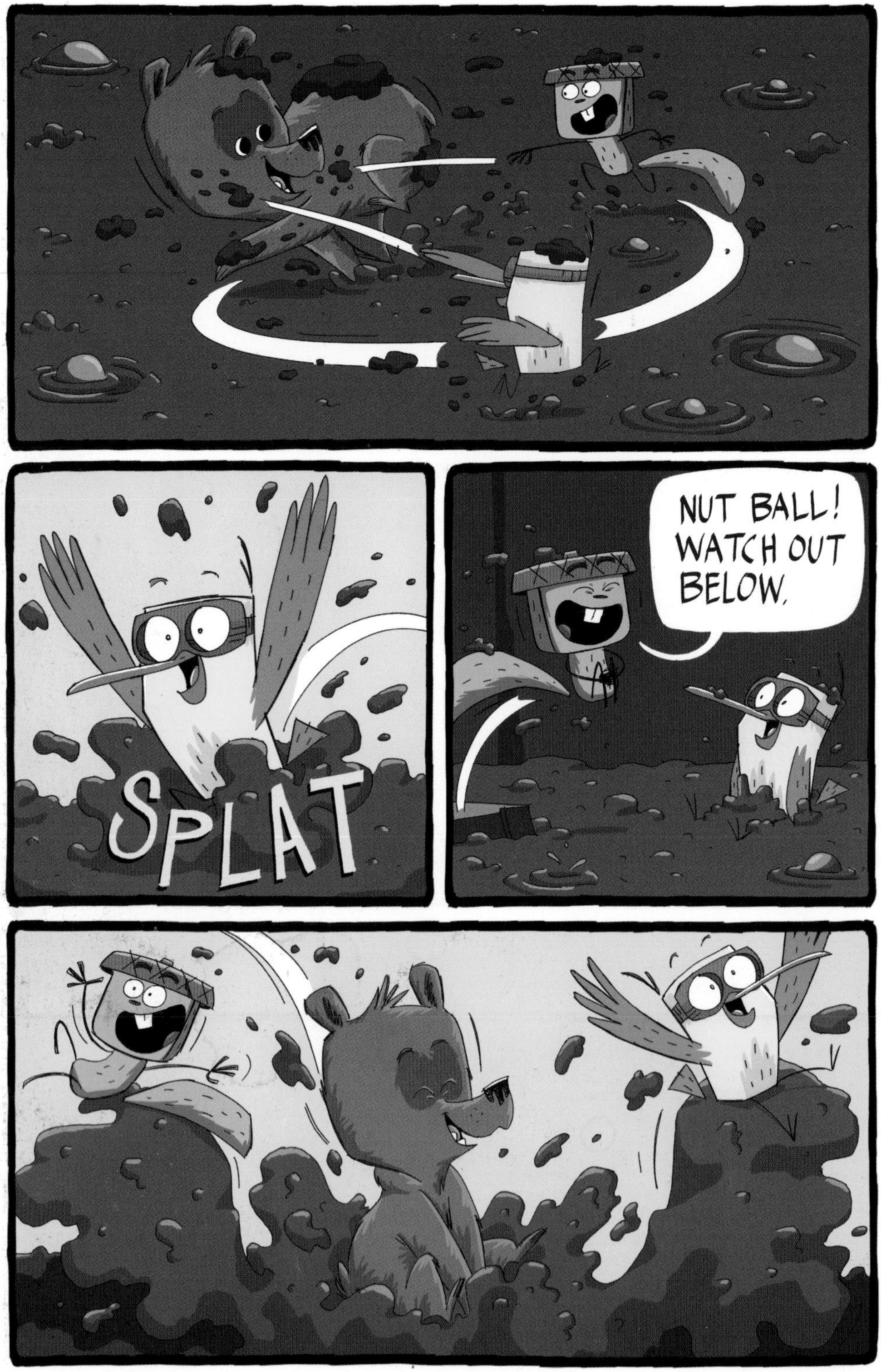
SPLAT
NUT BALL! WATCH OUT BELOW.

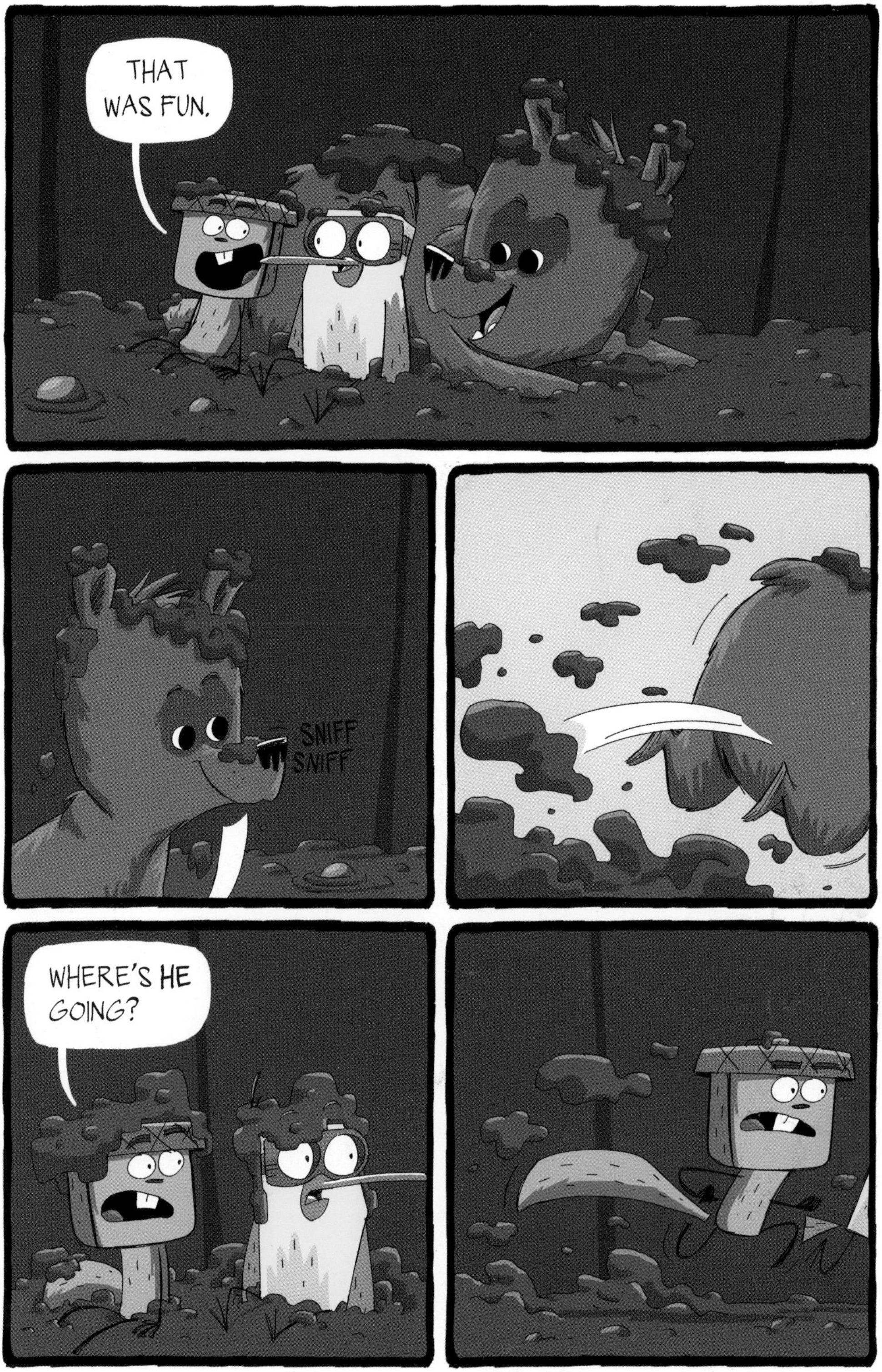
THAT WAS FUN.
SNIFF SNIFF
WHERE'S HE GOING?

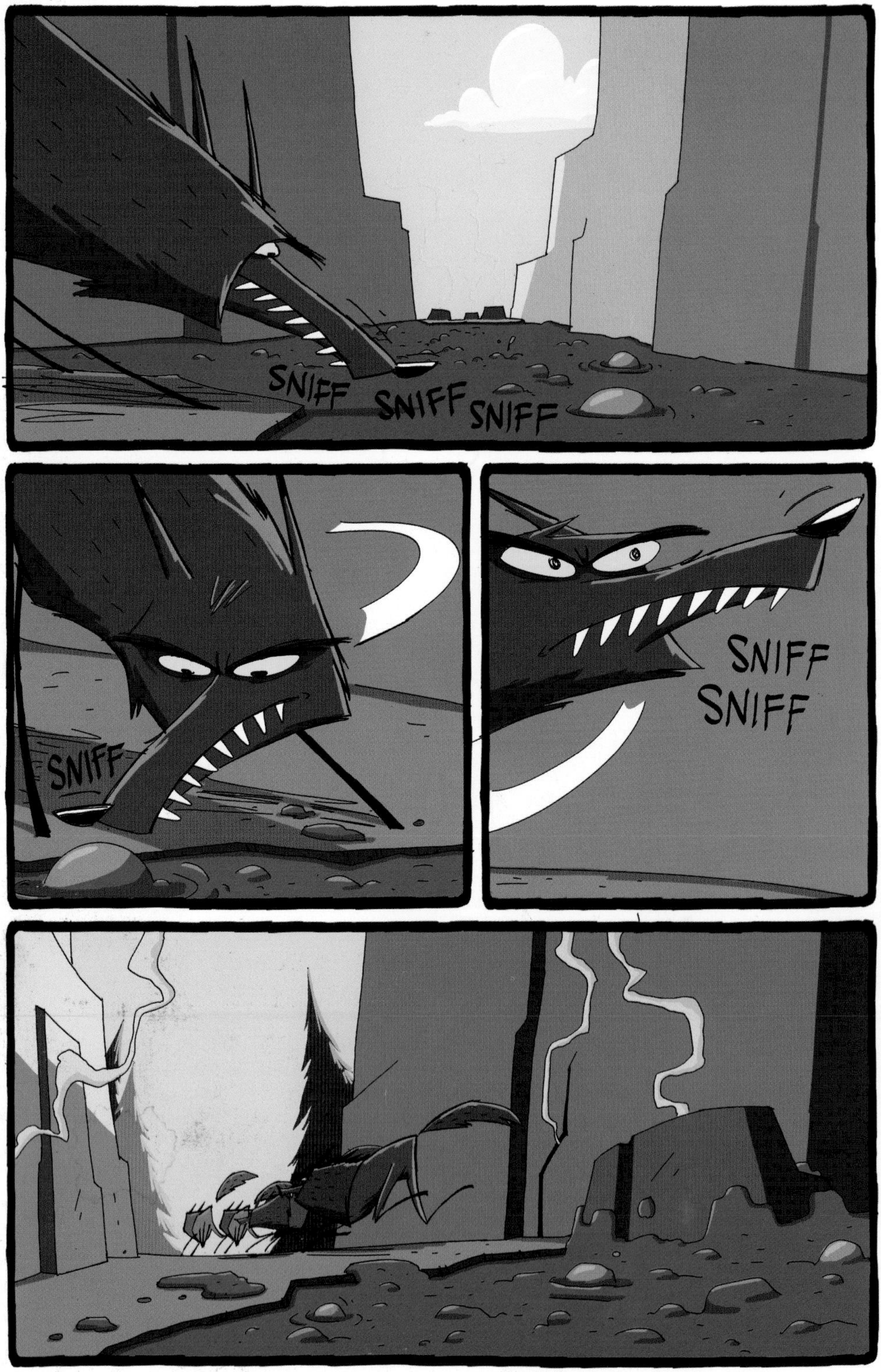
SNIFF
SNIFF
SNIFF
SNIFF
SNIFF
SNIFF

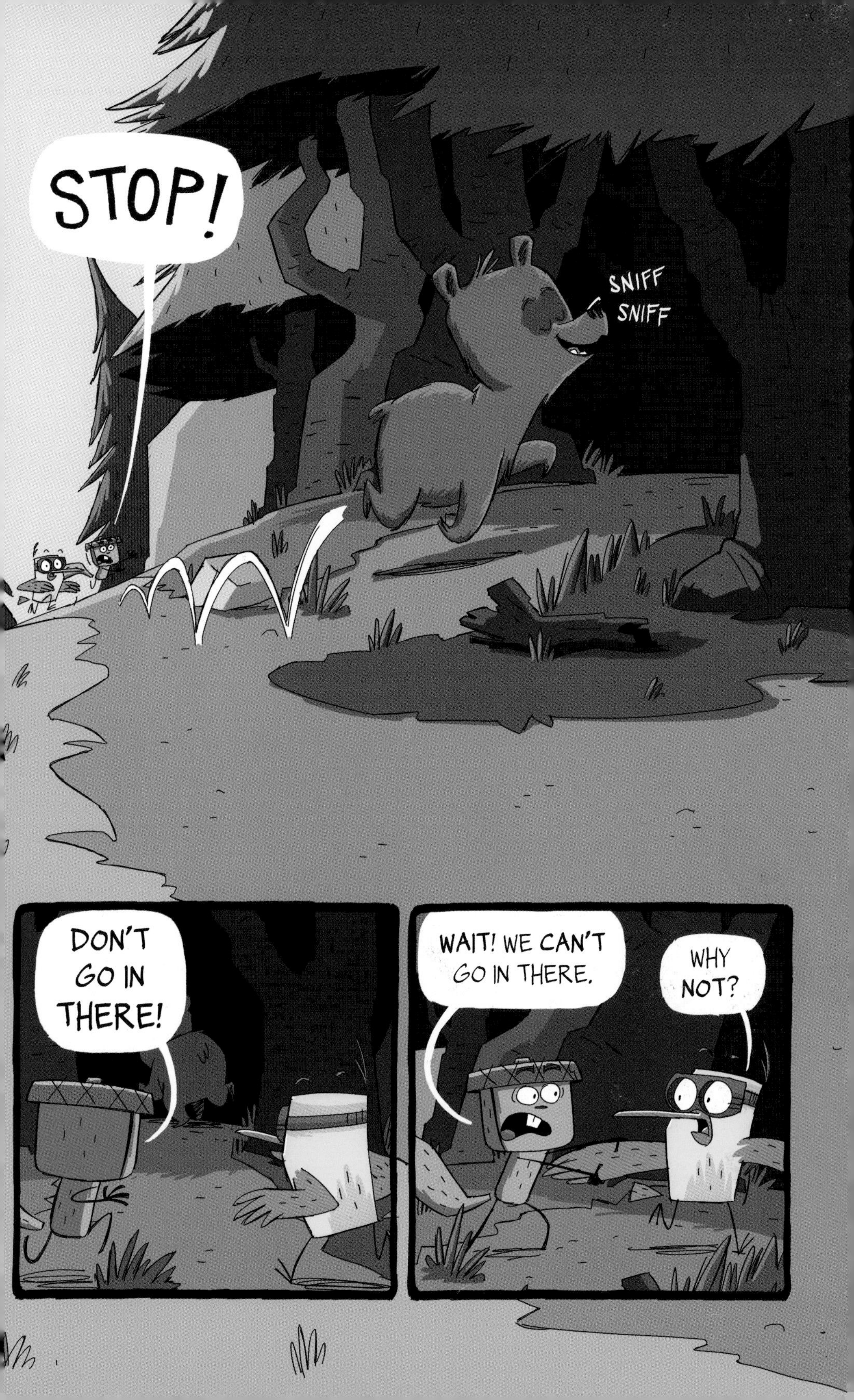
STOP!
SNIFF SNIFF
DON'T GO IN THERE!
WAIT! WE CAN'T GO IN THERE.
WHY NOT?

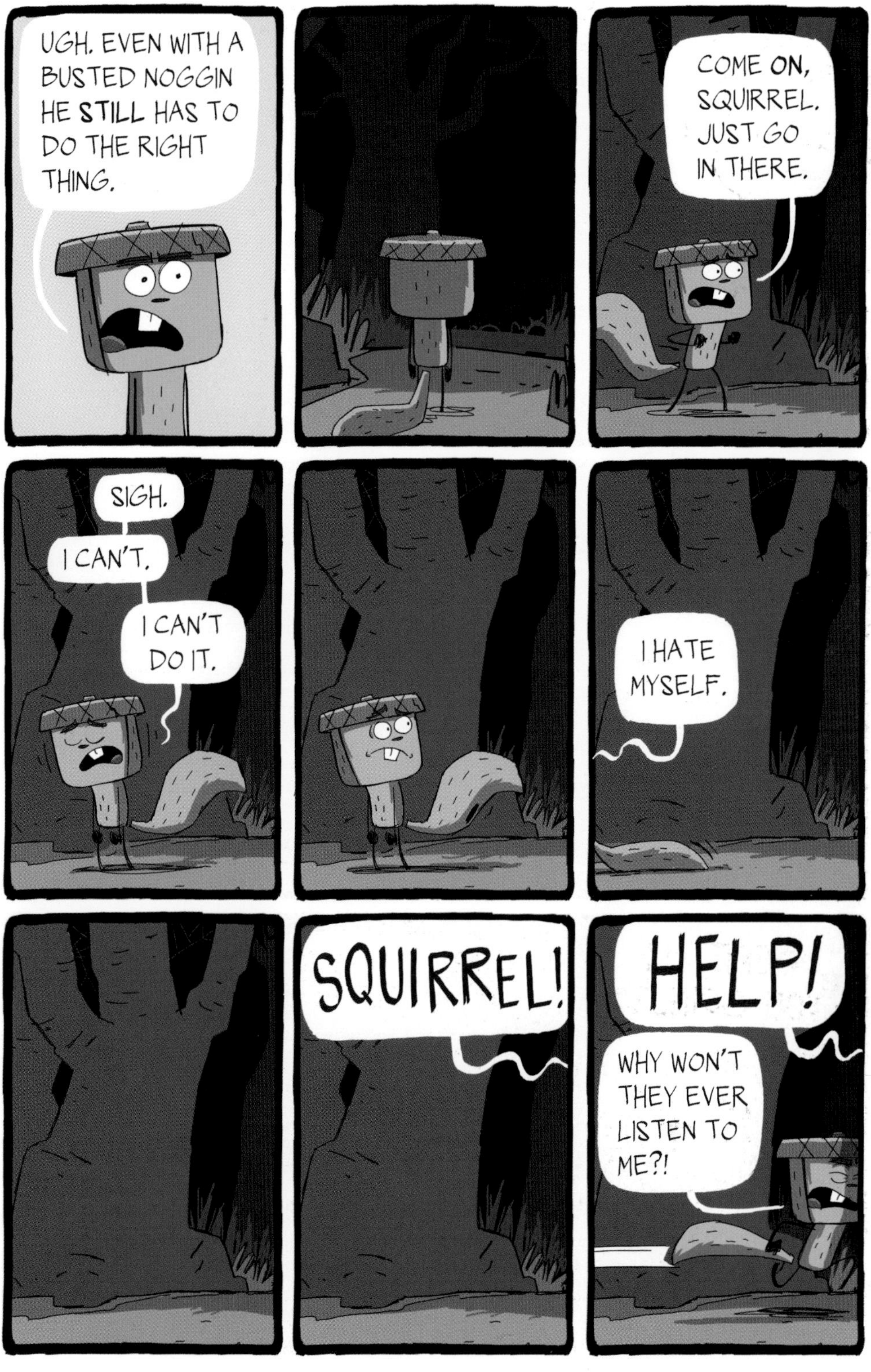
UGH. EVEN WITH A BUSTED NOGGIN HE STILL HAS TO DO THE RIGHT THING.
COME ON, SQUIRREL. JUST GO IN THERE.
SIGH.
I CAN'T.
I CAN'T DO IT.
I HATE MYSELF.
SQUIRREL!
HELP!
WHY WON'T THEY EVER LISTEN TO ME?!

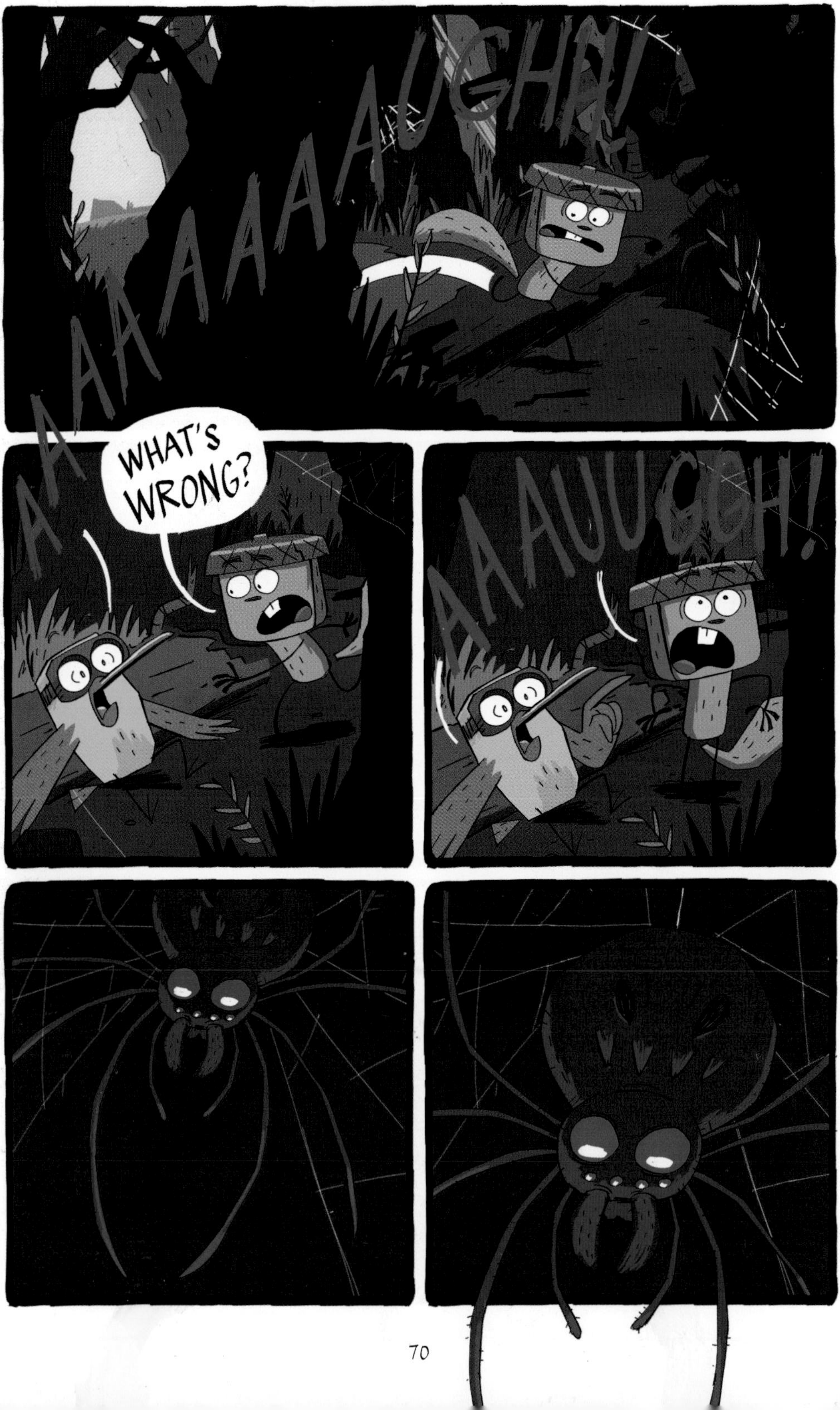
AAAAAAAAAUGHH!
WHAT'S WRONG?
AAAUUGGH!

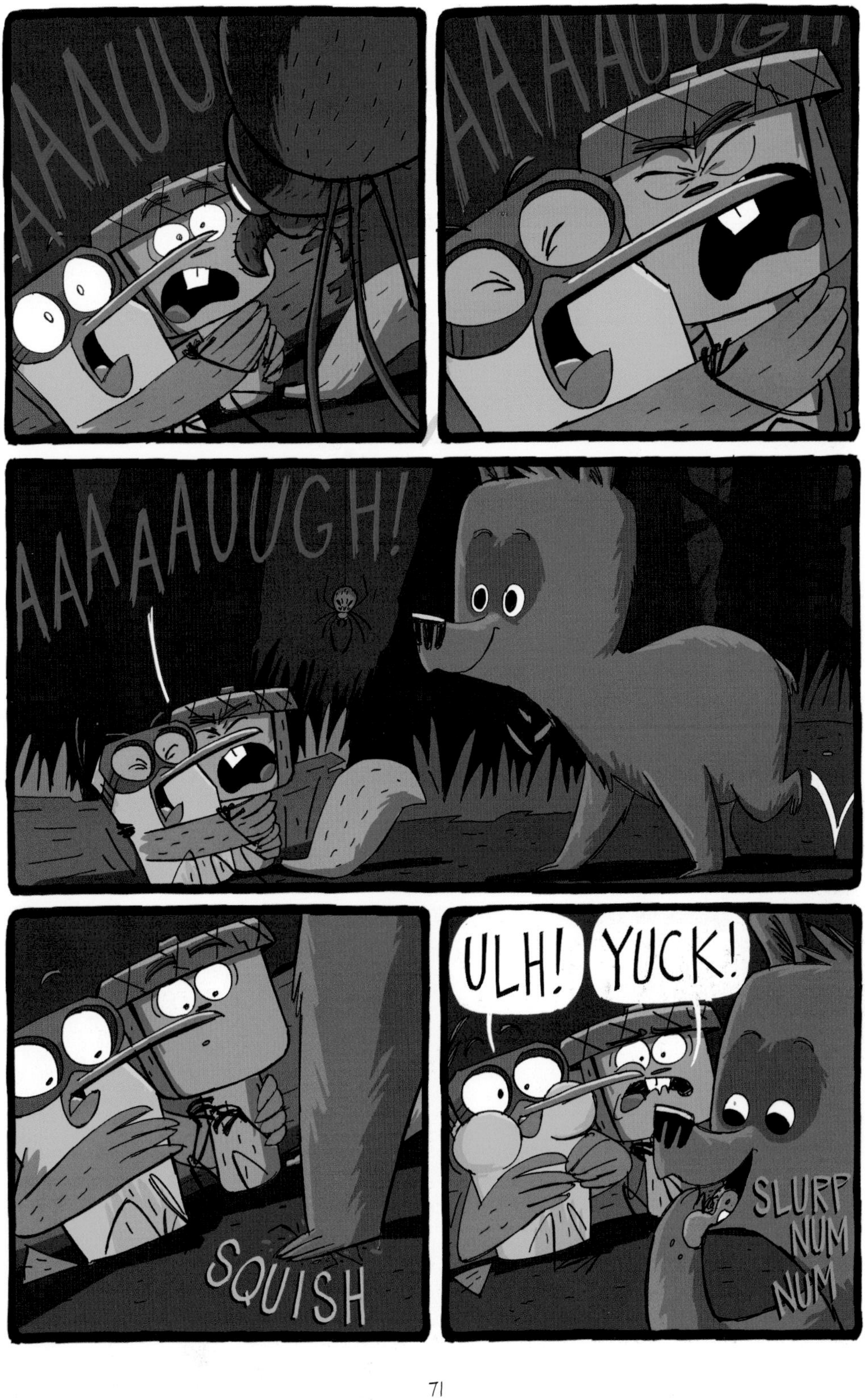
AAUU
AAAAUUGH
AAAAAUUGH!
SQUISH
ULH!
YUCK!
SLURP
NUM
NUM

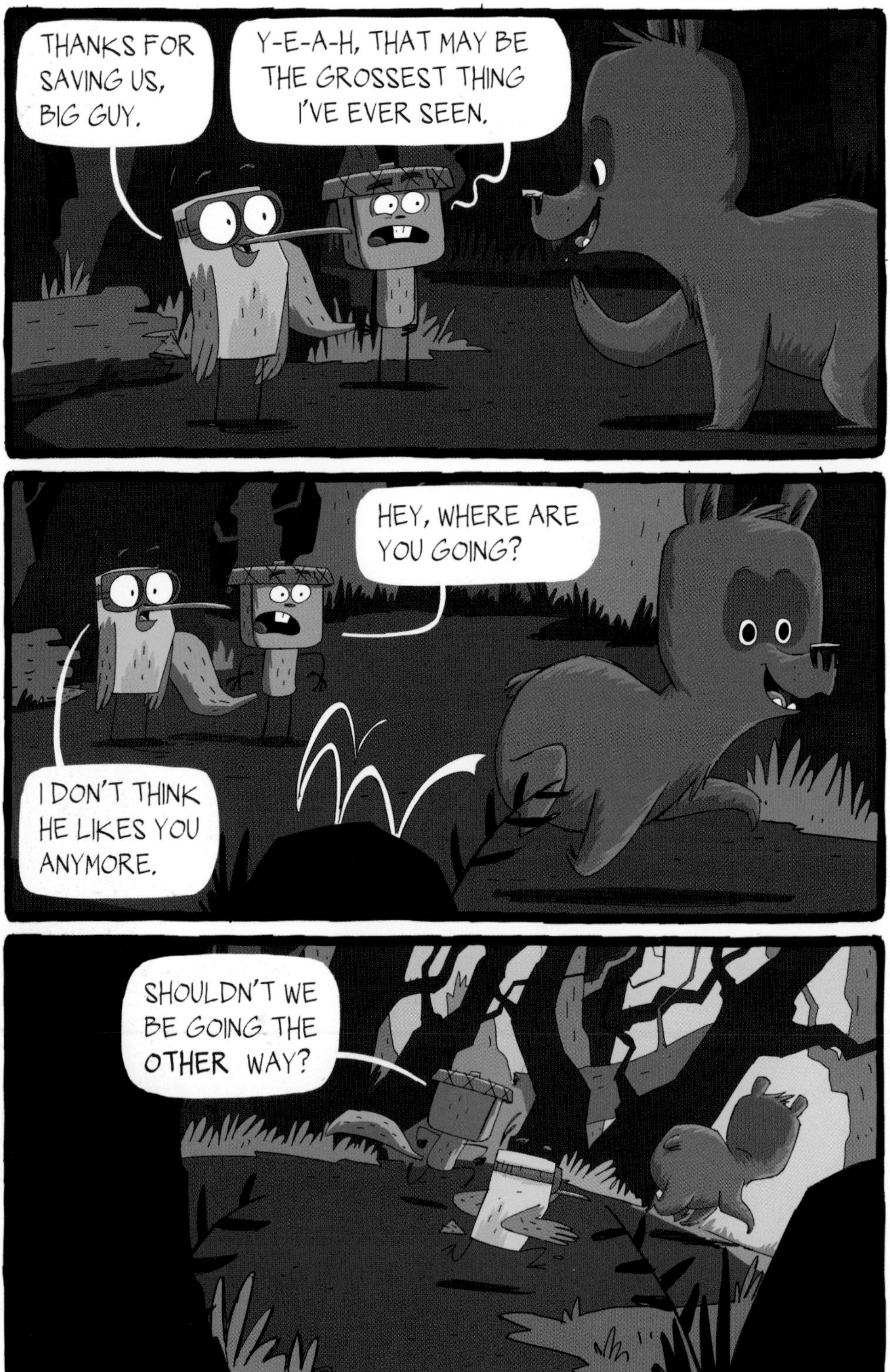
THANKS FOR SAVING US, BIG GUY.
Y-E-A-H, THAT MAY BE THE GROSSEST THING I'VE EVER SEEN.
HEY, WHERE ARE YOU GOING?
I DON'T THINK HE LIKES YOU ANYMORE.
SHOULDN'T WE BE GOING THE OTHER WAY?

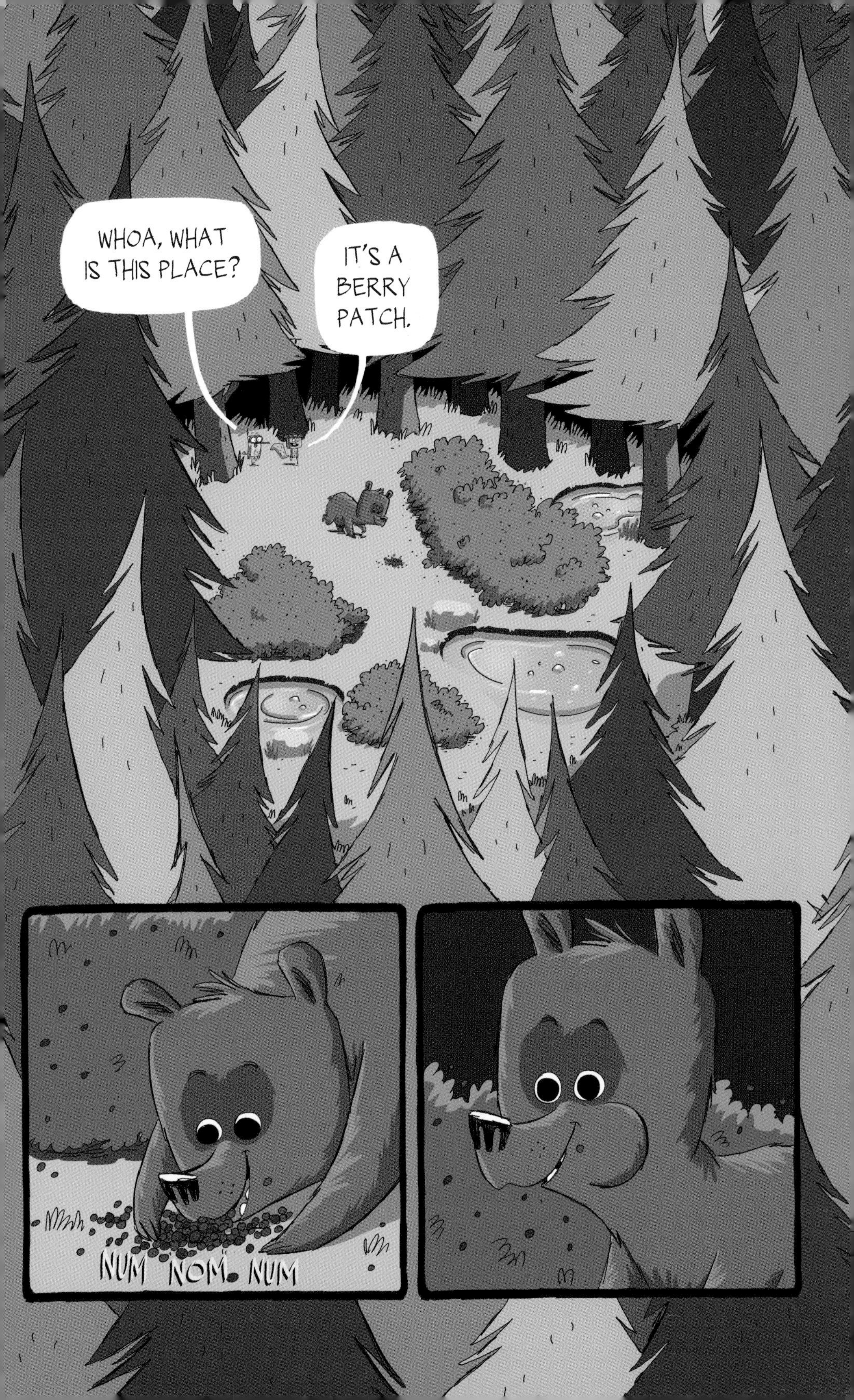
WHOA, WHAT IS THIS PLACE?
IT'S A BERRY PATCH.
NUM NOM NUM

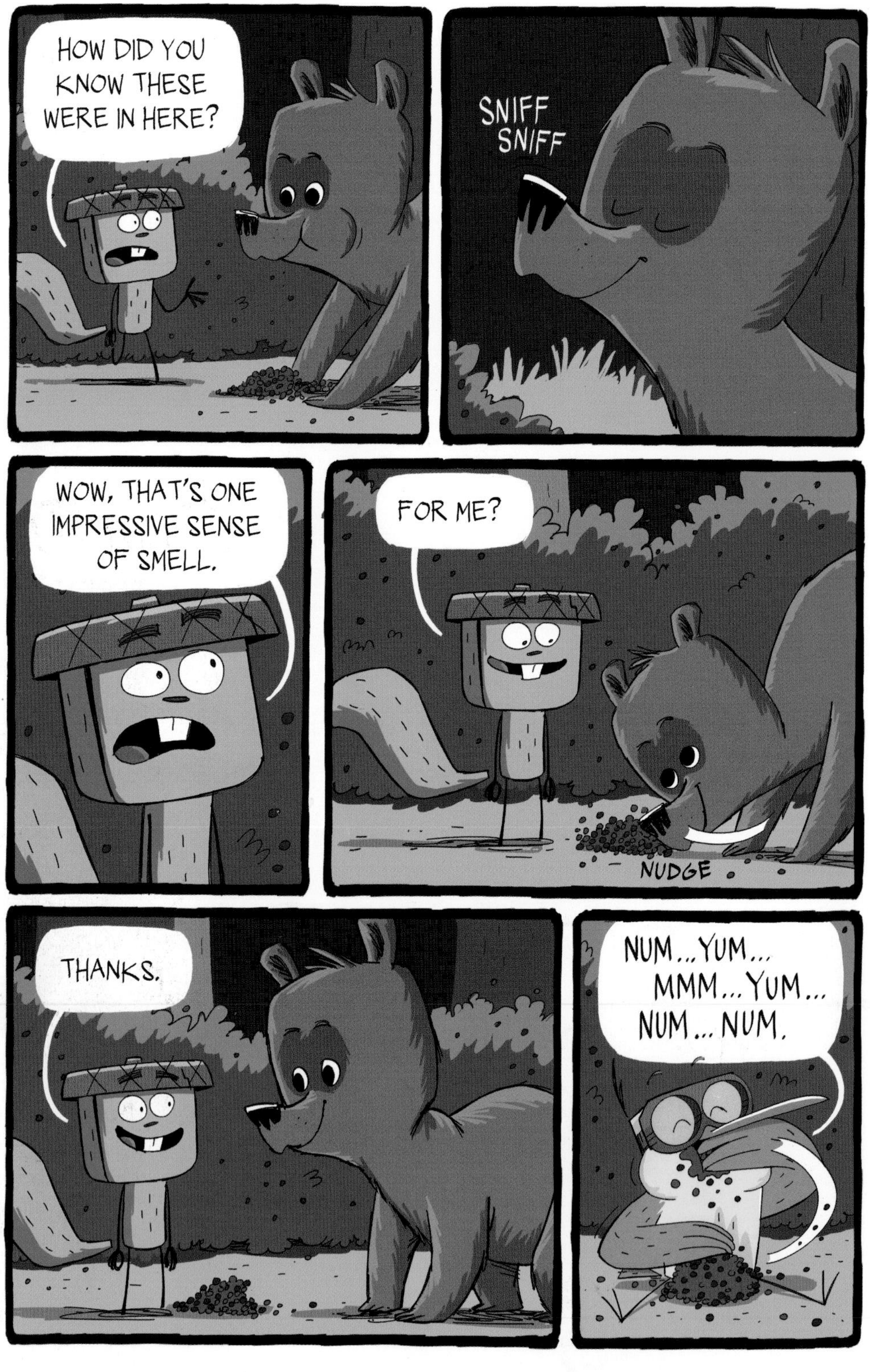
HOW DID YOU KNOW THESE WERE IN HERE?
SNIFF SNIFF
WOW, THAT'S ONE IMPRESSIVE SENSE OF SMELL.
FOR ME?
NUDGE
THANKS.
NUM... YUM... MMM... YUM... NUM... NUM.

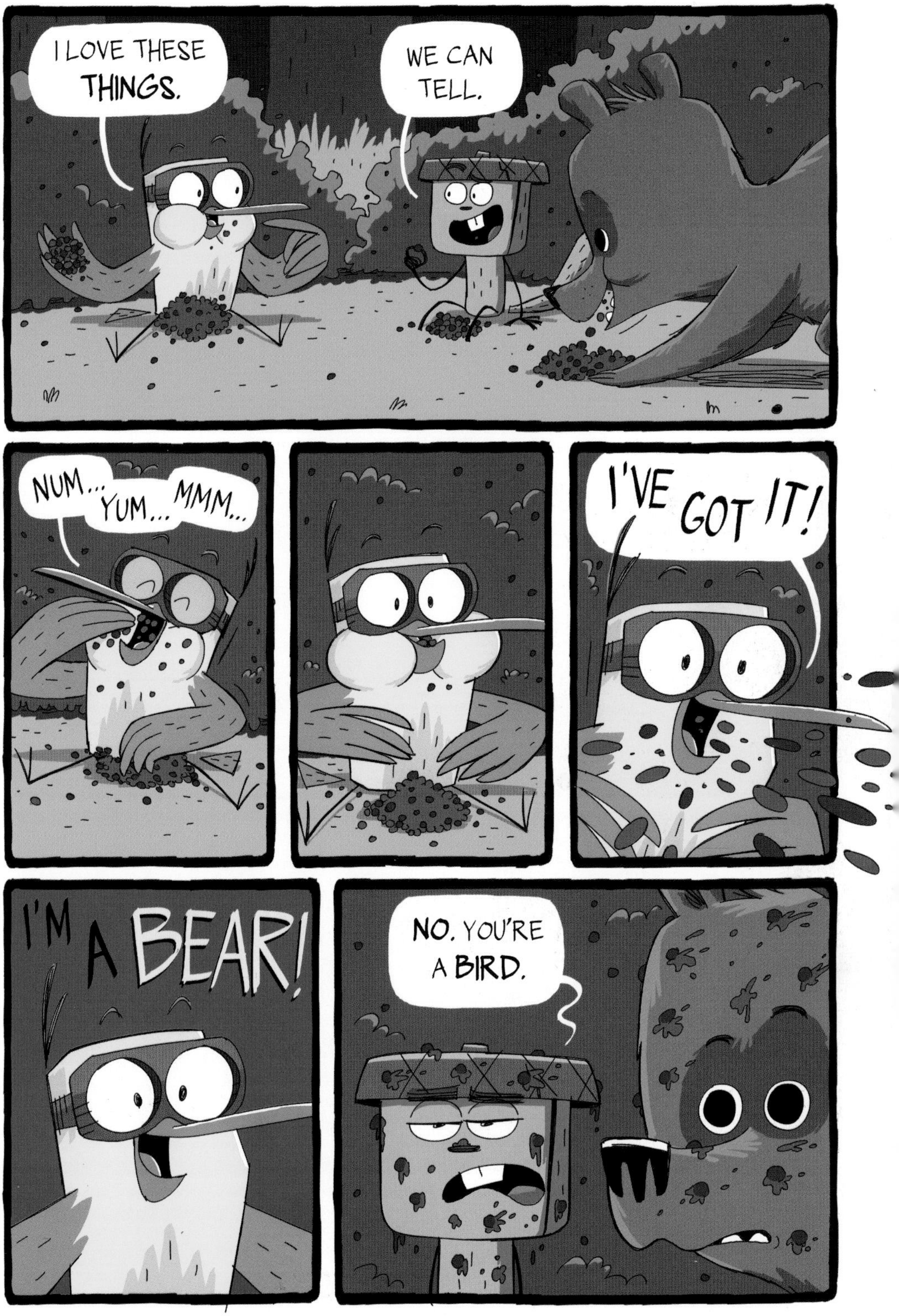
I LOVE THESE THINGS.
WE CAN TELL.
NUM... YUM... MMM...
I'VE GOT IT!
I'M A BEAR!
NO. YOU'RE A BIRD.

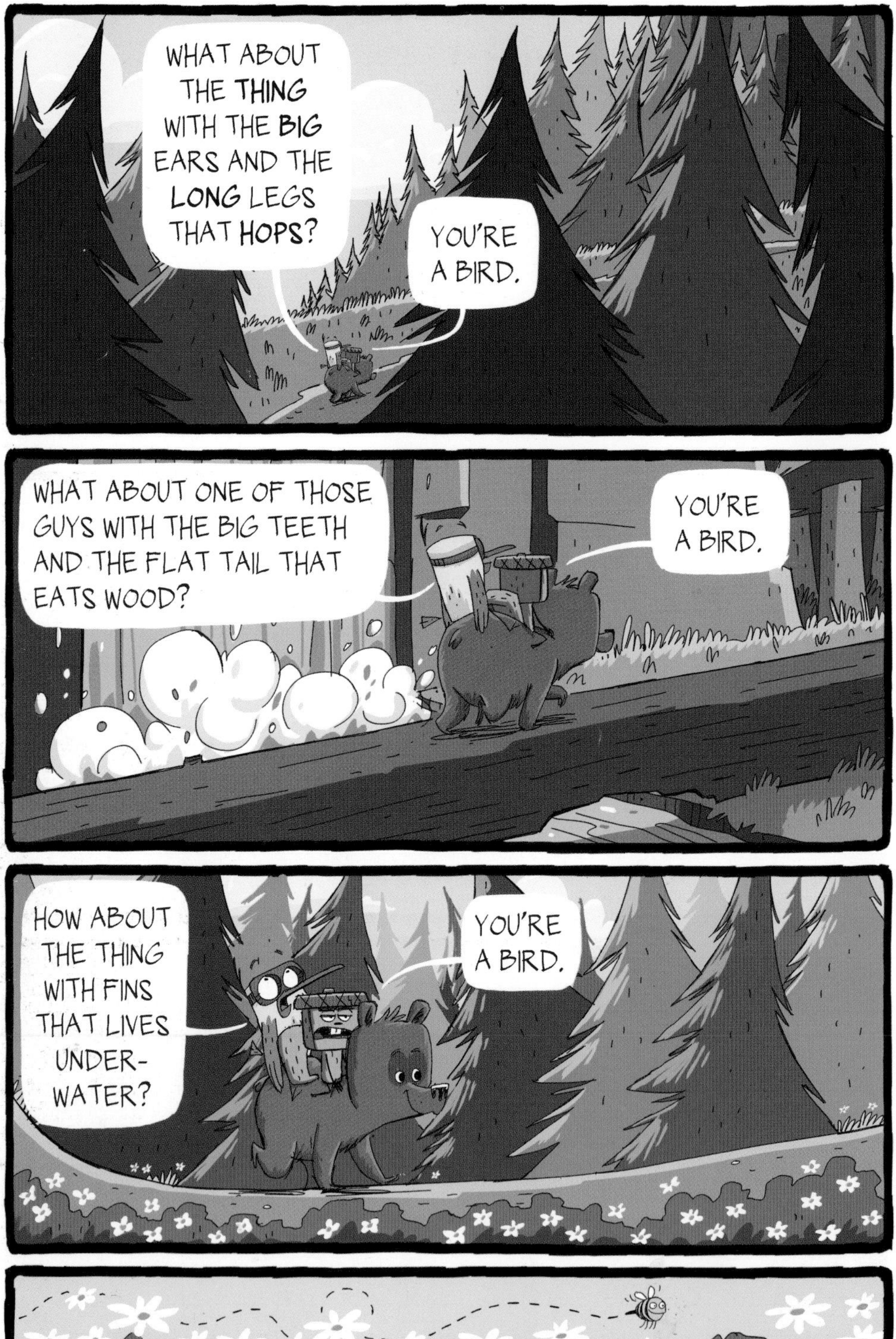
WHAT ABOUT THE THING WITH THE BIG EARS AND THE LONG LEGS THAT HOPS?
YOU'RE A BIRD.
WHAT ABOUT ONE OF THOSE GUYS WITH THE BIG TEETH AND THE FLAT TAIL THAT EATS WOOD?
YOU'RE A BIRD.
HOW ABOUT THE THING WITH FINS THAT LIVES UNDER-WATER?
YOU'RE A BIRD.

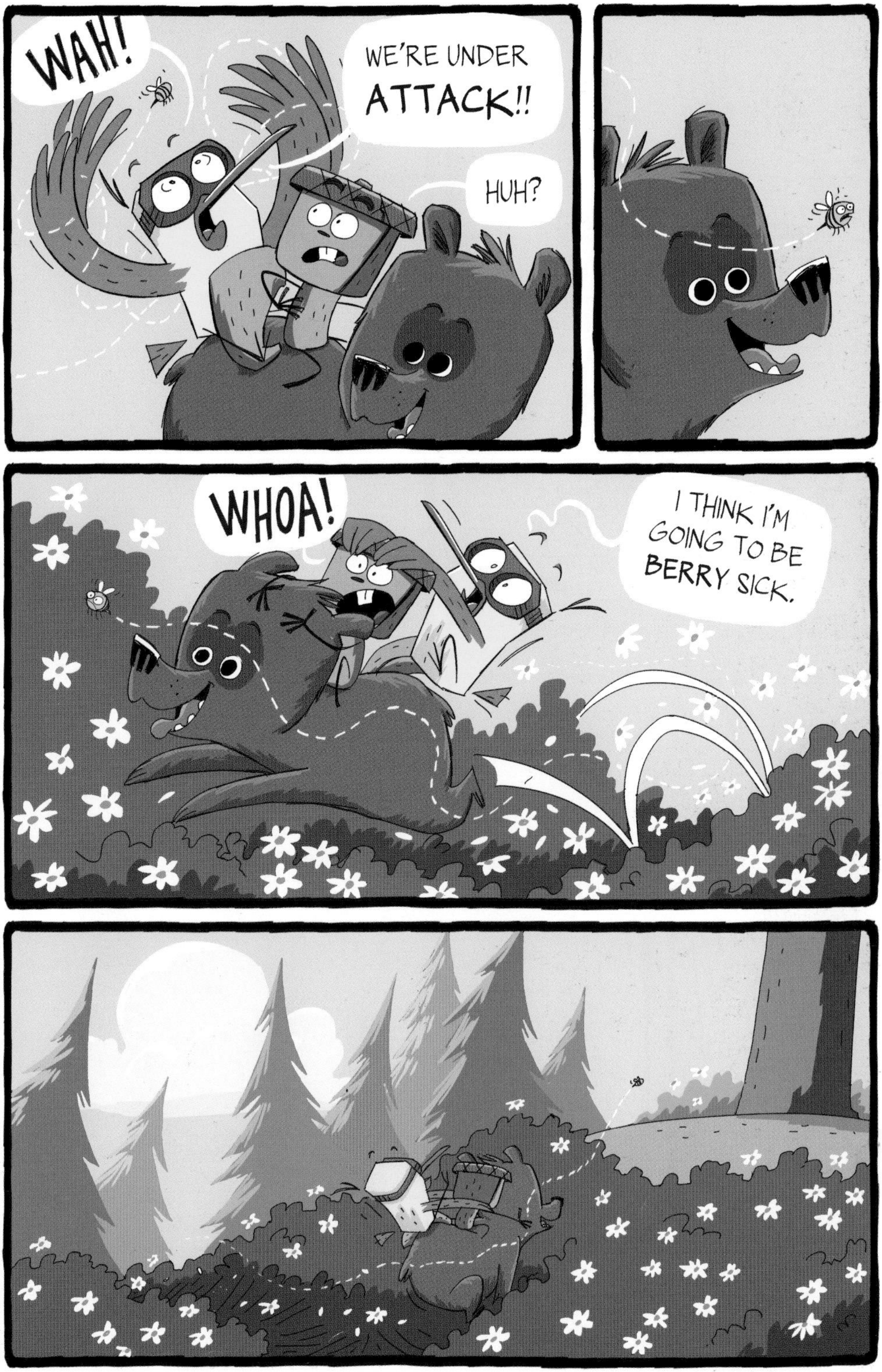
WAH!
WE'RE UNDER ATTACK!!
HUH?
WHOA!
I THINK I'M GOING TO BE BERRY SICK.

79

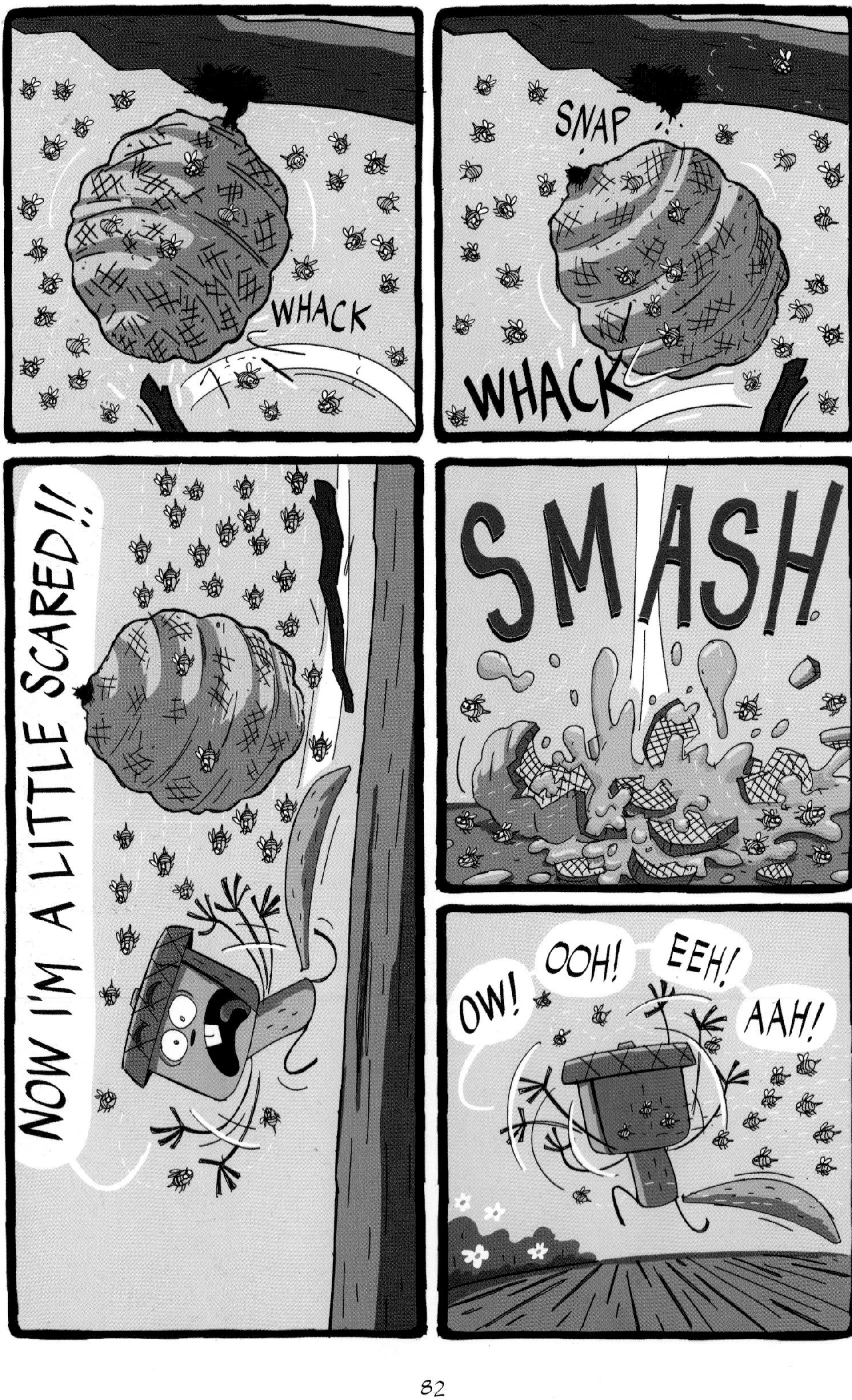
WHACK
SNAP
WHACK
NOW I'M A LITTLE SCARED!!
SMASH
OW!
OOH!
EEH!
AAH!

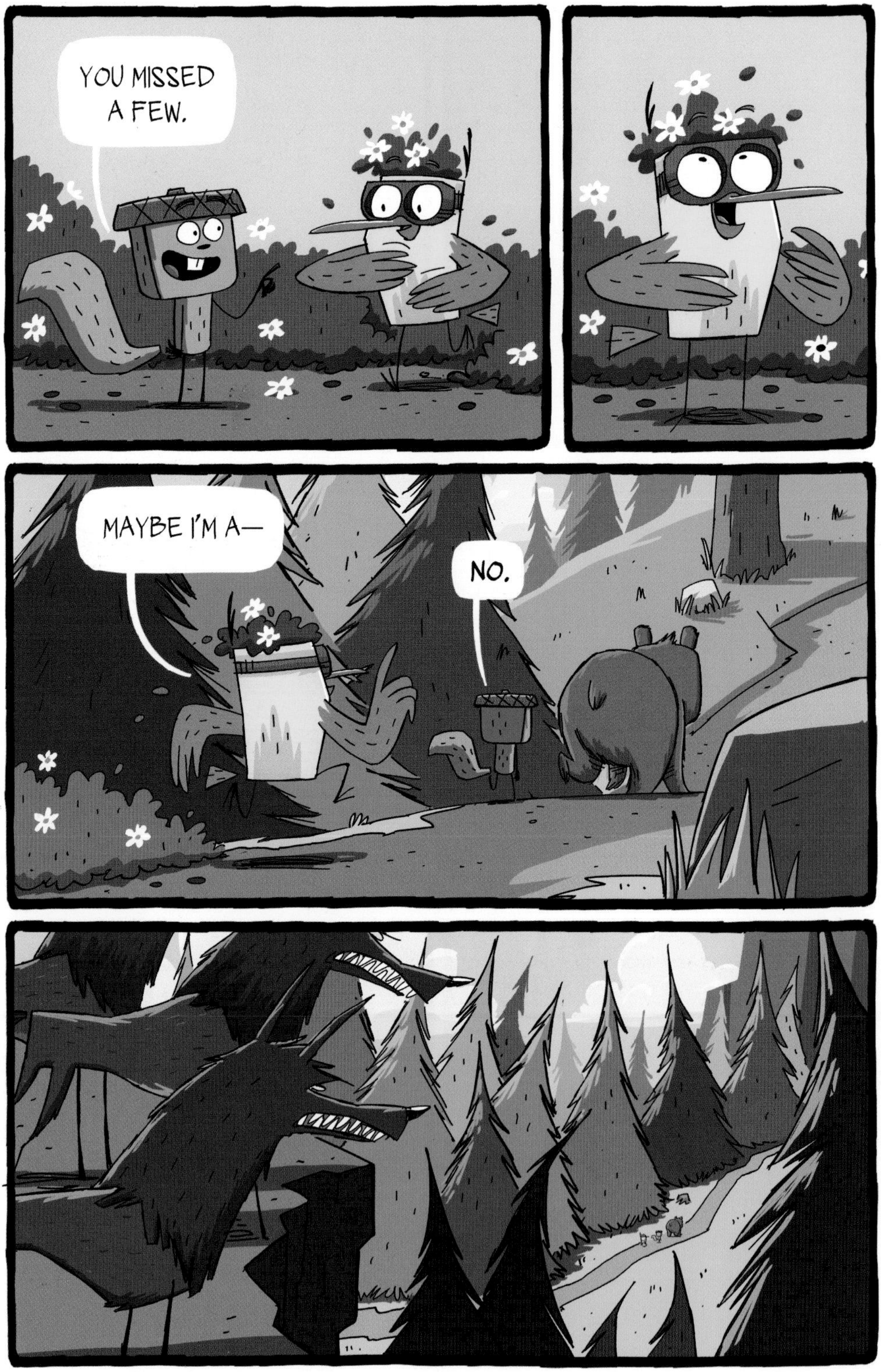
YOU MISSED A FEW.
MAYBE I'M A—
NO.

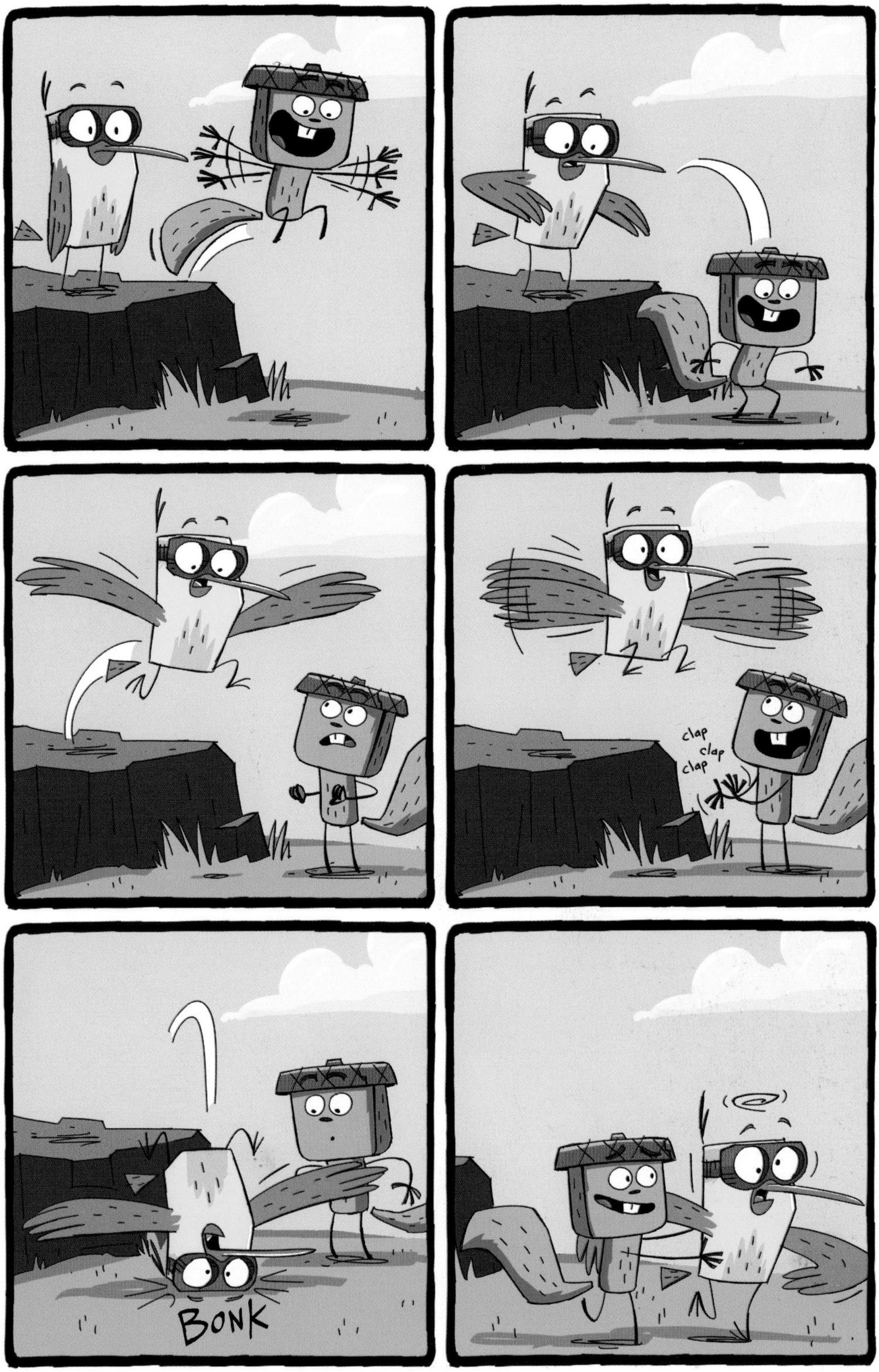
clap
clap
clap
BONK

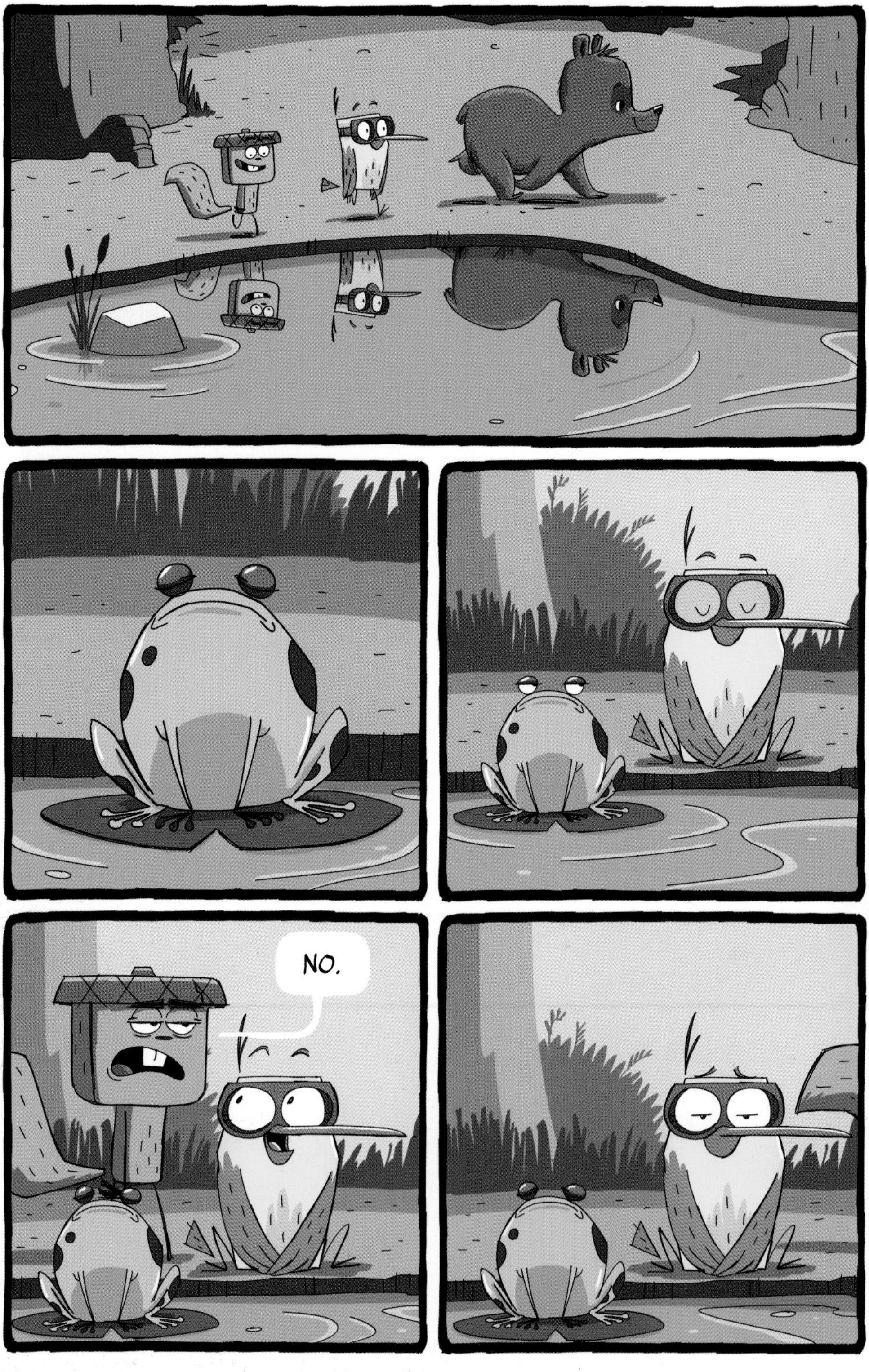
NO.

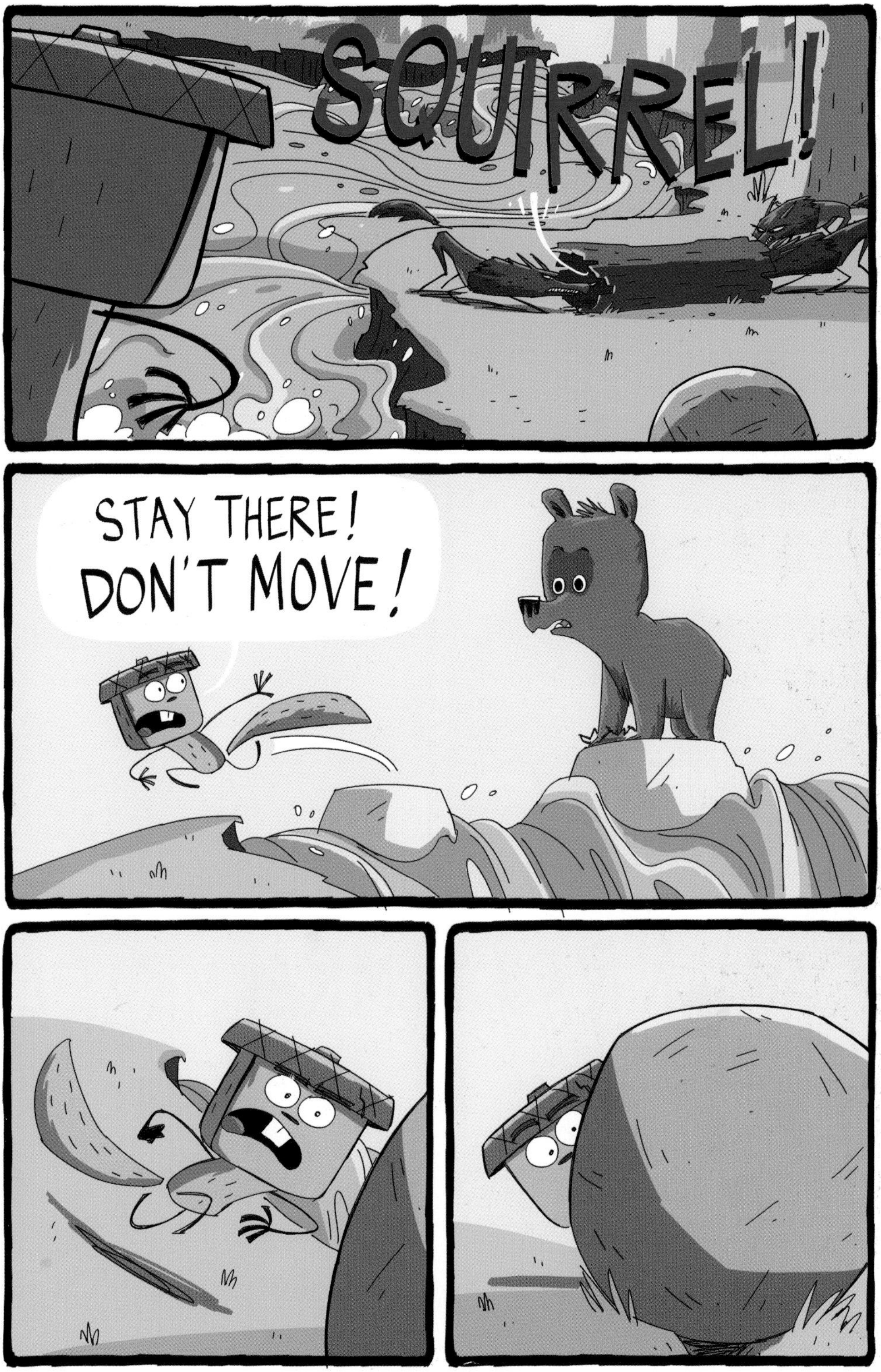
SQUIRREL!
STAY THERE! DON'T MOVE!

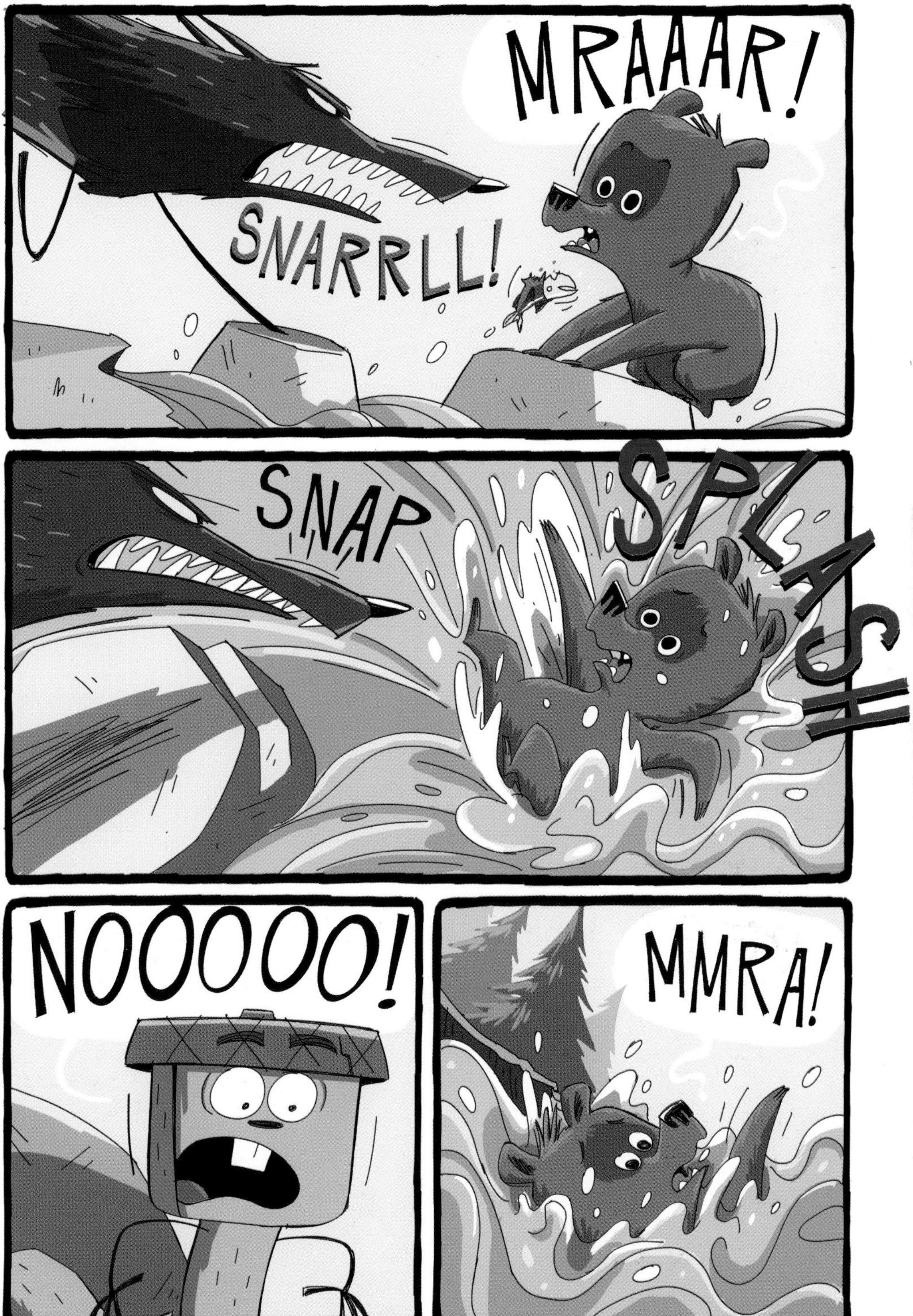
MRAAAR!
SNARRLL!
SNAP
SPLASH
NOOOOO!
MMRA!

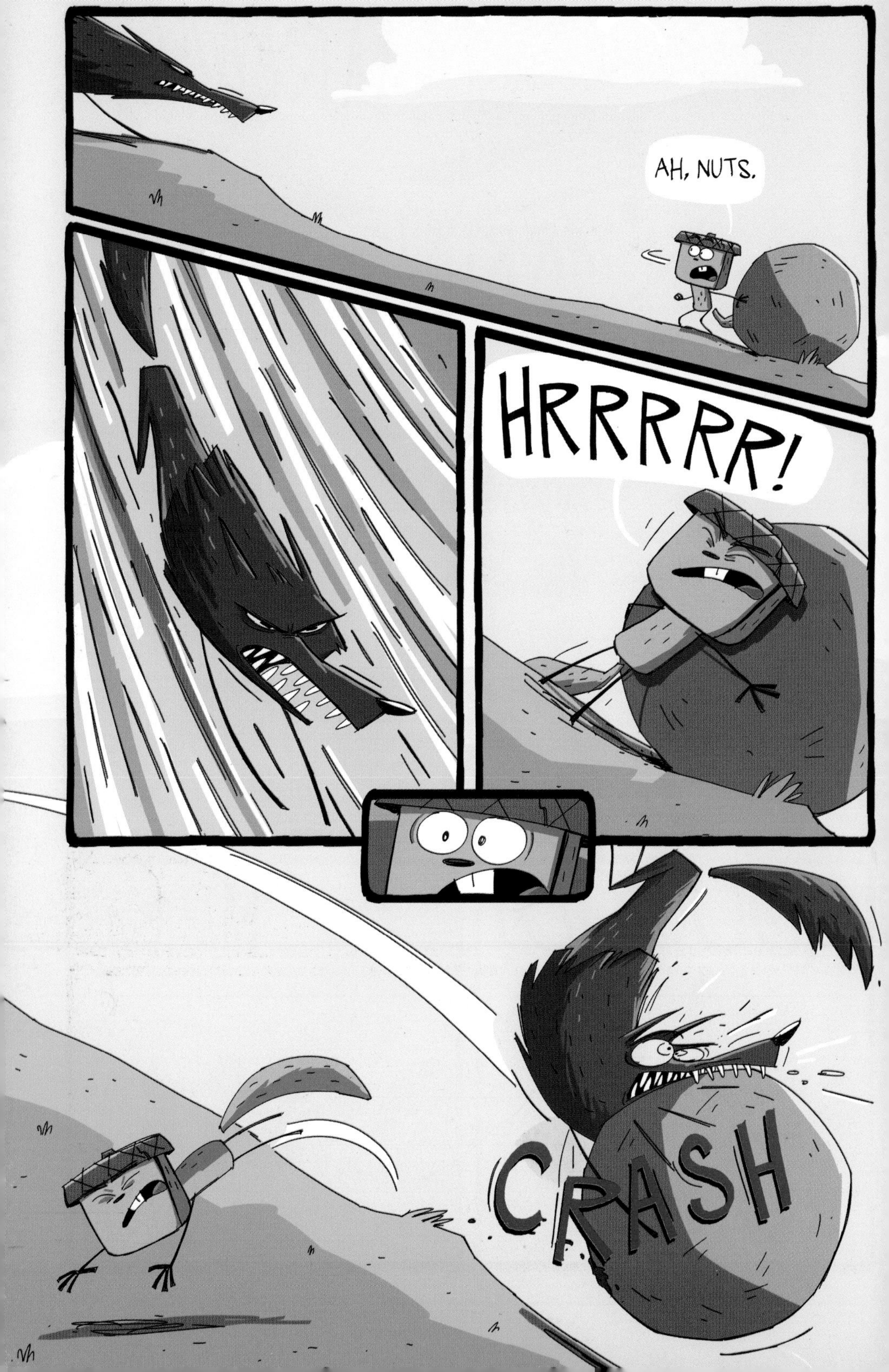
AH, NUTS.
HRRRRR!
CRASH

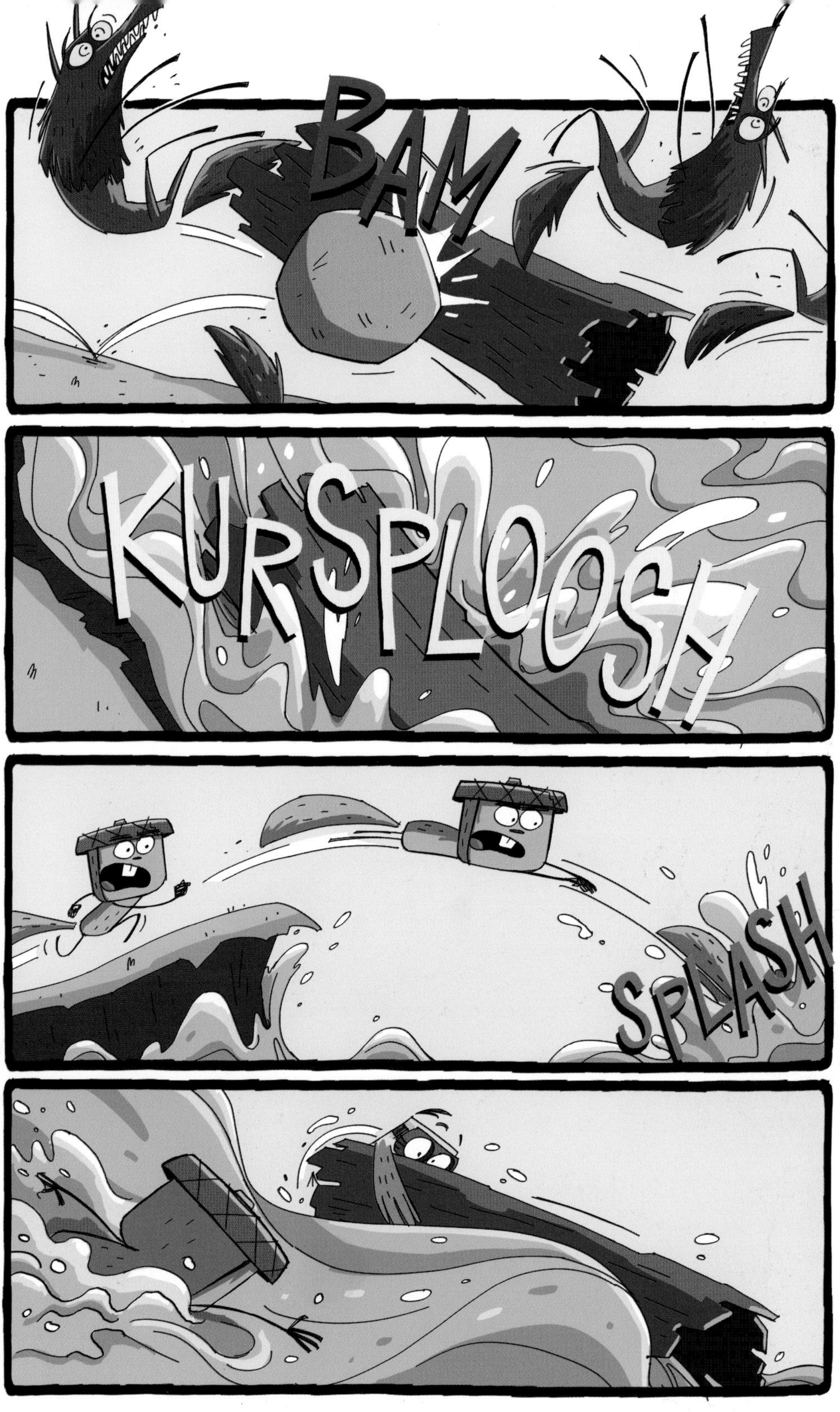
BAM
KURSPLOOSH
SPLASH

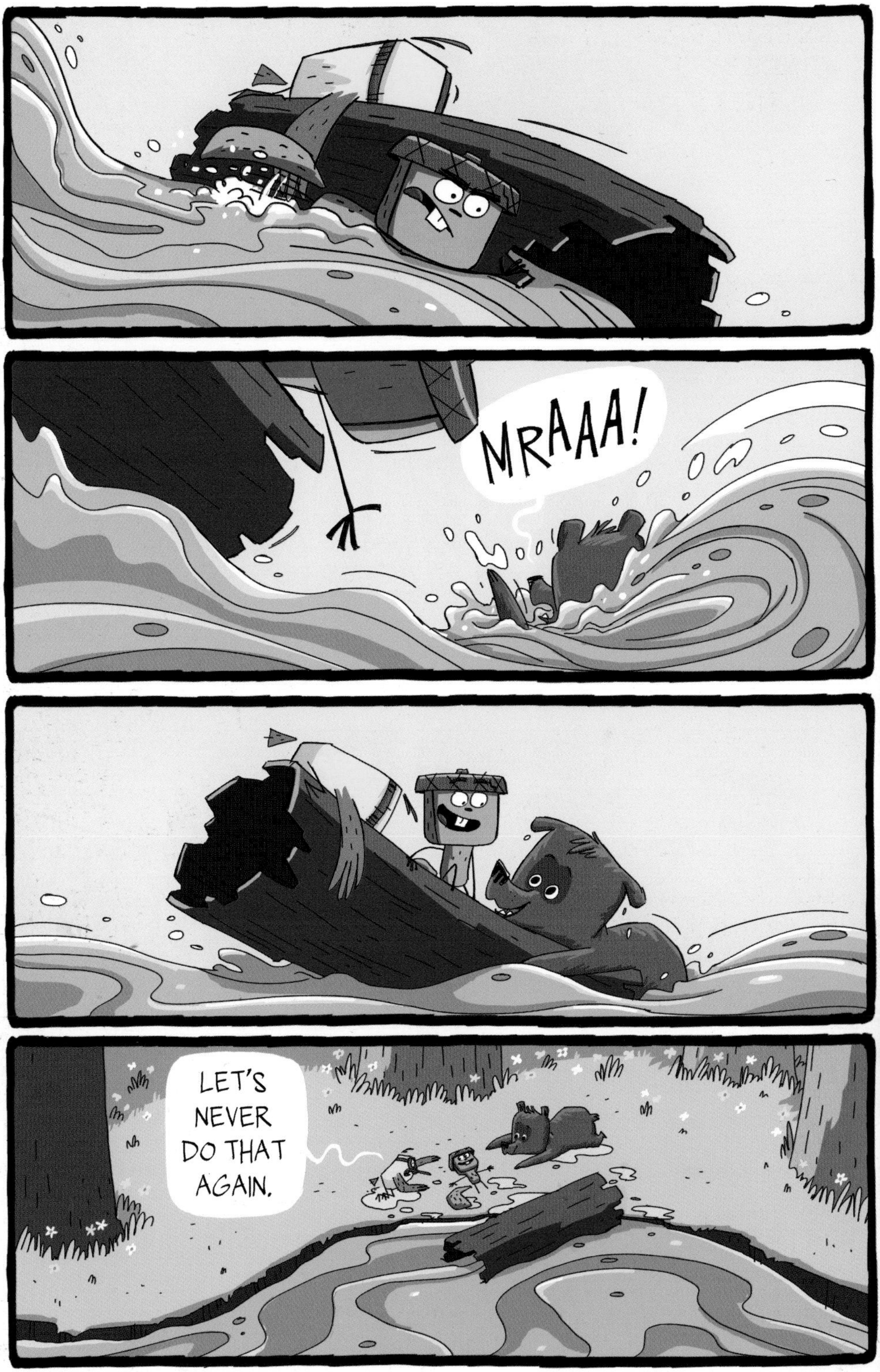
MRAAA!
LET'S NEVER DO THAT AGAIN.

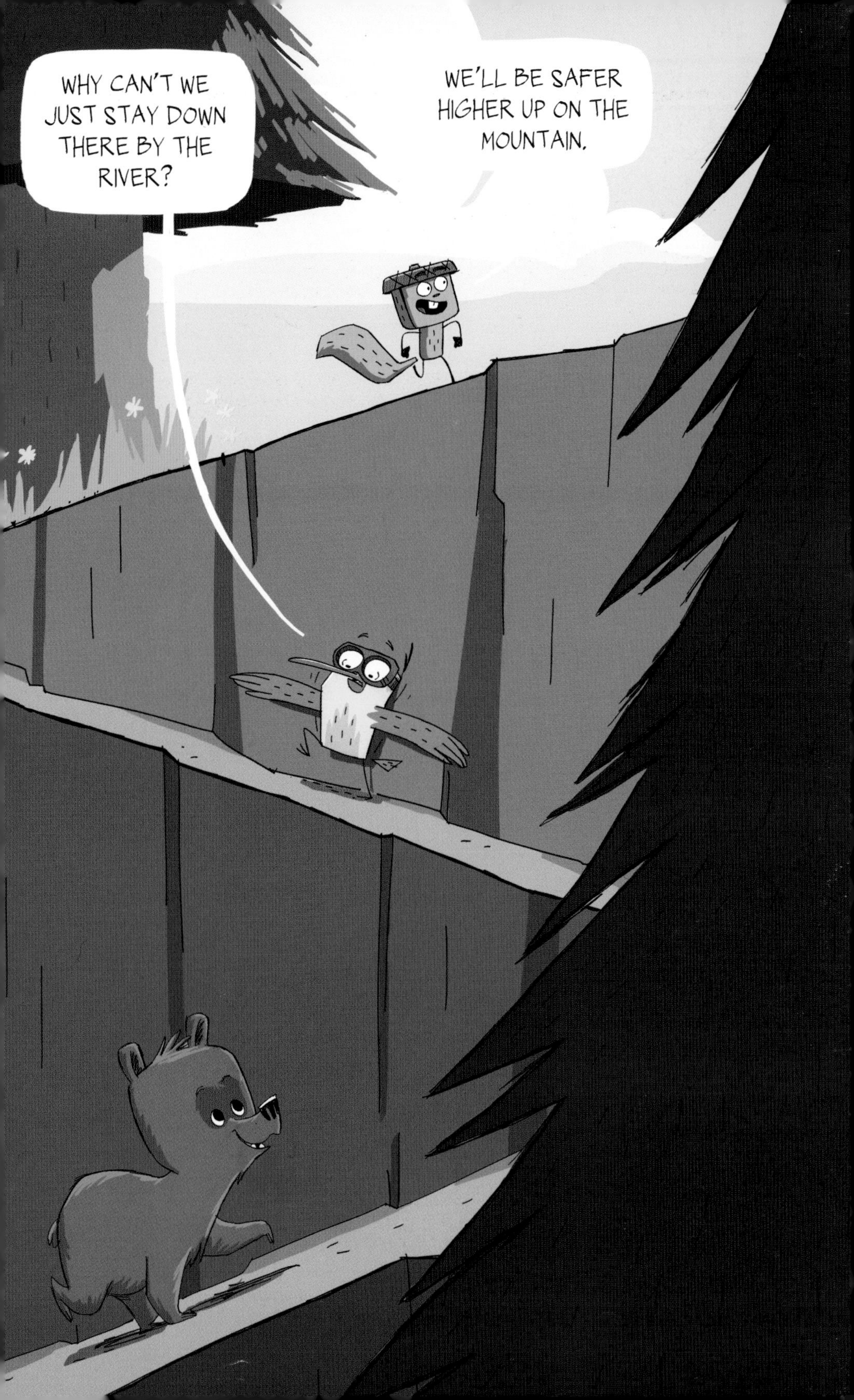
WHY CAN'T WE JUST STAY DOWN THERE BY THE RIVER?
WE'LL BE SAFER HIGHER UP ON THE MOUNTAIN.

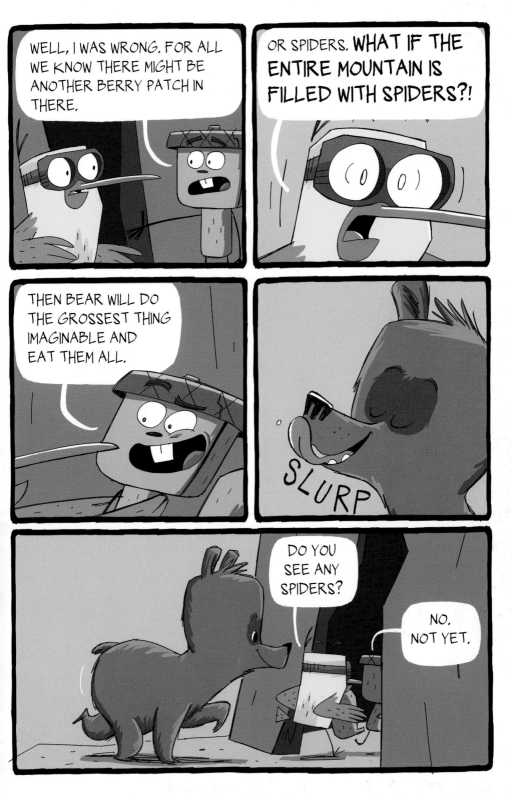

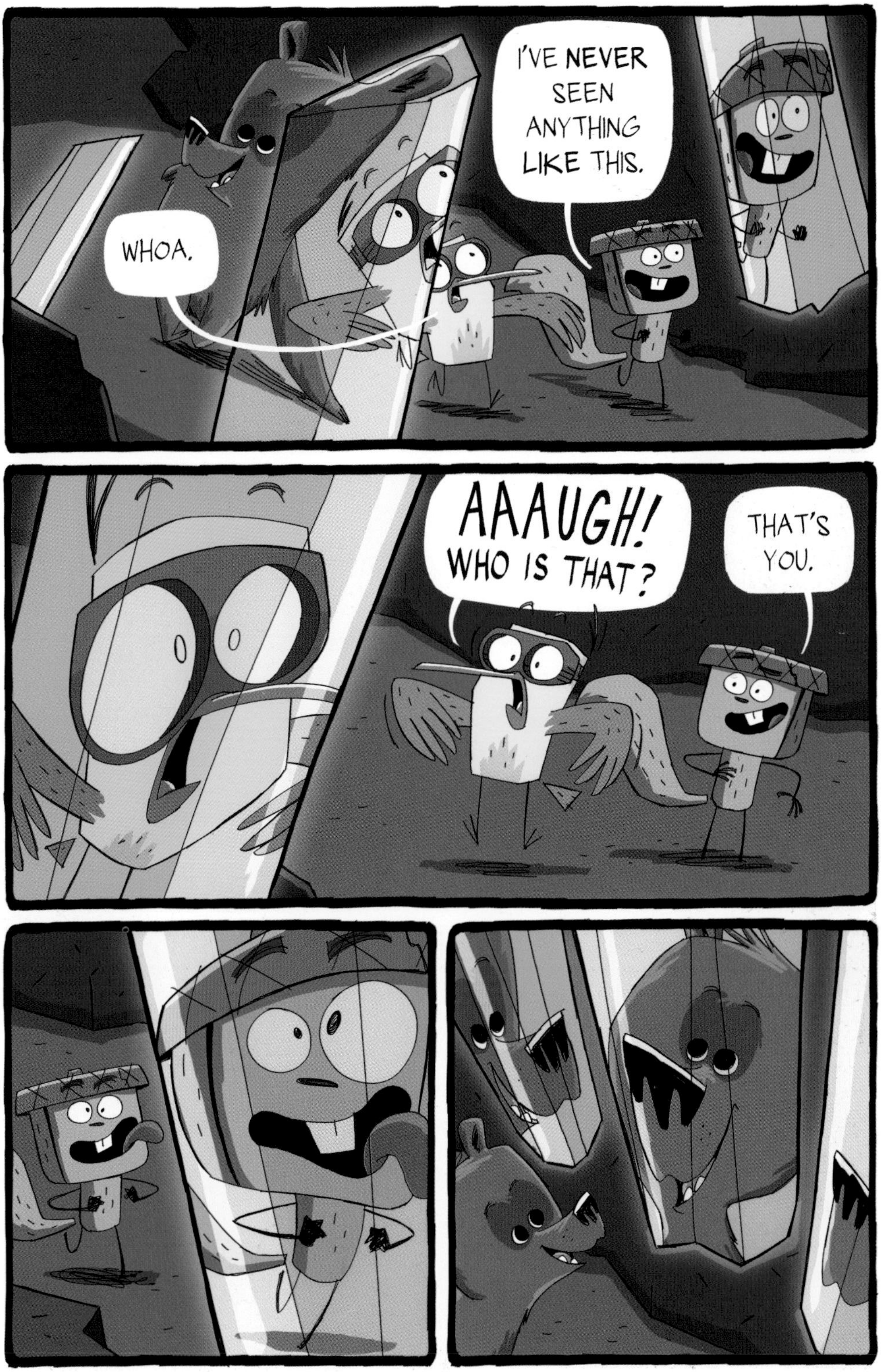
I'VE NEVER SEEN ANYTHING LIKE THIS.
WHOA.
AAAUGH! WHO IS THAT?
THAT'S YOU.

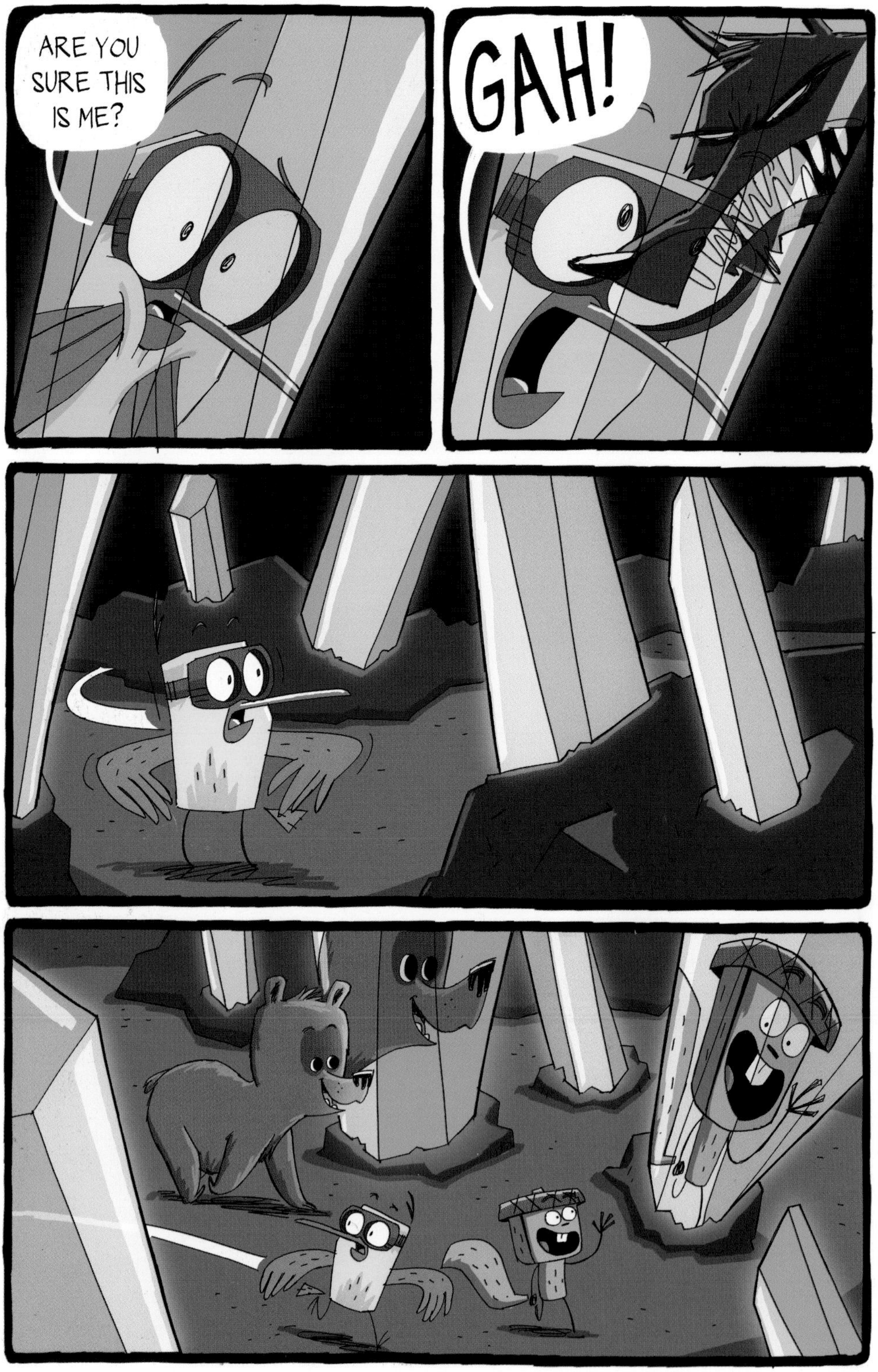
ARE YOU SURE THIS IS ME?
GAH!

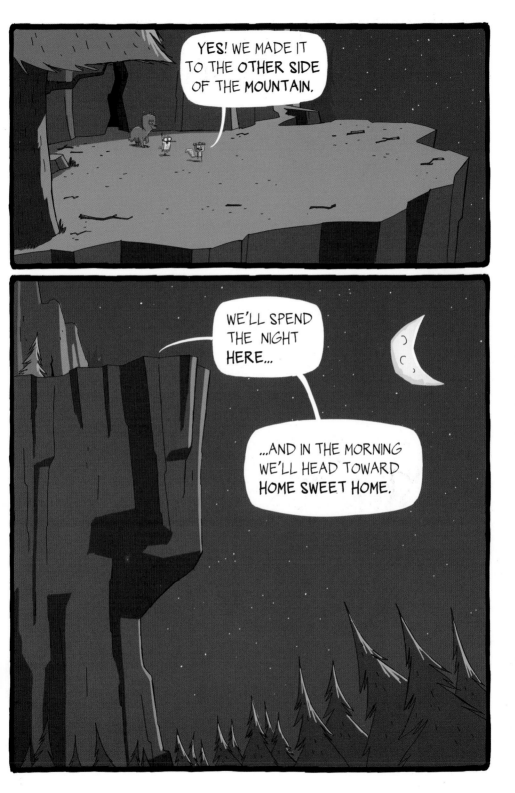

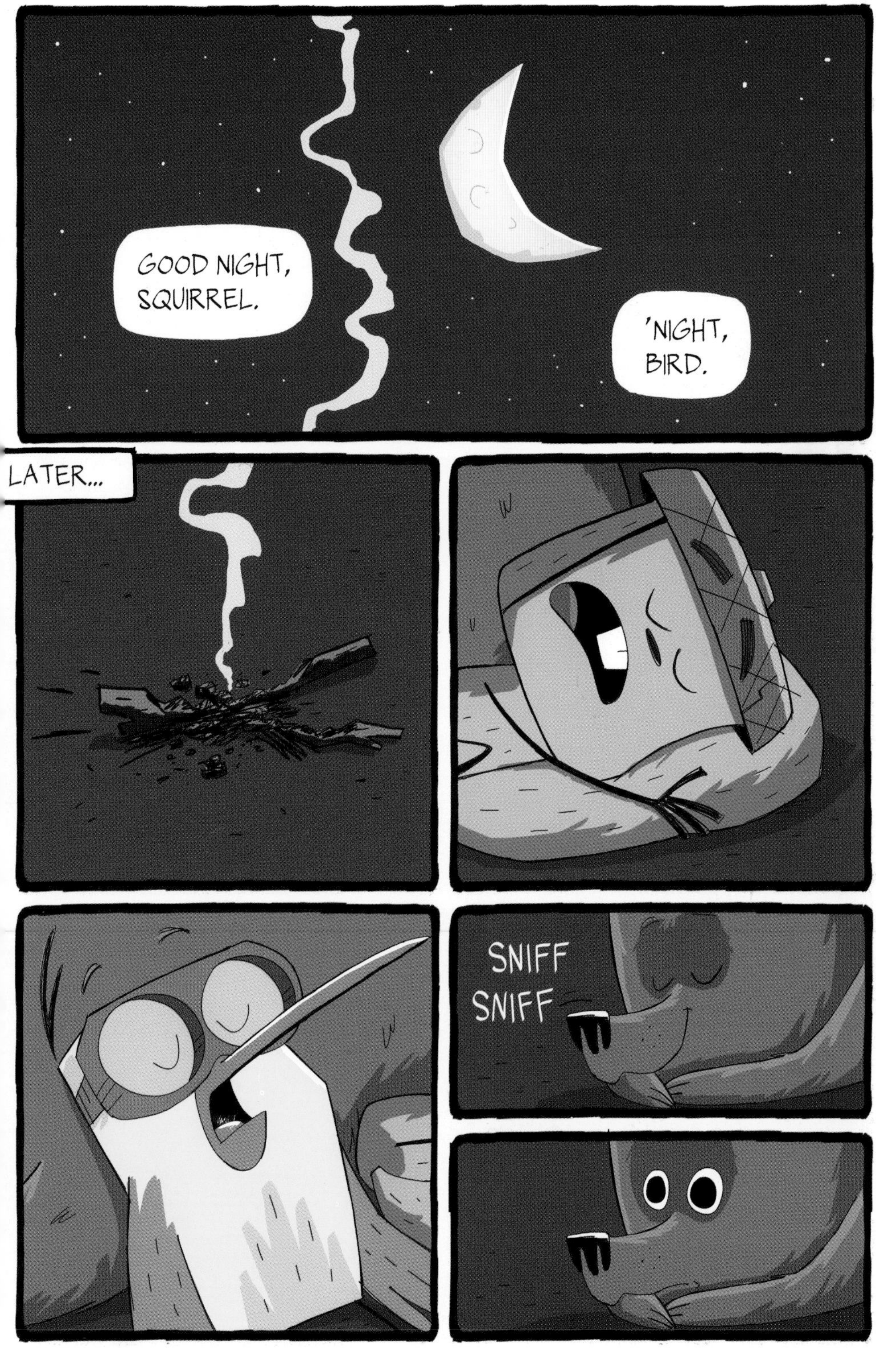
GOOD NIGHT, SQUIRREL.
'NIGHT, BIRD.
LATER...
SNIFF
SNIFF

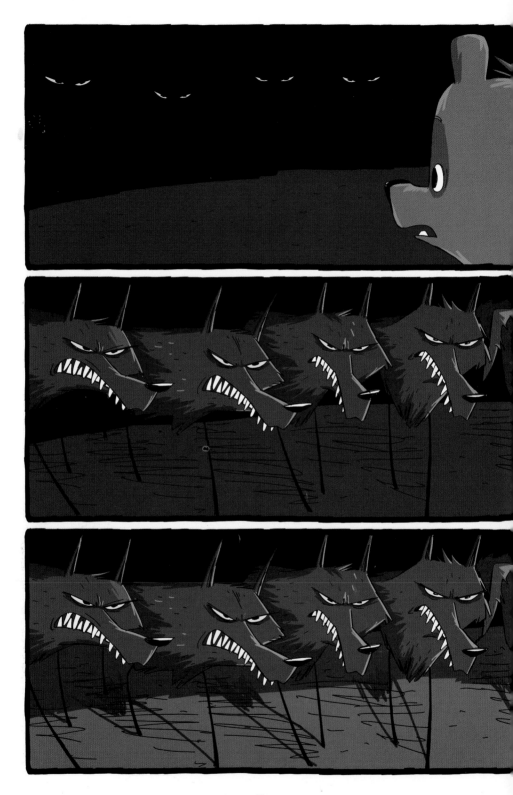

113

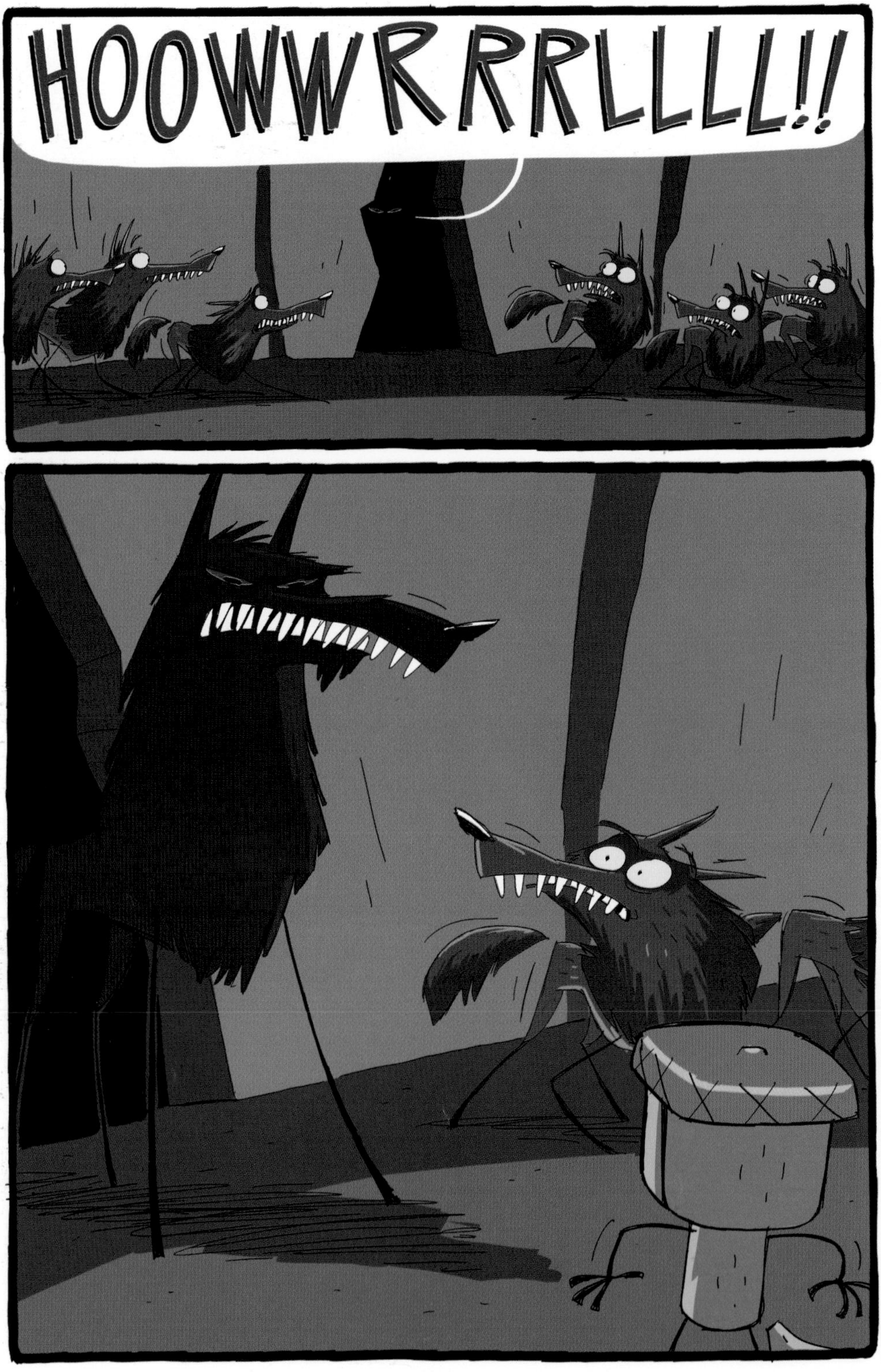
HOOWWRRRLLLL!!

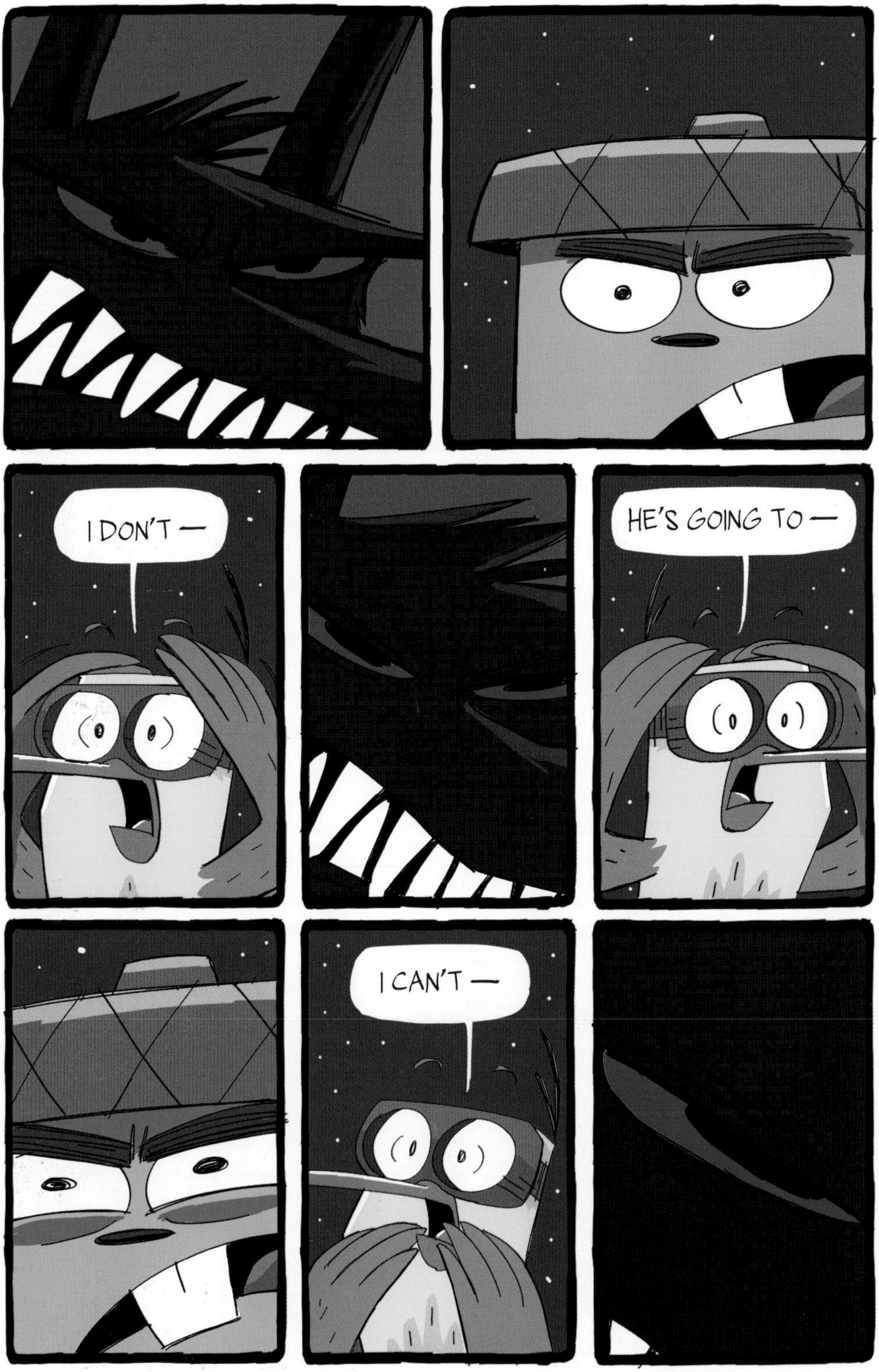
I DON'T —
HE'S GOING TO —
I CAN'T —

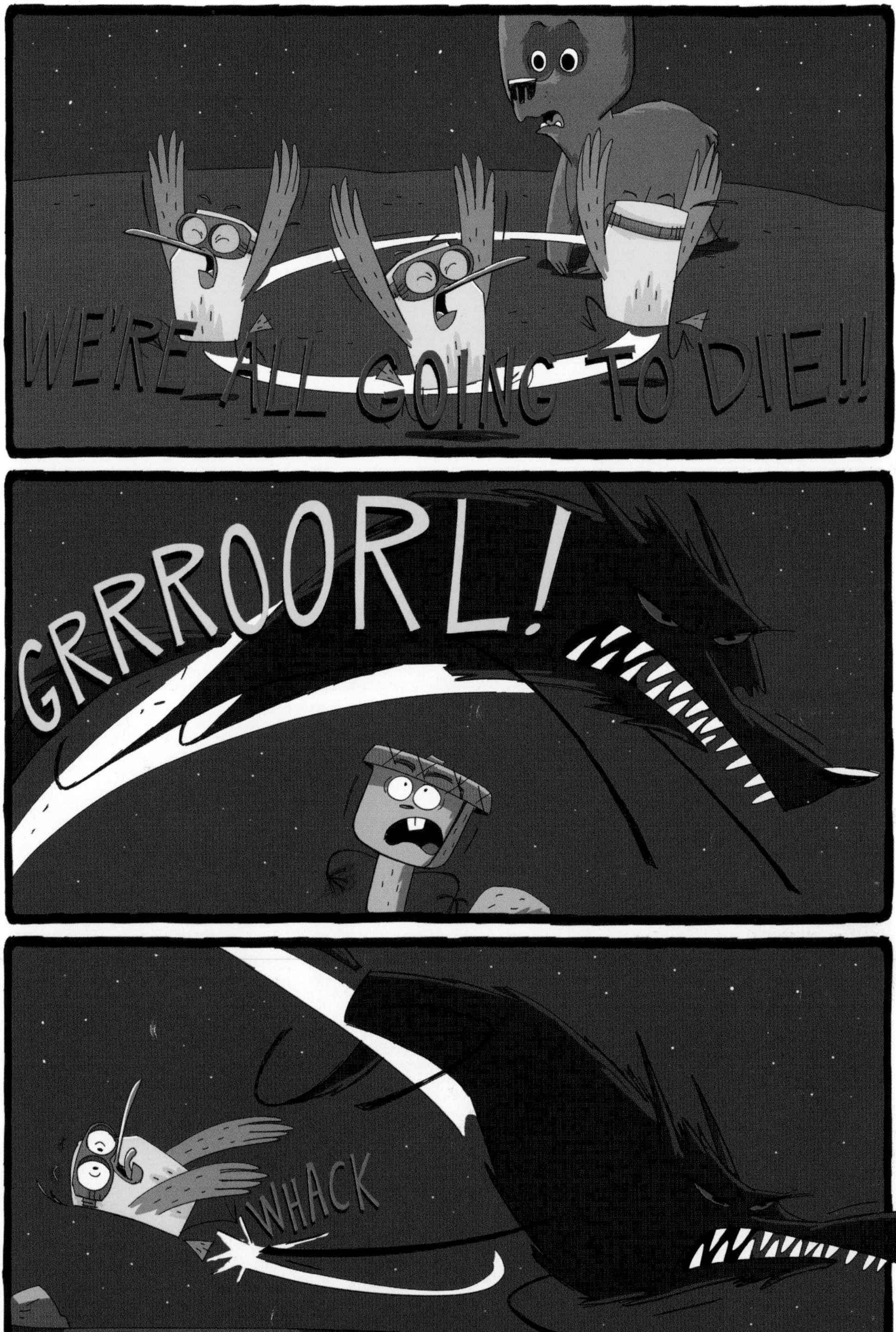
WE'RE ALL GOING TO DIE!!
GRRROORL!
WHACK

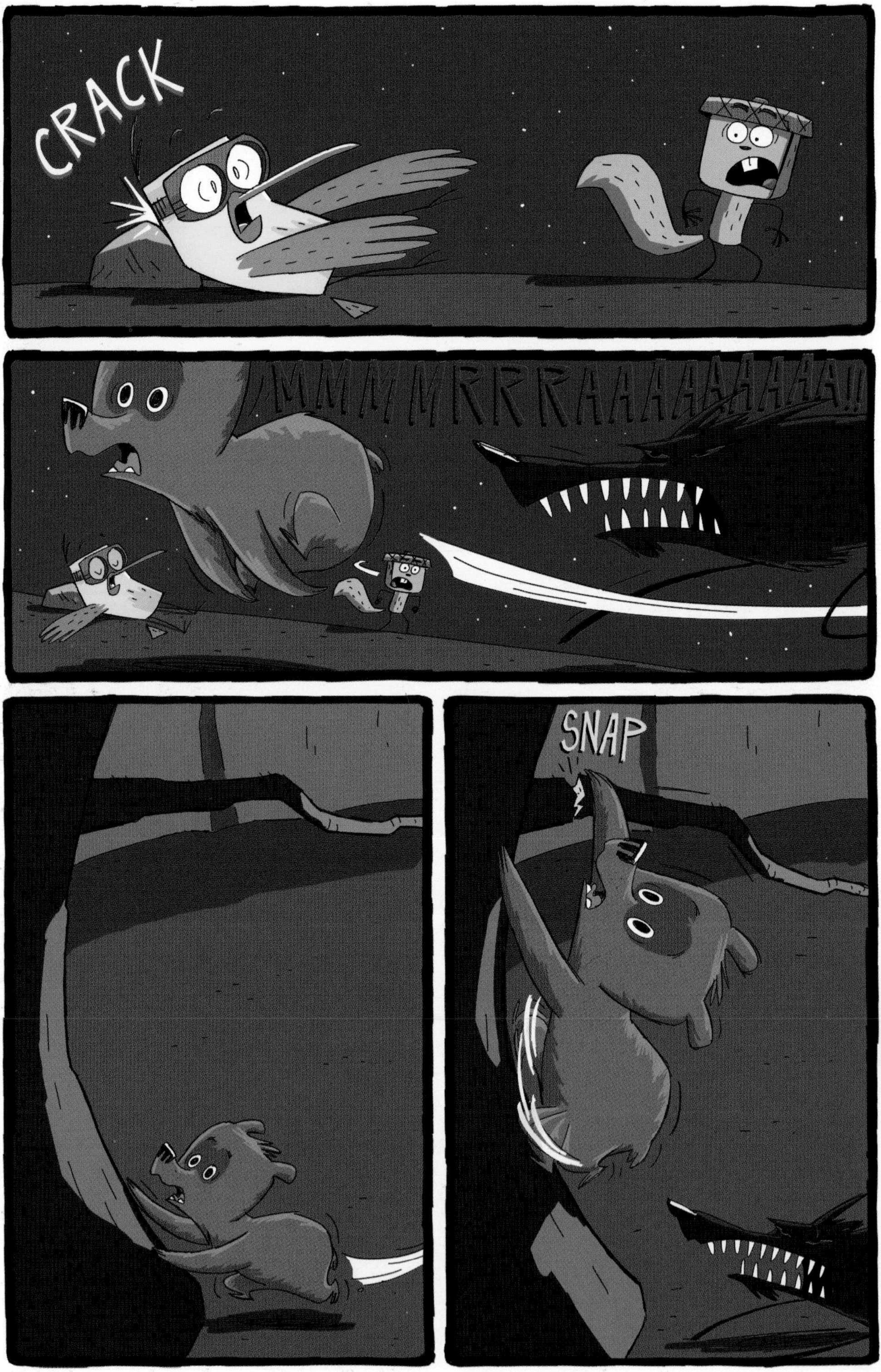
CRACK
MMMMRRRRAAAAAAAAA!!
SNAP

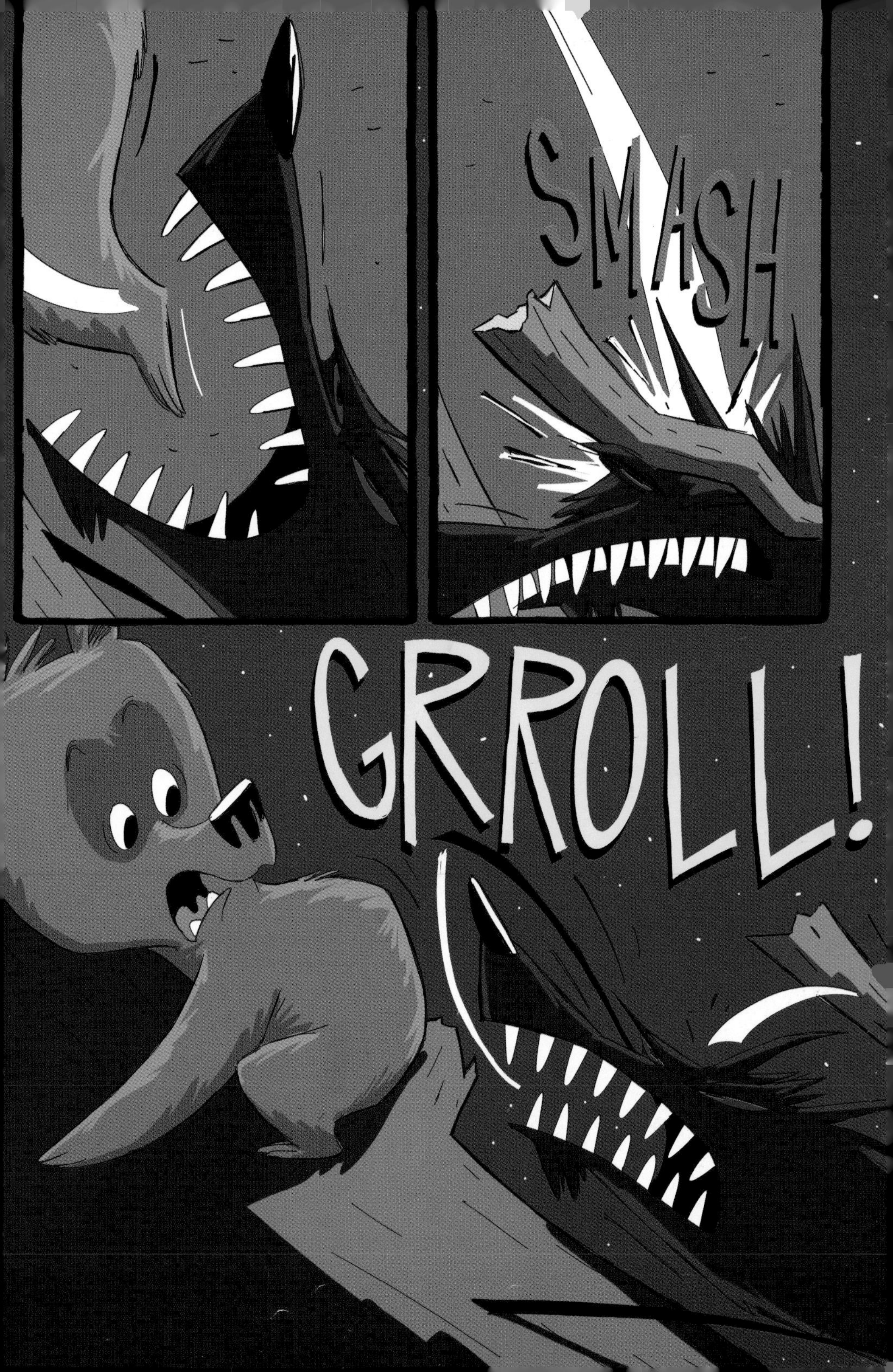
SMASH
GRROLL!

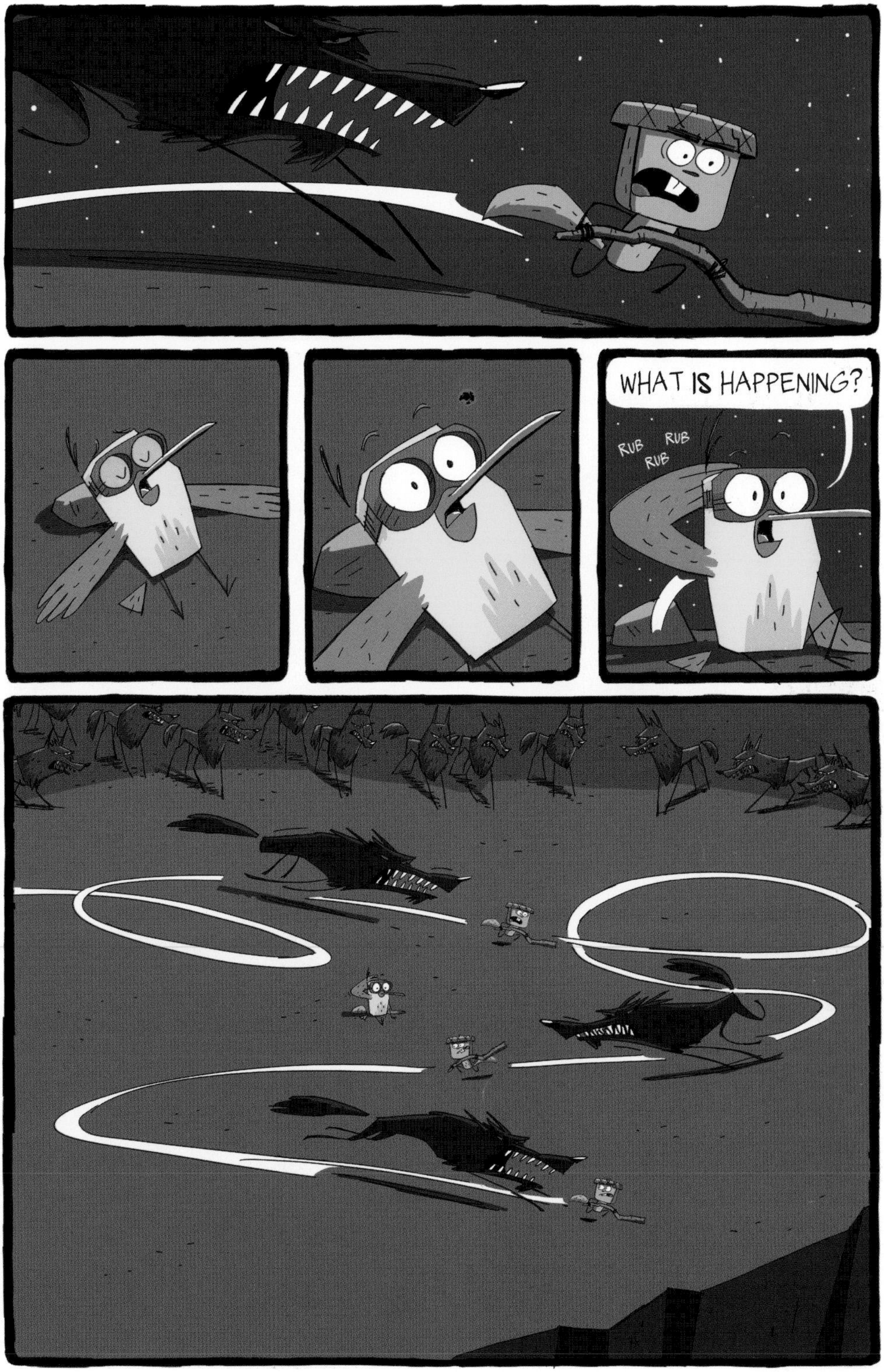
WHAT IS HAPPENING?
RUB RUB
RUB

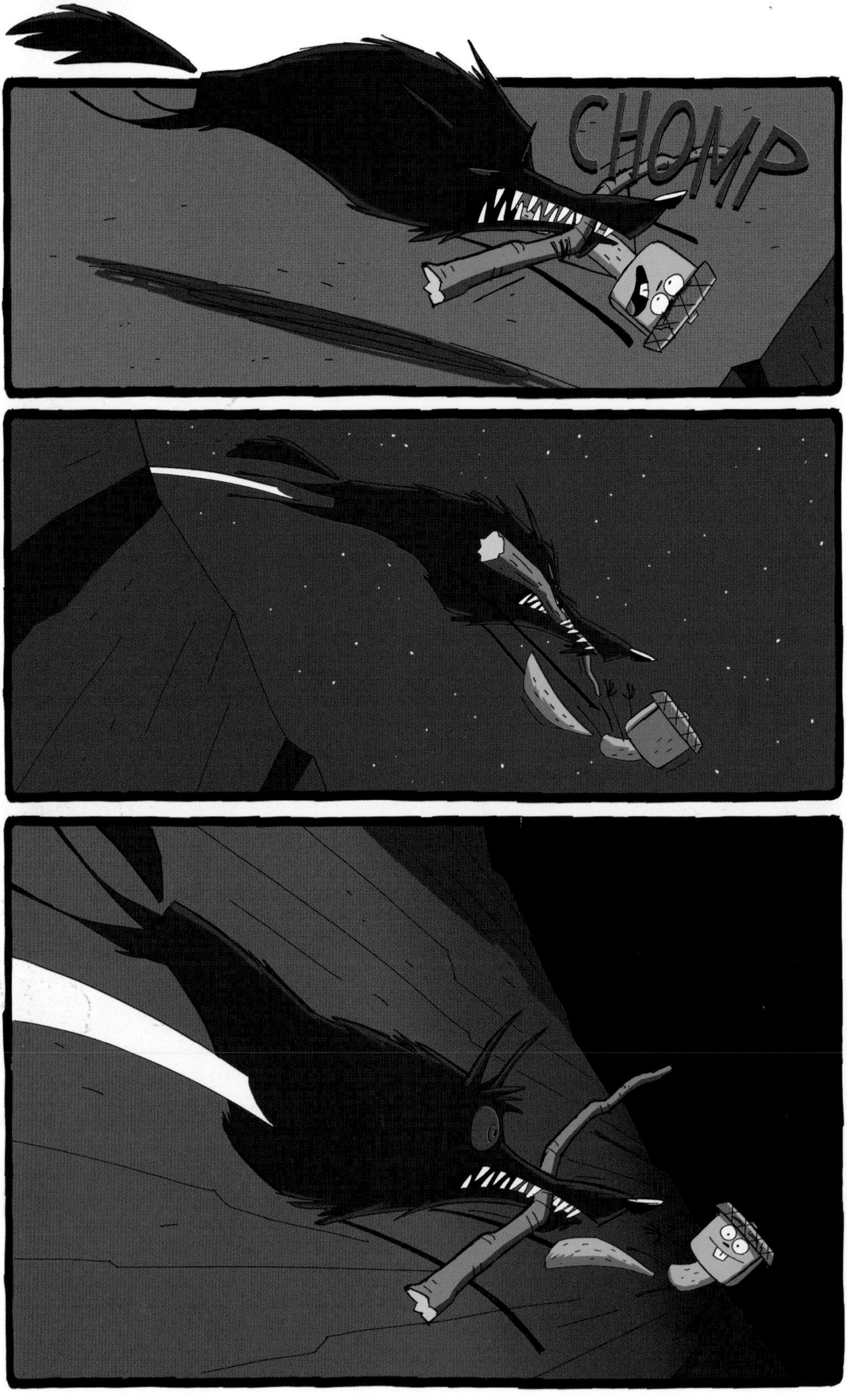
CHOMP

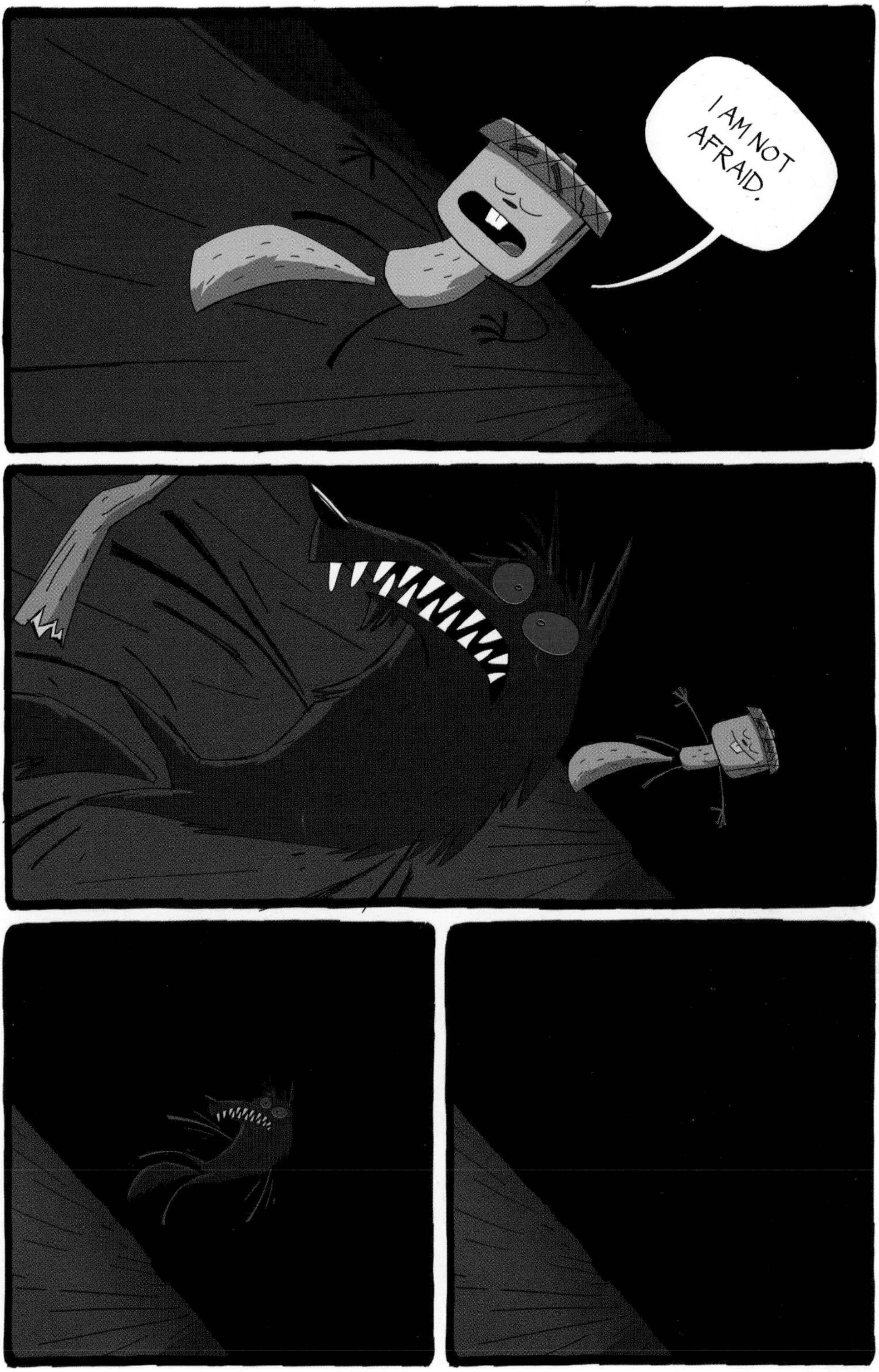
I AM NOT AFRAID.

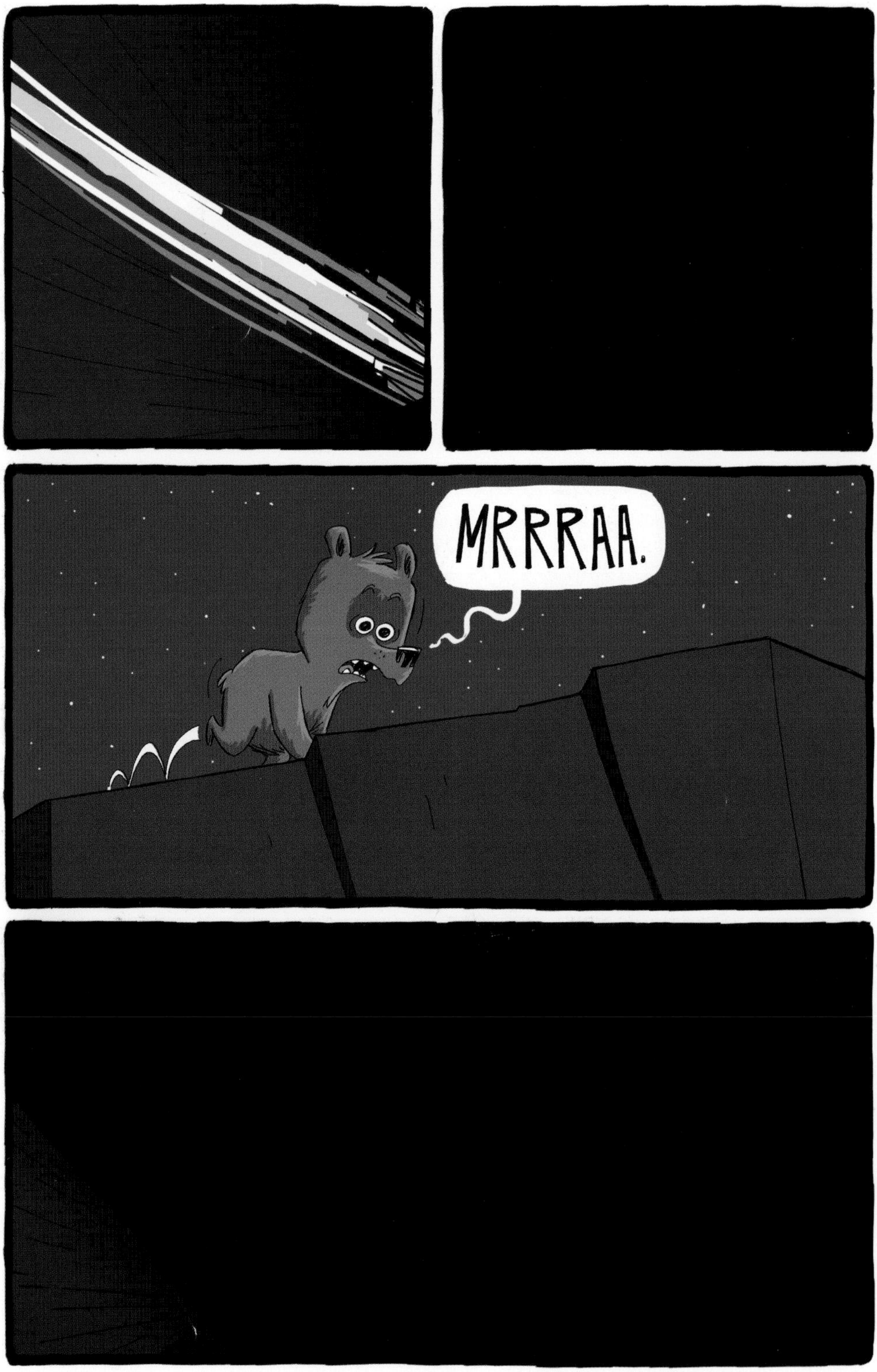
MRRRAA.

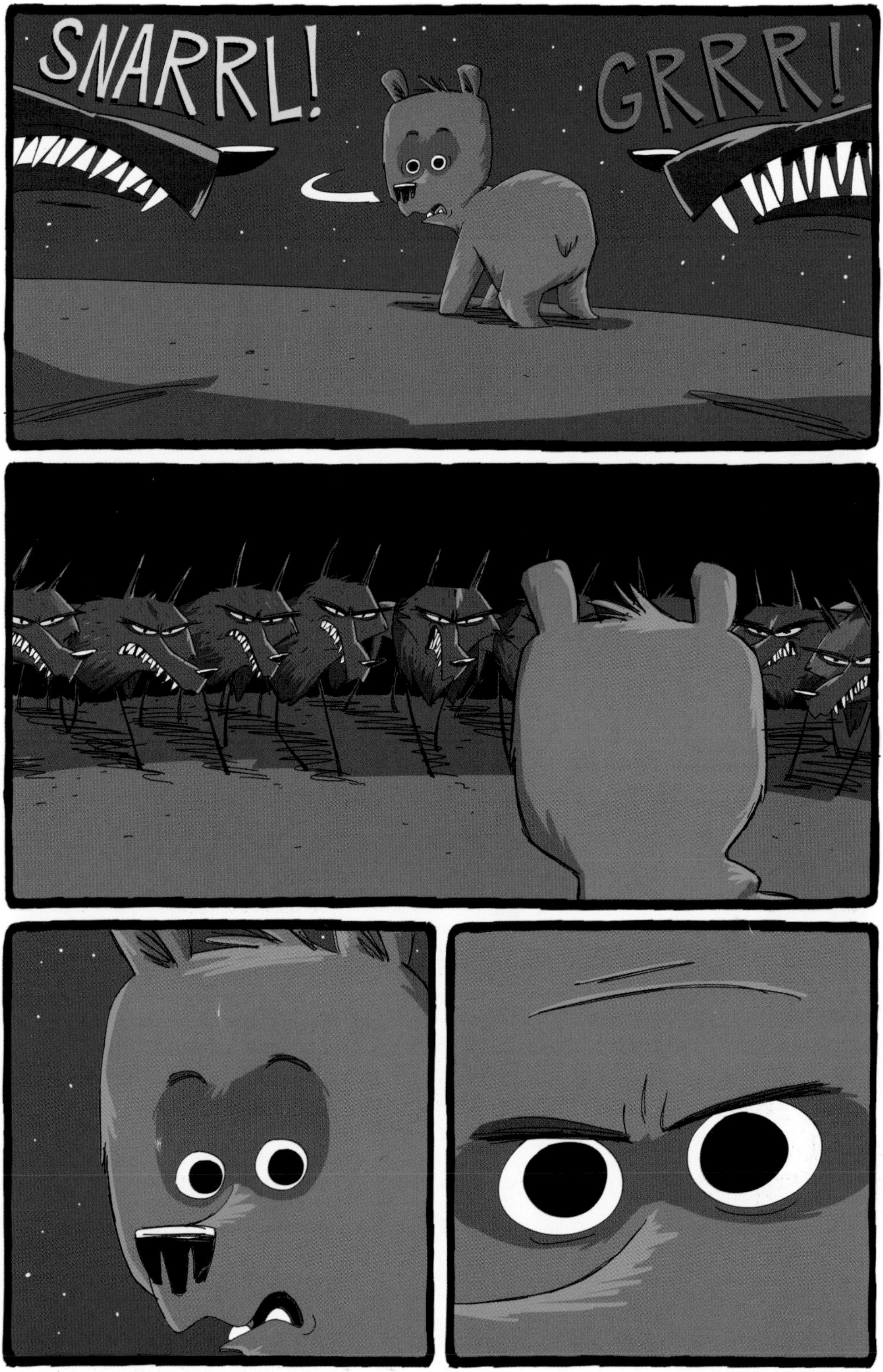
SNARRL!
GRRRR!

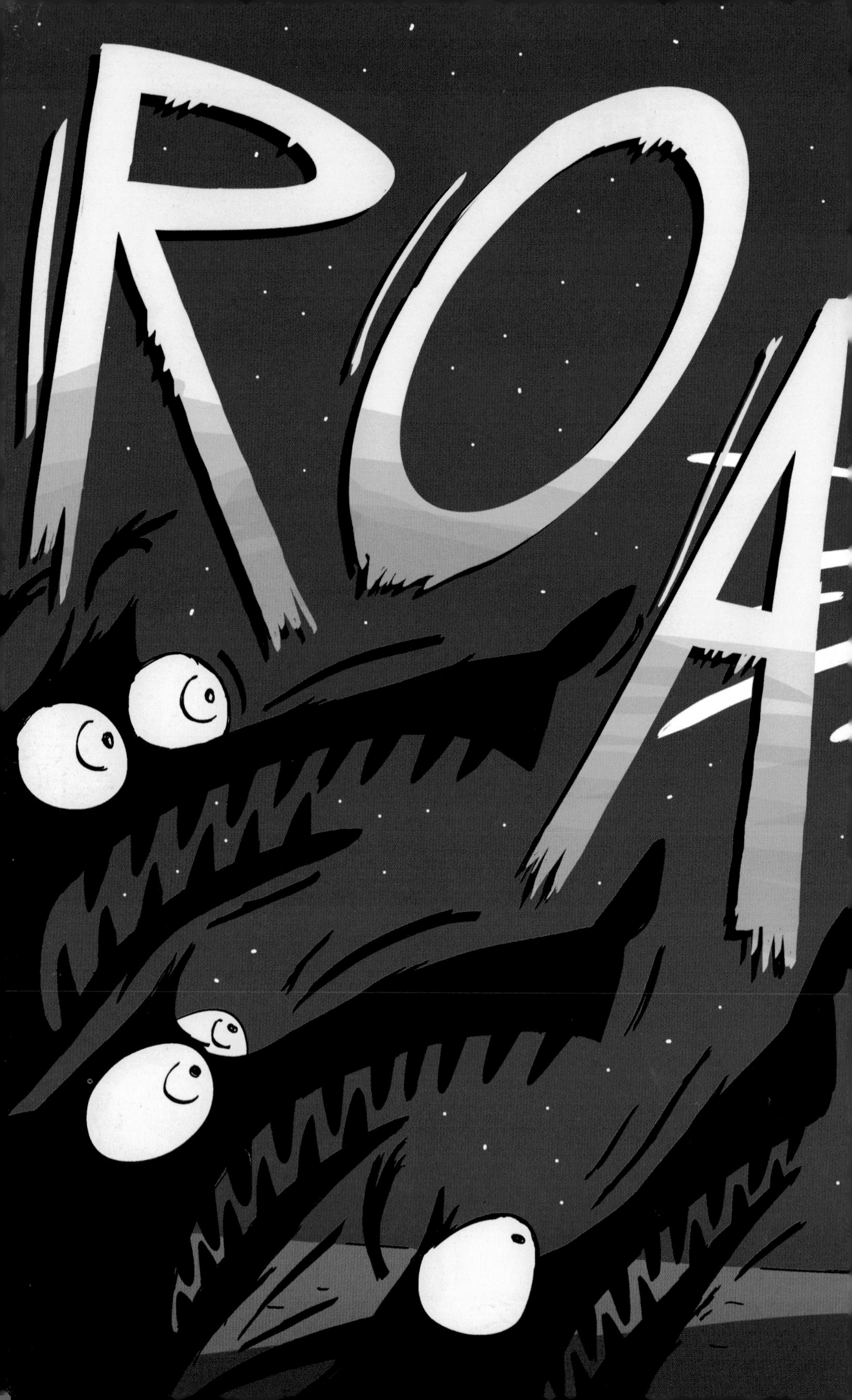
ROA

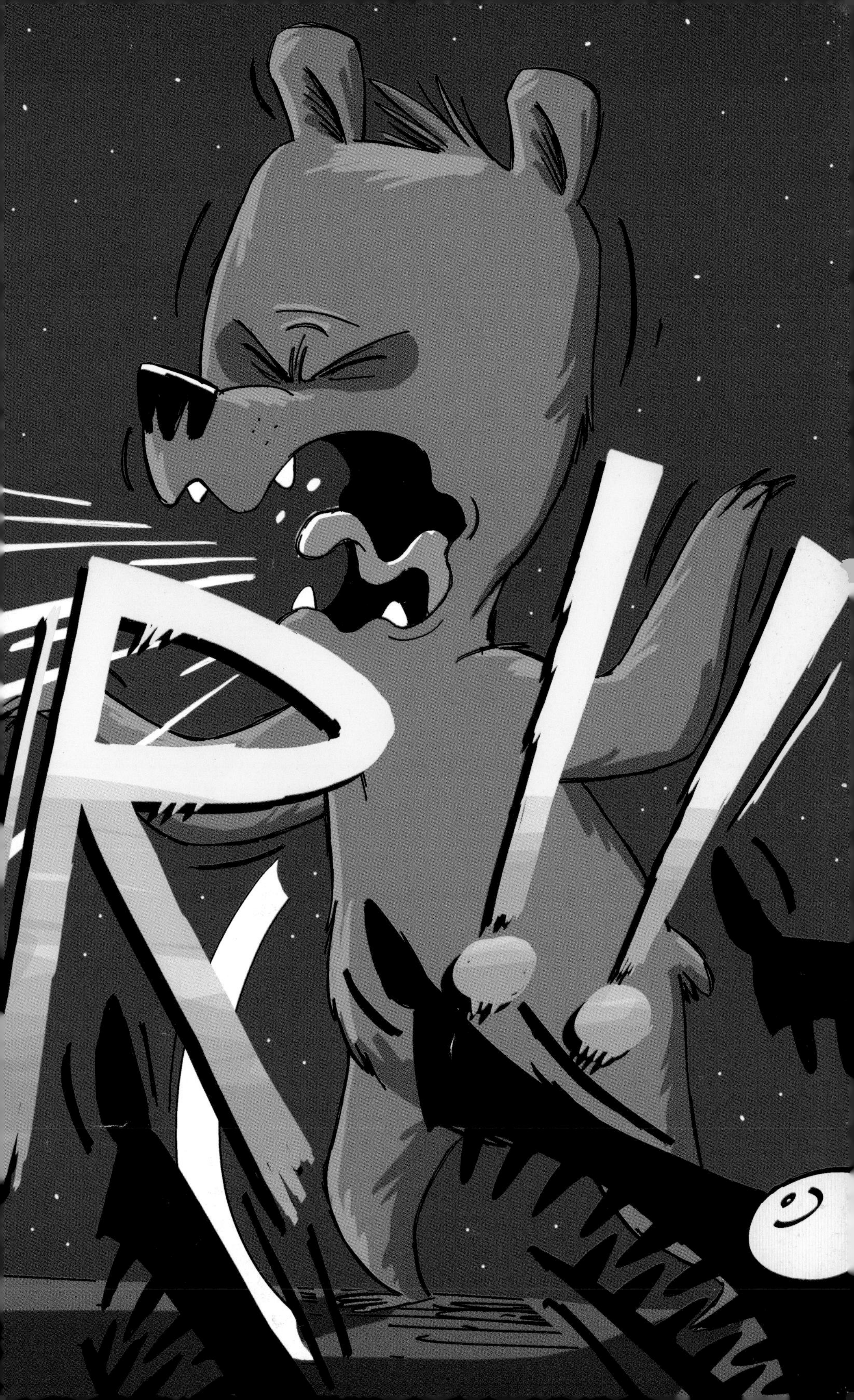
R!!

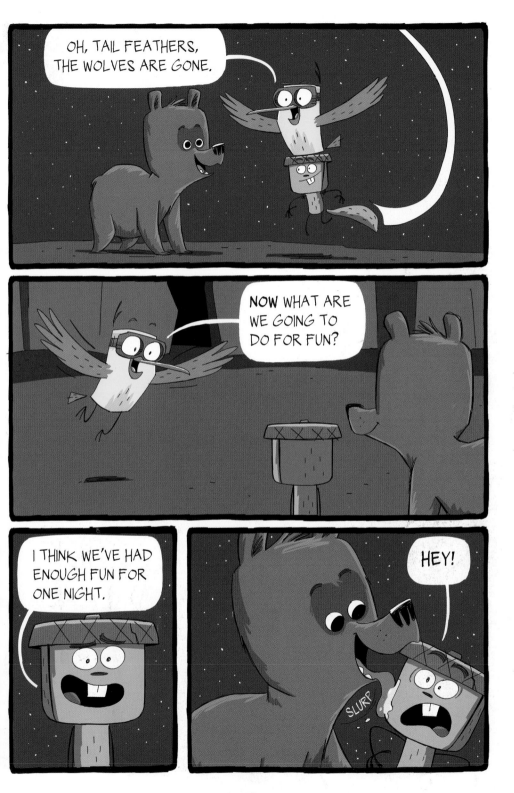

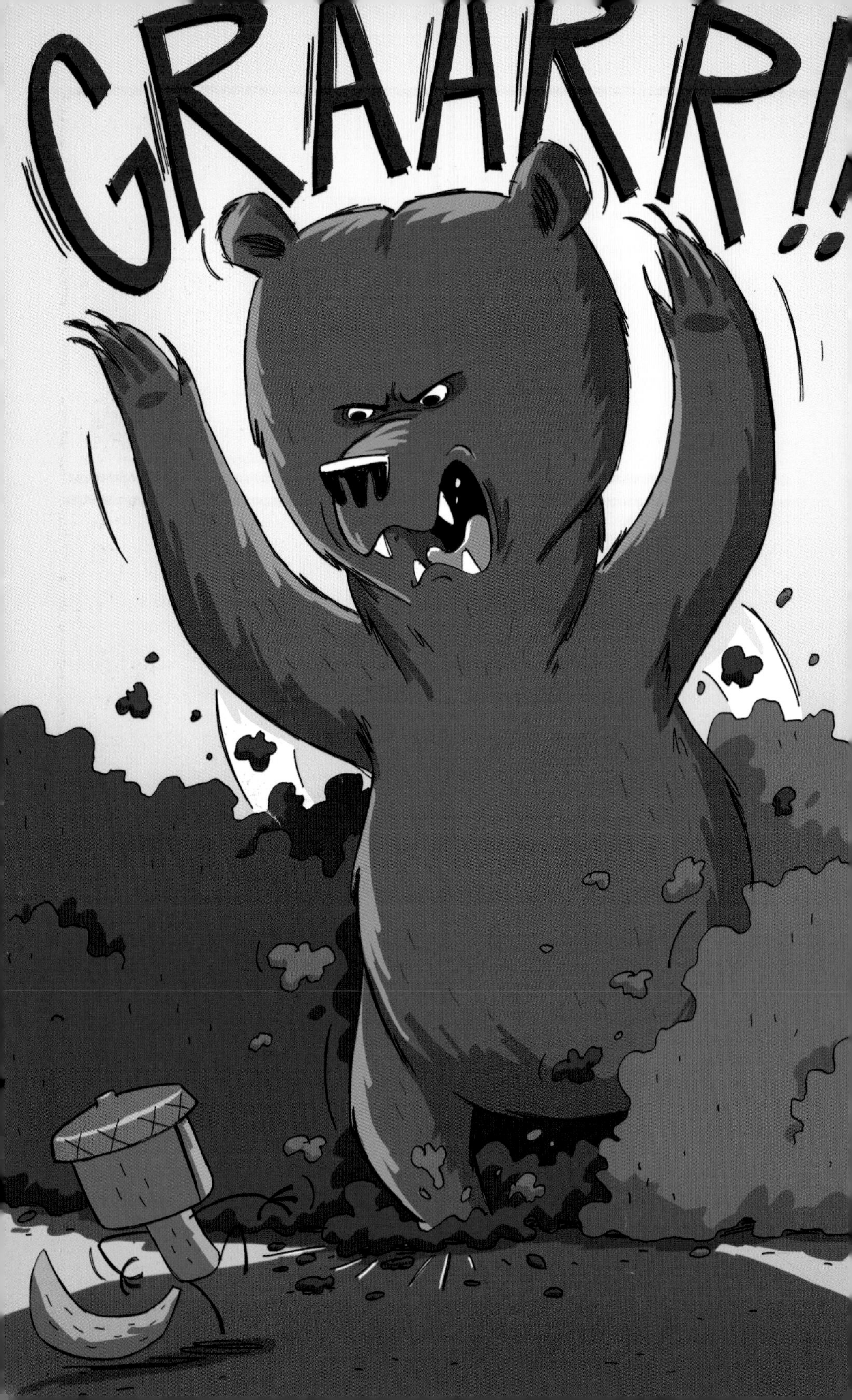
GRAARR!!

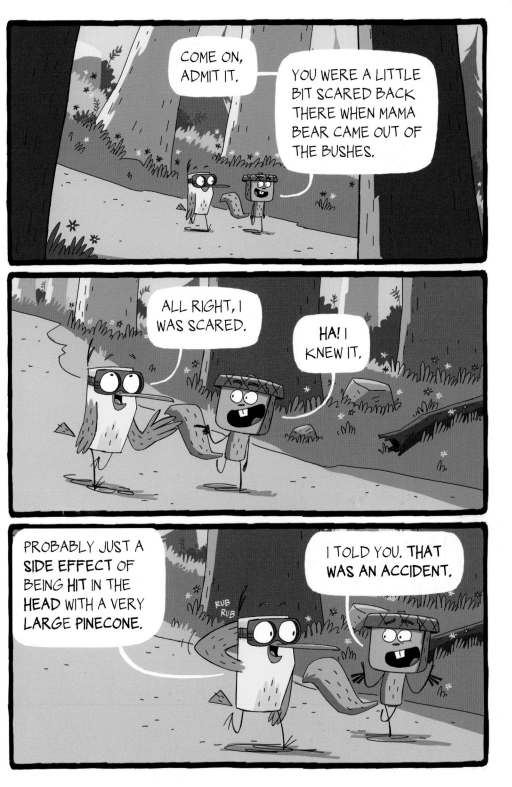

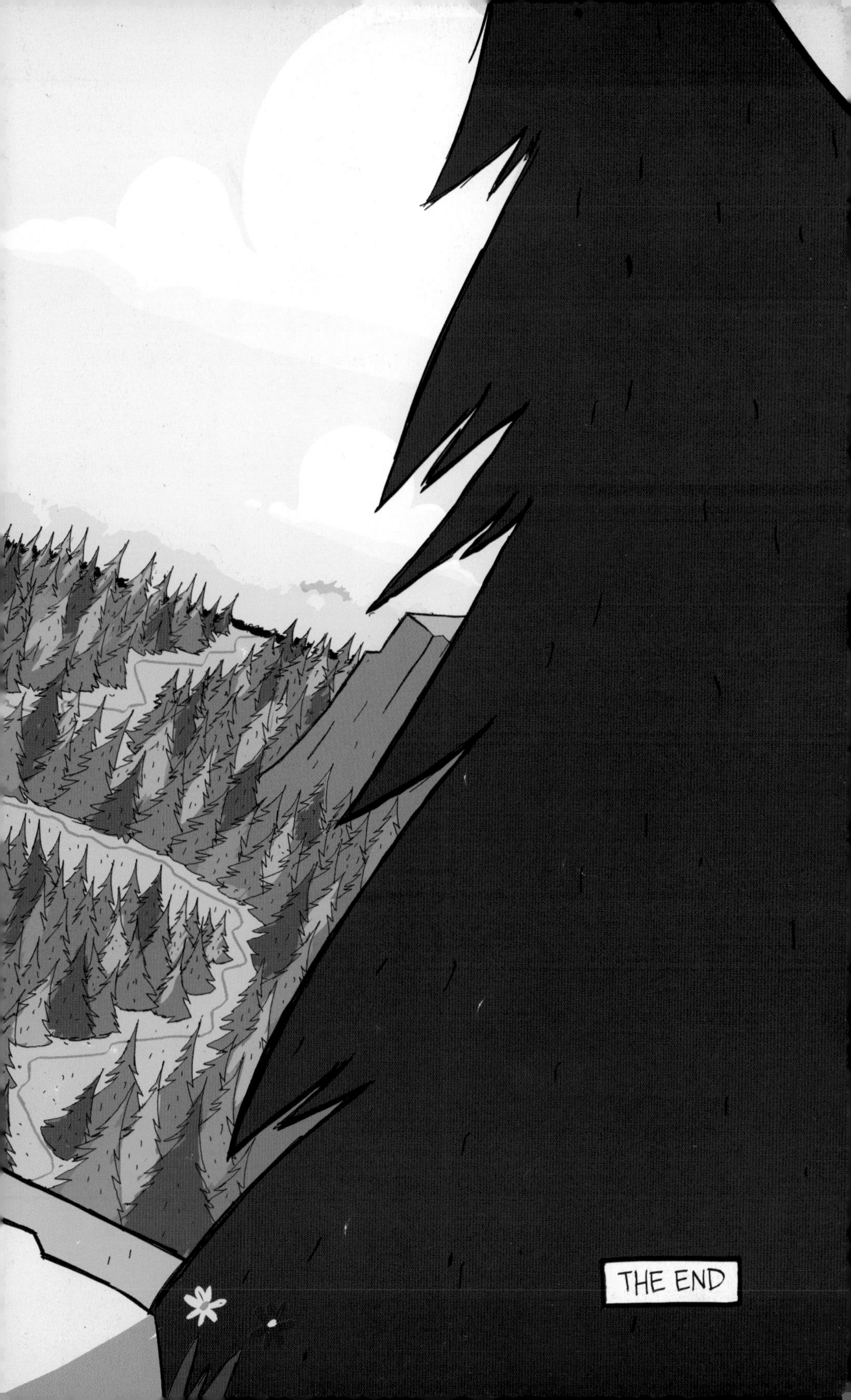
THE END

James Burks was a kid who always dreamed of being a light saber-wielding, truck-driving space pirate with a monkey for a first mate. But his parents refused to buy him a monkey! So he had to choose to be the next best thing when he grew up: a pen-wielding father of two with a lovely wife, two cats, one dog, a hunger for Mexican food, a love of running marathons, and a never-ending need to write stories and draw pictures about anything and everything he could imagine.

Go to www.jamesburks.com to see more art and follow James on Twitter at @jamesburksart.